EIGHTEEN
ROSES

SHANNON C.F. ROGERS

FEIWEL AND FRIENDS

NEW YORK

A Feiwel and Friends Book
An imprint of Macmillan Publishing Group, LLC
120 Broadway, New York, NY 10271 • fiercereads.com

Our books may be purchased in bulk for promotional,
educational, or business use. Please contact your local bookseller
or the Macmillan Corporate and Premium Sales Department
at (800) 221-7945 ext. 5442 or by email at
MacmillanSpecialMarkets@macmillan.com.

Library of Congress Cataloging-in-Publication Data
Names: Rogers, Shannon C. F., author.
Title: Eighteen roses / Shannon C.F. Rogers.
Description: First edition. | New York : Feiwel and Friends, 2024. |
Audience: Ages 13 and up. | Audience: Grades 10–12. | Summary:
Filipina American Lucia grapples with teenage angst, family
expectations, and friendship woes as she reluctantly
prepares for her debutante ball.
Identifiers: LCCN 2023048477 | ISBN 9781250845733 (hardcover)
Subjects: CYAC: Friendship—Fiction. | Family life—Fiction. |
Debutantes—Fiction. | High schools—Fiction. | Schools—Fiction. |
Filipino Americans—Fiction.
Classification: LCC PZ7.1.R6626 Ei 2024 | DDC [Fic]—dc23
LC record available at https://lccn.loc.gov/2023048477

First edition, 2024
Book design by Meg Sayre
Feiwel and Friends logo designed by Filomena Tuosto
Printed in the United States of America

ISBN 978-1-250-84573-3
1 3 5 7 9 10 8 6 4 2

For Lilah and Rowan

AUTHOR'S NOTE

A DEBUT (PRONOUNCED /DƐ'BU:/) IS A TRADITIONAL Filipino coming-of-age celebration of a young woman's eighteenth birthday. Given its elaborate and lavish nature, this ritual has long been associated with the Filipino elite. However, debuts have gained popularity with working- and middle-class families, and in the United States in particular.

"Immigrant families use debuts and quinceañeras to mark the passage of Filipino- and Mexican-American girls into 'not just any women' but ethnicized young ladies."
    —Evelyn Ibatan Rodriguez

"I'm not doing that."
    —Lucia Cruz

1

THE SUNSHINE, A TINY THEATER THAT SHOWS OLD movies for two-dollar tickets, is located, as all my favorite places are, in a strip mall.

I love strip malls. I love how you can tell when they were built based on the architecture and the fonts on all the signs. I love it when all the signs are in different fonts, but also when all the signs are the same font. I love it when the big sign by the street is really old but they just leave it there, year after year, even as the businesses shutter and turn over and change. I love the retro, neon signs all along old Route 66, of course, but even more so, I love the weird stuff. Like there's this one strip mall in the Heights that used to have a bowling alley in it, and even though the bowling alley isn't there anymore, the sign is still shaped like a giant red bowling pin, next to a giant red bowling ball. I love that it now says "Staples" and "Guitar Center" inside that giant bowling pin, and underneath, it says "Hot Pink Thai Cuisine" and "Southwest Financial," and I also love that the words *Hot Pink* are written in purple, not pink.

Albuquerque is full of strip malls—it's mostly strip malls, it's a sparkling grid of strip malls beneath a vast, open sky, blue and orange and dusty pink; strip malls with offices and storefronts and restaurants, vacant or shiny new, little brown low-slung buildings with bright murals splashed across their sides, carpeting the high desert from the Sandia Mountains to the Rio Grande and from the river to the horizon where the sun sets over the Three Sisters; strip malls as far as the eye can see, mirroring each other from across wide streets, lined with cactus, evergreen, and mesquite, all coursing between them like capillaries in the lungs, like veins, asphalt crumbling and cracking under temperature swings, blistering dry heat, numbing cold, crumbling, freshly paved, crumbling, neighborhood by neighborhood, and year by year.

The Sunshine Theater's marquee glows in the center heart of its strip. It shares a parking lot with Famous Pho restaurant, a Supercuts, Salazar's Taqueria y Carniceria, Milly and Manny's Comic Books & Boba Tea, and a titty bar called the Prickly Pear where all the dumbasses at school think it's funny to say they saw your mom last night. The Sunshine Theater is our most sacred, holy place—my best friend, Esmé, and me, who make a pilgrimage to this particular strip mall every day after school as soon as the last bell rings.

When we hop into Esmé's car in the school parking lot, I automatically subtract an hour from the dashboard clock she never bothers to change. Her grandpa left this car to her when he died. It's an old man's car, huge, boat-like, and smells like stale cigars, but it suits her, and she keeps his rosary and his Virgin Mary of Guadalupe air freshener hanging on the rearview mirror, thanking him every time she narrowly avoids a tree, or a curb, or another car.

"Señor Josh was in rare form today," I say, flipping down the mirror to confirm how rough I look after seven plus hours being run through the meat grinder of the public education system. I do, indeed, look like I got hit by an overcrowded bus. "He didn't even shave."

"I know!" Esmé says, turning west, away from the mountains, which are lined with newly yellowing trees at the crest. "He looks like he's going *through it*. What do you think is going on with him? It's only October."

Our Spanish teacher is this white guy whose name is not Josh, but we think it's funny to call him Señor Josh because he looks like Josh from *Blue's Clues*, if Josh from *Blue's Clues* was white. Which is funny because Josh from *Blue's Clues* is, of course, Filipino, like me, and Señor Josh at school is white, and Esmé is Chicana, and her dad's side of the family has lived here for hundreds of years since before New Mexico was even called New Mexico, and there we are, in Spanish I together, because according to Esmé she's a "no sabo" kid, conjugating verbs from an extremely old textbook that includes *vosotros*, and every time we ask Señor Josh about it he just says, *don't worry about that column, you'll never use it*, which pisses off Esmé, who said why does Señor Josh get to be the arbiter of what we will use and what we won't use? But then I said one less column of verbs to worry about is fine with me, and anyway I think he just meant that it's a Spain thing and maybe an Argentina thing? So why bother? And Esmé said it was the *you* that pissed her off, and the *never*, he said *you'll never use it*. It was the implication.

It's true that it's exhausting to spend your whole day trying to decode these little implications. Which is why by the time 3:00 p.m. hits, I'm basically catatonic from all the inane human interaction I've been subjected to at school and I can't wait to sit in the darkness at the Sunshine Theater, in my favorite strip mall, and not say a a word to anyone for at least ninety minutes. But, since Esmé's driving, and I'm in her passenger seat, it's like her job is to drive us to the Sunshine and it's my job to be the in-flight entertainment, not that either one of us has ever been on a plane before. If we ever do fly on a plane together, maybe we'll watch a movie instead, but until then, in her grandpa's car, every day, I try to make Esmé laugh. When she laughs, it's like I've earned my spot in that seat somehow.

Esmé Mares is my only friend. Nobody else likes me at school, probably because I barely say anything at all and then when I finally do it's weird or mean or both, and it's probably also about a movie that nobody else has seen, but Esmé likes me, because she laughs at those things. So even though it takes every scrap of energy I have left, when I'm sitting in her passenger seat, I pull out my best observations about Señor Josh, who seems to be in need of a Zoloft refill because his unshaven jaw today was giving blob, and Noah Bradford, who I hate, who said he saw our trig teacher at the Prickly Pear when *no he fucking didn't* and I told him so, and my sister's friends from the track team who all did their hair in identical ponytails today because of some dopey spirit thing we're supposed to care about, and how the Hot Silent Sophomore switched to using a *blue* Pilot G2 pen in AP World History making him even more elite than we thought previously, until the fifteen-minute drive across town is complete and we're safely swinging into the parking lot of the Sunshine.

"WATCH OUT!" I say.

Esmé has almost clipped our friend Mr. Marco, the movie proprietor, returning to this post with his afternoon coffee from the adjacent strip mall, which houses Chismosas Tattoos, a Golden Pride Fried Chicken and Burritos, Monologue Coffee, and two empty storefronts that used to be a Blockbuster and a Hollywood Video, respectively, their signs remaining despite their windows being boarded up for years.

Mr. Marco did *not* get his coffee at Monologue, which has vegan donuts in the glass pastry case and oat milk in the mini fridge by the paper straws—he got his coffee at Golden Pride Fried Chicken and Burritos for a dollar. He takes it black.

"Sorry, Mr. Marco!" Esmé calls out the window.

His coffee sloshes onto the pavement and he swats at the back of her car with his newspaper.

"Thanks, Abuelito," she murmurs in the direction of her grandfather's rosary, blowing cigarette smoke out of her driver's side window and tucking us safely into her preferred parking spot.

She stabs the butt into the ashtray. I wish she wouldn't smoke. My mom smokes and I feel like because of that when I see people smoking it doesn't look cool to me the way I think it's supposed to. It looks sad.

The marquee over the door boasts only two movies this week, their titles stacked on top of each other in such a way that they are scrambled and unreadable, but we were here yesterday, so we know that GLENGARRY GLEN GIRL FUNNY ROSS is actually *Glengarry Glen Ross* and *Funny Girl,* respectively. There's never any real rhyme or reason, from what we can tell, to the movies that old Mr. Marco chooses to screen at the Sunshine. It seems like he just goes off vibes, which is what I like about him. He does what- ever he wants. It's his place.

Mom gets mad at me every time I say Mr. Marco is old. He's at least as old as my lola, which I guess is not *super* old, but Mr. Marco *seems* super old to me, in his big glasses frames that look like they haven't changed since the premiere of one or both the films he's screening this week, and his old man sweater, which is actually cool and I'd wear it if I found it at Savers.

My mom gets mad at me for dressing "ugly," like today, which isn't even that bad, just a T-shirt and sweat- pants. Mom gets mad at me for a lot of things, like "ter- rorizing" Mr. Marco at the Sunshine every day.

He accepts our crumpled-up dollar bills and quarters and dimes with an eye roll—he loves us—and pushes two red-striped bags of popcorn across the chipped plastic countertop without us having to ask for them.

"Looks like we might get some weather tonight," I say.

Mr. Marco keeps a notebook next to the register where he logs the daily precipitation from a rain gauge he keeps in the planter out front. The daily precipitation is usually zero.

"Looks like," he grunts, turning back to this crossword puzzle.

"Let me know if you get stuck on five across," I say. "I'll give you a hint."

He grunts.

Esmé uses a straw inserted into the popcorn to make sure the fake butter is adequately distributed throughout the bag because she's a genius.

"Girls, not so much!" Mr. Marco calls out to us. "You'll get a hole in your stomach lining."

"For legal reasons, we'll pretend we didn't hear you say that," I say.

We take our usual seats, in the middle of the theater, with no problem as there are only two other people present, a couple who sits down in the front row for some reason.

The outsides of the popcorn bags are soon slick with oily fingerprints. With our feet propped up on the seats in front of us, we shovel palmfuls into our mouths while we roast the movie trailers for sentimental movies about dogs, *like they have souls*, the couple down in the front row having a whisper fight, *like we can't hear them*, and the way Mr. Marco said he wanted to switch to real butter, *like we want that*. Like we care. As always, we're clutching cramping stomachs by the time the lights dim, *we should have shared*, we groan, as if we should know by now.

Then the whole world fades to black.

Because we've already seen *Glengarry Glen Ross*, we're seeing the other movie, *Funny Girl*. It's the story of Fanny Brice, a young girl living in New York City in ye old-timey times, except she's a young Barbra Streisand looking very much like it's 1968 when the movie came out, per the opening credits. I know that Esmé is loving her eyeliner and she's going to try to replicate it tomorrow and possibly even try to replicate it on me even though she's going to look like a Chicana Barbra Streisand and I'm going to look like I have two bruised eye sockets because that's how I always look in makeup. It just doesn't sit right on me.

Fanny Brice is a funny girl who wants to be on the stage even if it means auditioning for the chorus when she can't dance because she just *knows* she's a star.

The joke seems to be that somebody who looks like her could never be a star even though she's the most beautiful woman on screen and maybe quite literally the most beautiful woman I've ever seen, so I don't get it. It's probably racism because she's Jewish.

That eyeliner, and the lighting. She looks amazing.

"They just don't make movies like this anymore," I whisper in an old-timey-radio, mid-Atlantic-adjacent accent, and Esmé laughs.

Esmé laughs a lot at movies, and she cries sometimes, too. I feel like movies give people permission to feel things that they don't always let themselves feel in regular life, but I still can't cry at them. I never cry at the right times, only when I really, really don't want to.

Esmé grabs my arm when she laughs really hard at one of Fanny's jokes and I start eating her popcorn once I finish mine, even though I'll get a hole in my stomach lining, and even I *almost* cry when Fanny's dream comes true but it doesn't feel like she thought it would—and somehow, somehow, the two hours and thirty-five minutes are done and the credits are rolling and I feel like my molecules have been rearranged.

It feels so weird, every time, when we step through the

exit door after the movie is over, and our eyes adjust to reality. What time is it, what day? Not to be all Nicole Kidman about it, but I love that about the movies. About this place. It's a time machine. It's a portal. It's not home, it's not school, it's a space in between. Esmé's car feels like that, too, and as we talk about the movie the whole way home, our sentences overlapping, the desert and the mountains a blur outside the window, strip malls, strip malls, Esmé laughing and smacking the steering wheel as I make my dumb jokes about Barbra Streisand's eyeliner and the jumbled marquee and how GLENGARRY GLEN GIRL FUNNY ROSS would be a bittersweet tale about a bunch of real estate agents trying to close an audition in the chorus line, it feels possible that things will always be this way. If I can just keep her laughing.

2

YOU'RE NOT A CHORUS GIRL, FANNY BRICE'S FRIEND told her when he saw what she could do onstage. *You're a comic.*

But *why* was Fanny Brice funny?

The movie doesn't go too much into it, it focuses a lot on the romance storyline instead, but I feel like it must have something to do with her mother. Her mother and her friend Mrs. Strakosh, who told Fanny that she was fine for a regular girl but not beautiful enough to be a star.

When your mother says stuff like that to you in front of all her friends while they play cards in a Brooklyn saloon, you kind of have to say something funny, don't you, to take the heat off you? But then she ran straight into the heat of a different spotlight. At least it's one she chose, she was saying.

Lucky for me, I have developed a solid method for when I need to redirect my mother's heat, which is to focus her attention instead on my little sister, Ali.

Ali's side of our bedroom, at our mom's apartment, is a mess. Which is annoying because everyone assumes *I'm* the messy one, just because Ali always looks so *together*, and I look, well, how I look. Not that I care what everyone assumes. Most people, famously, are stupid, and they are even dumber in groups. It's been studied.

It's an ungodly hour to be awake right now, but I have to get to school early for detention, because schools are institutions designed to punish you for not being stupid enough to comply perfectly with all the stupid rules they invent.

When I trip over a pile of Ali's dirty clothes in the dark, all her perfect, stupid, matchy-matchy clothes, I scream silently at her sleeping form.

YOU'VE NEVER EVEN HAD *DETENTION, HAVE YOU?*

She lets out a little cherubic sigh, our tuxedo cat curled up beneath her arm, and I briefly consider sweeping her hoard of body sprays and moisturizers and various other sundry potions, which are completely covering what is supposed to be our desk for doing homework, but she has now claimed as her *getting ready station*, onto the floor. Instead of doing that, I scoop her dirty clothes off the floor and shove them in the laundry hamper.

We've shared a room our whole lives, or, I guess, just Ali's whole life. My reign as an only child totaled a mere eighteen months, so it kind of just feels like she's always been there. Long before our parents divorced and Mom moved us all into this apartment, we've been elbowing each other for space in front of the mirror before school. In our room, when we were kids, it used to be that her stuffed animals were everywhere, staring at me. Now it's clothes. Ali's side of the closet has been slowly, steadily encroaching on my side for the last several years. Track team jerseys, little flowery dresses that slip off the hangers and onto the floor, and piles and piles of the same pair of jeans over and over, even though Ali swears up and down that each one is actually a *distinct wash*. Even the walls are papered with her posters, they seem to multiply overnight.

And I let them. I let them because at Dad's new house, with Dad's new wife, she's not allowed to leave her stuff everywhere. There, Ali acts like a guest, neatly unpacking her many hair products from her duffel bag when we arrive, and then dutifully packing them up when we leave. And she doesn't complain, or ask if she can store her mousse or her leave-in conditioner or her double-barrel curling iron there. Not even a brush. She does this because she just somehow knows that it's not our house.

And it's kind of breaking my heart.

That's why it always works to redirect Mom's heat on me to Ali. Any conversation radiating in the direction of my unwashed hair or my unplucked eyebrows or my too-baggy clothes can be derailed by a strategically deployed *Mommy. I'm worried about Ali*. Because Ali is the baby. Ali is so sweet. Ali is so sensitive. *Watch her for me*, Mom pleads, my insufficiencies always forgotten in the face of my utility. I'm there to watch Ali, so I do.

Our bedroom at Mom's apartment still feels like our old bedroom, sometimes, right before I open my eyes in the morning. The one we shared growing up. But then when it isn't, when my vision rights itself, I get this pang, like *I want to go home*, and it stays with me throughout the day. I'm zoning out in Physics but then suddenly, *pang*, when the last bell rings, *pang*, and I walk to meet Esmé at her car in the parking lot, *pang. I want to go home.*

But the thing about wanting to go home is that you can't. What even is home? A place that isn't there anymore, a place that, sometimes, feels like you invented it, that you can go back to only when your eyes are closed, when you've slipped into that space between sleep and waking. Someone's fingertips are at the crown of your head. You're wearing warm socks. The sharp smell of garlic and onions browning in the kitchen. The sound of people who love each other laughing easily together in the other room. There's nothing that you have to do. There's nothing that you need to say. Your stuff is everywhere. It's always been there and it will always be there.

It's just an idea, though.

It's a place that doesn't exist. A place where things stay the same.

In the kitchen at Mom's apartment, the soft light of morning falls over the chipped countertops crowded with too many appliances. There's the rice maker that works and the rice maker that doesn't work, which Mom keeps saying she is going to return as soon as she finds the warranty, but I know she never will so I now call it her emotional support rice maker. The apartment itself is extremely generic, everything from the carpet to the bathroom tile is the same vague color that can't decide if it's cream or sand. According to Mom, that's what builders do, so as to not put off renters and buyers. *People want to make their homes their own*, she told me once, looking up from her real estate textbook at the kitchen table, *they want a blank slate*. It's weird to think about all the people who used to live here and who will live here after we are gone. For now, Mom has made this home her own by covering the walls in wooden crosses and the refrigerator with magnets and pieces of paper to remind her to do things that she will forget to do. There are layers and layers of bills and envelopes and notes to herself. Peeling back the pages of fridge archaeology, you can find invitations to weddings from five years ago from couples who are now divorced.

I'd hoped she'd be long gone before I have to leave for detention, but alas, Mom is still here, and in fact, has fallen asleep standing up in front of the coffee maker. It burbles ineffectually—it's on its last leg—and I give it a good smack to get it going again.

Mom startles, her hand going to her heart.

"Ay naku," she says. "You scared me."

She's freshly showered after her night shift at the hospital and changed from the scrubs she left the apartment wearing last night into a wrap dress and a blazer.

I pour coffee first into her travel mug, and then into mine. "What kind of psychos want to look at a house this early in the morning?"

"Psychos who want to buy it, hopefully," she says.

Mom just got her real estate license a few months ago, and this would be her first sale. The market's not so great right now. That's what Esmé's mom says anyway. After many painful hours of me trying and failing to teach Mom to use Excel—*Luz, help, all the numbers went crazy again!*—we figured out there is an actually depressing number of sales needed before she could actually let her job at the hospital go, for good, as planned. But she doesn't seem deterred by that.

Nothing deters her, really. Not Dad leaving us in the tepid, half-assed way that he did, leaving but not really leaving, as in, Mom legally changed our last names to hers but we still see him, sometimes, whenever he feels like it, whenever he feels like being a dad, or at least looking like one. Not losing the house where me and Ali grew up, not the period of time when she was living out of her car before saving up enough for the deposit plus first and last month's rent on this place, not Dad marrying his basically-a-child bride, calling Mom to tell her about the wedding plans after not seeing us for months, *I'd love to involve the girls in the ceremony*, nothing. Undeterred, she just laughed and said, *of course.*

Mom projects a kind of relentless optimism. That's why she's got this Maxxinista blazer look going on today, like she's trying to be on HGTV or something, and when I see it, I want to scream out the window, *that's my mom, she tries so hard,* and also, simultaneously, I want to scream in her face, *what are you doing?*, because it all seems so tenuous, so far-fetched that any of this is going to pan out. I don't do either thing. I don't scream at all. I just run the formulas in Excel and edit her résumé and help her with her taxes and pump her up before she leaves to try to make a sale.

"Always be closing," I say, saluting her.

"What?" she blinks.

"*Glengarry Glen Ross?*"

No recognition crosses her face, so it must be one of those American movies that she hasn't seen. She's seen a lot of them, of course, but not everything. She used to get really irritated when Dad looked at her incredulously and asked her *how it could be possible* that she hadn't seen this movie or that movie, or hadn't heard of this band or that band, which was simply dumb of him because it's not like he'd ever seen or heard of *any* of her references. And he never asked about them and that's his loss because he's really missing out. But then again, Dad thinks the U.S. is the center of the universe. Just like him.

"It's a movie about *real estate agents*," I say. "I thought you said that was a reputable school you attended, Mother, I can't believe this important text wasn't on the syllabus."

She rolls her eyes. "Must have been sick that day."

"Well, it's playing at the Sunshine this week."

Mom reaches into the fridge for her disgusting coffee creamer that tastes like chemical Christmas. "I hope you girls aren't still terrorizing the poor old man."

"I don't know what you mean," I say, blinking innocently.

She sighs, leaning against the counter, looking exhausted. She swallows a big gulp of coffee and then points with her lips at a big pile of mail on the table.

"It came," she says.

My heart drops at the sight of the sparkly pink envelope resting at the top of the pile.

"Do we *have* to go?" I ask.

She clicks her tongue and furrows her brow. "Palagi na lang, of *course* we have to go. Why can't you at least act like you're excited to see your family and celebrate your cousin?"

"Yeah, monumental accomplishment," I say. "Maricel's turning eighteen. How special. Let's have a ball about it."

Ali appears at the edge of the kitchen, yawning, in her pjs. Her straight black hair is piled on top of her head in a messy bun.

"What's going on?" she asks sleepily.

Crouton, our tuxedo cat, pads into the room silently following behind her, her ears perked and curious. Crouton is the name she came with from the shelter and it's a horrible name for a cat but it felt wrong to change it.

"We got the invitation for Maricel's debut!" Mom says.

"Alert the media," I say.

"Oh!" Ali says, lighting up and leaping for the envelope. "Can I open it?"

"Of course, baby," Mom says.

Ali rips the bright pink paper with gusto, and a burst of pink glitter falls out onto the kitchen floor.

"ARE YOU SERIOUS?" I ask, recoiling at the glitter bomb. "THAT SHOULD BE ILLEGAL."

Crouton bolts out of the room, terrified. Crouton is scared of everything.

My mom smacks my arm and shoves past me in order to read the invitation over Ali's shoulder. She puts an arm around her and their heads tilt gently toward each other as they admire the piece of cardstock in front of them like it's the *Mona Lisa*.

"Wow," Mom whispers, almost to herself. "Tingnan mo ang ganda niya."

Look how beautiful she is, or something like that. Me and Ali can't speak Tagalog, but I know enough to know that mom is always calling *somebody* ganda-ganda, and it's never me.

Ali holds out the invitation to me, and I gingerly take it by the corner.

"You don't have to make your face like that," Mom says.

"Like what?"

"Like you're smelling a dead rat," she says.

"You *do* look like that," Ali snorts. "A lot. It's your dead rat face."

"Dead rat face!" Mom says, laughing and pointing at me.

"Glitter takes *one thousand years* to biodegrade, okay?" I shake the cardstock as the glitter remnants fall to the floor.

YOU ARE CORDIALLY INVITED

TO JOIN CONCEPCIÓN CRUZ DIAZ
& NELSON BAUTISTA DIAZ

IN CELEBRATION OF THEIR DAUGHTER

Maricel Magdelena Rosalia Cruz Diaz

ON THE OCCASION OF HER 18TH BIRTHDAY

Under the text, which is in a loopy font so over-the-top that it's nearly illegible, there's a professional photo of Maricel, her long dark hair tumbling down her shoulders, in a soft white dress, standing on a boardwalk, palm trees and blue ocean softly out of focus behind her. She has a flower in her hair. She looks like Miss America, like María Clara de los Santos, like every other older girl cousin has looked on her debut invitation. Feminine. Perfection.

I flip it over to the back, where we are asked to RSVP with our enthusiastic attendance or deepest regrets, and I briefly wonder what kind of confusion would ensue on the family WhatsApp group if I sent it back with both boxes checked—because I already know I will be forced to attend and yet I will also deeply regret my attendance.

My shoulders tighten as I try not to crumple the thing up in my hands.

"Can I bring Esmé?" I blurt out. *As my emotional support plus-one.*

Her being there is the only way I'll be able to survive *yet another* endlessly long debut program—the welcoming remarks, the prayer, the dinner, the titas gossiping, talking shit to your face while pretending they're just being nice, the Eighteen Roses ceremony, the Eighteen Candles ceremony, the toasts, more toasts, more praying, the crying, the gushing, the sparkly dresses, the father-daughter dance—it's all so excruciating and even though it's the last one I'll have to attend because after Maricel's debut is over we're finally, *finally* out of cousins turning eighteen, that somehow makes it harder, like why can't it just be *over* already?

I'm seventeen now, but I'm obviously not having one. If Ali wants a debut when she turns eighteen, at least it will be on our home turf, and we won't have to drive all the way across Death Valley just to get there, only to arrive all sweaty and dusty, just for me and Ali to get laughed at by the snotty California cousins for not having cars and not knowing what a dance crew is or never having tried In-N-Out before. Whatever. Blake's Lotaburger is better.

Green chile anything > Animal Style fries.

"Would her parents be okay with her coming?" Mom asks.

"*Yes*, Mommy," I snap. "I'm sure Esmé's parents are fine with her going to a *family birthday party.*"

Mom clicks her tongue. "Well, it would mean staying overnight."

"In terrifying, crime-ridden San Diego! Oh no!"

She shakes her head at me and clicks her tongue again, wanting to reprimand me for talking back, for always talking back, but too tired to do so, taking the invitation from me and avoiding my gaze as she magnetizes it to the fridge, its top layer currently comprised of debut invitations and debut save the dates and last year's Christmas cards from our family in California, lots of smiling brown faces in matching pajamas and Santa hats.

I know that if the reverse were on the table, and Esmé's family was taking a road trip for a Fiesta de Quince Años in California with a bunch of family that Mom had never met, there's no way she'd let me go, even though she's close friends with Esmé's parents. It's just that, for my mom, there's a far greater chance of bad things happening in this world than good. Basically, she's seen some shit in her life, especially pulling graveyard shifts in the ER. And when she's seen something new, some new horror, some new possible fate for me or Ali that she hadn't yet considered, and I wake up in the morning and she's not in the apartment and I look out the window and I see that she's leaning on the hood of her car down in the parking lot, smoking, staring at the sun as it comes up over the mountains, well, I know there's probably one less normal teenage thing we will be allowed to do going forward because she saw what she saw and she can't unsee it.

Mom's constant, palpable anxiety fills me with shame and rage almost simultaneously. Yes, I'm acting like an asshole. No, my cousin Maricel would never, never talk back, would *never* speak to her mother like this, and neither would Shaira or Shaylene or any other of my perfect cousins whose perfect debuts I was forced to sit through, even after what happened at Cecelia's debut when I was ten, which we strictly *do not talk about*. Even so, I'm so obviously dreading this, and I don't understand how Mom couldn't see that.

"Please, Mommy," I say.

Right then, her phone rings. She snatches it from the counter.

"It's your lola," she says. "*Don't* mention the debut. And also, she thinks I already sold a house. Okay?"

After a stunned moment of processing, Ali and I exchange a baffled look.

Lola is the guest of honor at every family event, with every tito, tita, kuya, and até pulling out chairs for her and fixing her plates as she waves them away in order to dance with all the little kids, swinging them around and letting them climb all over her. Why wouldn't we mention the debut to her?

And what's this about selling a house already? Why would Lola think she'd already done that?

Mom answers the video call before we can ask any follow-up questions.

"Nanay, kamusta po?"

"Magandang umaga, Ren," Lola says in her gravelly voice. "Are the girls there?"

"Yes, but they just woke up, po—"

I take the phone from my mom before she can stop us from talking to Lola just because Ali hasn't brushed her hair yet and because I don't plan on brushing mine at all. Lola doesn't care about stuff like that. She's cool.

"Hi, Lola," me and Ali say simultaneously. "Kamusta po?"

Lola's short, thick hair is black-from-a-box-black, and she's wearing a T-shirt that says Gucci, but the font is a little off.

We talk to Lola on video call pretty regularly, and Mom does almost every day, sometimes on her break at the hospital when it's daytime there and nighttime here. These days, Lola is really into mahjong, but only when my titos can get her to take a break from working on my Tito Nando's coconut farm or at my Tito Choy's sari-sari store. She's about that age where everyone's trying to convince her to stop but she just won't. She says she never will. She's *that* Lola. Snaps the heads off shrimps and sucks out the brains and eyeballs Lola, *that's where the good stuff is, apo.* Sews dresses for Ali from nothing Lola. Manifests meals when the cupboard had only three things in it Lola.

Lola lived with us for a while, almost a year, when Mom and Dad split up and Mom first got this apartment. She brought us a karaoke machine for the living room that plugs into the TV, the kind that gives you a score at the end, and they sang duets and we made up dances to all their favorites, and we all went crazy when they got a one hundred, a perfect score, and it felt like that one hundred belonged to all of us because we were all so in sync. They taught us to love songs like "Halik" by Aegis, "Ang Huling El Bimbo" by the Eraserheads, and "Guhit ng Palad" by Verni Gonzalez.

But Mom and Lola fought all the time, because Lola was lonely here—she was used to big family parties, to titas dropping by unannounced, to somebody handing you a baby to hold for a minute while somebody else tells you the really good tsismis. We knew she wasn't happy, so Ali and I practiced and practiced "Ang Huling El Bimbo" by the Eraserheads with special choreography to surprise her with our performance on her birthday. But then she and my mom shut themselves into their room, because they were fighting, and so Ali and I sat on the couch with the song queued up, ready for them to come out, ready to change everything with our dance, but they never did, and we fell asleep there in the glow of the TV screen.

Eventually she went to live with Tita Concepción, Maricel's mom, called Connie, in San Diego before going back to Cavite for good to live with Mom's oldest brother, our Tito Ferdinand. She said he needed her help with the little kids. And there were still trees down from the last typhoon to clean up. And the roof was blown off. And it was time to go. She's been living with Tito Nando since then.

Tito Nando is Tito Ferdinand. Keeping track of my

millions of titos and titas and cousins is made harder by the fact that everybody has at least two names and sometimes they make sense like Tita Concepción, called Connie, and sometimes they make no sense, but that doesn't stop Mom from yelling at us for asking who the heck she's talking about when she started talking about Tita Cecil and all of a sudden she's talking about Tita Weng and how are we supposed to know they are the same person, when we've never even met any of the family who lives in the Philippines, besides Lola?

Mom has not returned home to the Philippines since she left it. Meaning me and Ali have never been there. She keeps saying she wants to go, and take us, *soon*. For a long time, it was *not until you guys are bigger* and then it was *not until Ali proves she can eat shrimp with the heads on*, still pending, then it was *not until I get my real estate license*, and lately it's been *not until I sell a house* and now it's *not until I sell enough houses to quit the hospital.*

Maybe this new lie about selling a house already when she hasn't yet means she wants to plan a trip to go see Lola? Mom lies a lot. It's almost a compulsion with her, actually. Mostly she lies to protect other people's feelings— *your dad called, he said happy birthday!*—and sometimes to save face with the California family—*Luz is so busy with her studies, we just can't make it this year*—but I've *never* heard her lie to Lola, directly, and to implicate me and Ali in the lie seems even weirder.

I try to make eye contact with Mom to figure her out but she is laser-focused on Ali, who is still talking to Lola.

"Ali, when is your next race on the track?" Lola asks.

"Next week, it's at another school in—"

"Nanay," Mom says, taking her phone back. In Tagalog, she says, *something something* Western Union. So, *something something* about money. It's always *something something* about money.

"Yes, thank you for the money, Ren," Lola says. "Girls, your Mommy is a fancy-fancy top-notch Realtor now, di ba?"

Ali laughs nervously and glances at me. She'd fold so quickly under questioning, it's scary.

"Apparently!" I say.

My mom shoots me a death glare.

"Sorry, Lola," I say. "I have to get to school, po. Love you."

"Wait," Mom says, her head snapping to me. She drops her voice low and hands the phone over to Ali. "Why are you going to school so early?"

Mom follows me to the front door as Ali walks away with the phone, resuming the thrilling conversation with Lola about her upcoming track meet against the famous Portales High School Rams.

Mom looks like she doesn't want Ali to talk to Lola without her, but she also doesn't want to let me go without an explanation. I pull on my backpack. One of the straps is being held together by duct tape, and I close my fist over it so that Mom doesn't see it and burst a blood vessel in her eye. It's happened. *People are going to think we're poor!*

"I joined a club at school," I say.

"You did *what*?" she asks.

She doesn't have to react *that* strongly.

"Yeah, it's really cool, our mission is to sit silently in a classroom and reflect on our decisions and their impact on other people."

"You got detention," she says.

"Yes, I did."

"*Why*, Luz? In the first week! Of your senior year."

"Why are *you* lying to Lola about selling a house?" I whisper. "And why can't we talk about Maricel's debut?"

She squeezes the bridge of her nose like she's getting a migraine.

Her wedding ring is still there, on her hand. She says people respect married women more so she keeps it on. She told me once that when she was a kid she used to pinch her nose like that twenty times a day because she hated how flat it was. When she pinches it even now, I want to push her hand away. She is so beautiful that I wish I looked more like her, but Ali is the one who is her twin, down to the identical beauty mark on their round cheeks. And, more and more every day, I look like Dad. Which is just—whatever.

"Do you need me to drive you?" she asks, ignoring my insolent questions.

A car horn blares outside.

"Nope," I say. "I'm good. Got a ride."

She glances nervously at Ali, who is still talking to Lola. I see an opening.

"And so it's okay?" I ask. "To invite Esmé to the debut?"

"What?" she asks, distracted. "Oh. Sure."

Before she can change her mind, I'm sticking my feet

into my sneakers by the front door and raising my travel mug to toast her.

"Coffee's for closers, Mom. Remember that."

"Wait, are you wearing *that* to school—?!"

I slam the door and run down the stairs to meet Esmé.

3

MY MOM SAYS IT ANNOYS HER WHEN SHE SEES COUPLES sitting on the same side of the booth in restaurants, and that's exactly how Esmé and I sit in the school cafeteria, where we talk over the cacophony of a hundred conversations echoing and crashing into one another between attempts to shove food into our mouths and feel human in the twenty minutes before our next scheduled *learning module*. It's nearly unbearable to know that on top of all this, the desert sun outside is pouring its warm, abundant light onto everyone lucky enough to not be trapped inside a concrete box with no windows, like we are.

We keep our backs to the wall, at the corner table, with all our shit strewn out in front of us to claim space for our Pinay/Chicana coalition of two. And how else could we fully survey the panorama of human misery on display during B Lunch? Not that the A Lunch crowd is any better—by now, Esmé and I know pretty much everybody, unfortunately, and there's not exactly anybody worth knowing.

Except her.

"Dude, I forgot to tell you," Esmé says. "A *bird* got in the house last night. Dad finally trapped it with a broom he duct-taped to a pasta strainer."

"Oh my God, *gross*. I hate birds."

"I know you do."

"It's just like, why don't they have hands?"

She snorts into her water bottle.

"Did you throw away that pasta strainer?" I ask. "Or burn it?"

"Please. You know Linda never throws anything away."

"Well, I had a thrilling evening, too. I watched *The First Wives Club* again," I say.

"I swear, at heart you are a forty-something divorceé who lives in New York," she says. "You're obsessed."

"With *revenge*!" I say, pressing my empty Tupperware closed. I've inhaled my tortang talong and rice in record time.

"And how was detention this morning?" she asks.

"I've fully reckoned with the consequences of my actions and I'll be a menace to society no more." I bump my shoulder into hers. "Thanks for driving me."

"It was just nice to beat the traffic," she says, her eyes smiling from behind the wire-frame glasses resting on her round cheeks.

She has such a cute face, my mom always says. *And she looks Filipina to me.*

Meanwhile, Esmé's mom says I look like a Mexican telenovela villain.

I'm telling you, Bombilla—Linda's nickname for me, it means light bulb—*you look exactly like this actress in a telenovela I used to watch with my mom. She was awful. Man, we loved hating her.*

"I've been thinking a lot about Fanny Brice," I say.

"Did you notice my homage?" she says.

She blinks exaggeratedly to emphasize the Fanny Brice–style eyeliner that I knew she would attempt and inevitably pull off flawlessly.

"Hello, Gorgeous," I say. "But why do you think it was that she was such, like, a *funny girl*? Like, was it *because* her mother didn't think she could be an actress? So she felt like she had to do it to prove her wrong?"

"I think it was probably because she was a Leo," Esmé says.

"Okay, don't look now," I say. "But Ethan is literally splitting a string cheese in half, like, lengthwise, into a stringier string, and, *oh God*, now he's giving half to Cat Iwamoto."

Things are just funnier when I'm telling them to Esmé.

"Jesus Christ," I continue. "Now she's *eating* the string cheese. Don't look. It's just so . . . stringy. And his fingers were all in it. There's something about this that's shaking me to my very core. Are you shaken?"

Esmé is shuffling her deck of Tarot cards, the ones where all the major arcana are depicted as Simpsons characters, so she's not even looking.

"Is it Libertarian Ethan or Cool Ethan?" she asks.

"Libertarian Ethan," I say. "Who the hell is *Cool* Ethan?"

"Ethan Montoya."

"What?!" I ask, shocked at this suggestion. "Do you not remember that time he asked Mr. Neuser what NPR was?"

Esmé lowers the lids of her wing-tipped eyes at me.

"Because *listening to NPR* is cool now?"

I snort. "Fine, not cool, but my point is, he's an idiot. Just like Libertarian Ethan."

Just like everyone.

Esmé's many bracelets jingle softly as the cards pass beneath her palms. She doesn't comment one way or another on my assessment of Ethan Montoya, or on my silent assessment of everyone else, and since she's kind of psychic I'm certain that she knows I made it.

Shuffle. Shuffle.

"Okay, so I have a favor to ask," I say, shifting the conversation away from the tableau of morons in front of us. "And I will literally die if you say no."

"It will be my absolute pleasure to be your escort to your cousin's coming-out party," she says.

"How did you know?"

"Because you've had *two* nightmares about Maricel's debut since you received the save the date."

"Three. But it's not likely that I'll *actually* vomit rose gold glitter everywhere or grow scissors for hands like Edward Scissorhands, go berserk and shred the balloon arch during the grand entrance, or whatever I did in the third nightmare that I can't remember, the one where I just woke up with a vague sense of dread around the *conceptual idea* of a debutante ball. So we're probably good."

"Probably. And, I've never been to San Diego!"

"Well, it is the Paris of Southern California," I say.

Chuckling, Esmé fans out the cards in front of her in an arc.

Thank God she's coming with me.

"Okay, I'm ready," she says, squaring her shoulders. "Let me pull a card for you."

I swallow. To be honest, I'm a little afraid of Esmé and her powers.

"Fine."

Her black nail polish glints in the fluorescent lighting as she draws out my card, flips it around to show it to me.

"Aha," she says. "The Fool."

"Rude."

Esmé contemplates the card in her hand. Her eyebrows come together.

"Not necessarily."

"How is that not rude?" I ask.

She slides the card, face up, across the table toward me. The character depicted on the card is Homer Simpson, dressed like a medieval court jester, strutting jauntily, as if on his way to ruin Marge's life yet again, with a placid, dopey grin on his face.

"The Fool," Esmé begins, with an eerie air of authority gathering around her, like a storm cloud, "is the first card in the major arcana. It's number zero. This card represents a new beginning and, necessarily, the end to something in your old life."

"Well, that's not ominous at all—!"

"Hey, Até?"

I jump, startled by my sister, who has appeared at the edge of our table, a blue and gold ribbon tied into her high ponytail. She is flanked by a group of other high ponytails with ribbons. Blue and gold are our school colors, all the metal surfaces of our campus are shellacked with chipped, sky-blue paint, muted gold thread fraying at the edges of white jerseys.

Ali smiles at me, the smile of someone who believes she will be taken care of, and always is. It's a little sister's smile that makes me want to shove her away and hug her close to me all at once because yes, Mom takes care of her and I take care of her, but the world won't, and I know it.

Ali wants to have a debut. And debuts are extremely expensive. It's like a wedding. And Mom would never ask Dad for help with it. She's stubborn about not needing him anymore. Let her sell a few houses, save up some money, and quit the hospital, and maybe she'll be able to save enough for Ali's debut. Ali *loves* shopping for clothes, and she'd have no problem pulling together *eighteen* friends who are willing to wear matching formal outfits and spend *weeks* orchestrating a dance routine after school, with her at the center, in a ridiculous ball gown. She's made for this kind of thing. Some people are. And some people aren't.

"What's up?" I ask, not making eye contact with any of the Ponytails, because I feel it's best to maintain dominance by feigning indifference to any of Ali's friends.

I know she won't say anything about what happened this morning. We'll debrief later when we get home, dissecting every possible theory of Mom's latest weirdness, but she never talks about anything like that in front of her friends.

She slides in next to me, breaking the invisible barrier around our table. Somehow she smells like home, I can't explain how. Maybe it's our shampoo. And the hardness around me begins to melt. The school-version of me flickers in and out as the older-sister-version of me comes into focus.

"Can you sign this for me?" she asks, pulling out a permission slip from her backpack. "Mom forgot to."

I roll my eyes. It's for that track meet in Portales next week, and there's an associated fee for the trip. It's fake anyway, so Ali should just sign it, but she's such a terrible liar that her attempts at Mom's signature looks like they're sweating and trying way too hard, so she always asks me to do it.

"Did you already pay?" I ask, clicking my pen and scrawling out Mom's signature on the line for *parent/guardian*, as I have hundreds of times before.

"No," she says.

"Here." I open my wallet and give her the money, which Mom had given me to run some errands later—we need vinegar for cleaning and vinegar for cooking and a phone charging cable because Crouton bit through another one. One day we figure she'll get a real good shock and stop but until then she's just chomping cables like candy.

Ali tucks it into the little white envelope stapled to the permission slip.

"Thank you!" she says. "Esmé, that's such a pretty lip color on you."

Esmé has all these like potions and tools and steps to her skin care and makeup routine that all need to go in a certain order. Ali puts makeup on every day before school, too, hogging the bathroom mirror for upwards of an hour, but with Esmé it's more in line with her whole witchy aesthetic, so it's cooler.

"Thanks, Al," Esmé says. "Want me to do a reading for you real quick?"

"Actually," Ali says, sitting up a little straighter. "There was something we wanted to ask you."

She glances at the Ponytails. One of them clears her throat.

"We're doing a fundraiser for the team," Ali continues, leaning forward. "And we wondered if you could help out. Esmé, maybe you could do a tarot reading booth? Or donate a makeup consultation or something?"

Esmé glances at me.

The Ponytails collectively shift their weight from one foot to the other.

"And Lucia, you could do . . . something," Ali says. "We need someone to—"

"No thanks," I say. "We have plans."

Esmé reshuffles her card deck.

"But I didn't say what day it was."

"We always have plans," I say. "And they do not include school functions."

Ali leans her head on my shoulder, a puff of that shampoo smell envelopes me.

"Come on," she says.

I take a sip of my soda and remain silent for so long that the Ponytails begin to shuffle their feet.

Dominance successfully asserted. School-version of me reestablished.

"Okay," Ali says, shrugging. She's smiling, light, like always. She's fine. She doesn't need me. "Let me know if you change your mind! See you at home."

Esmé taps her deck gently against the table as I watch Ali and her friends cross the cafeteria, back over to their side, ponytails swishing.

See you at home, she'd said. Now I'm trying to remember which day it is, and whether we're supposed to go to Dad's or Mom's.

We're almost always at Mom's, so the going-to-Dad's days sneak up on me in this incredibly jarring way. I feel that tug in my chest again, *I want to go home*, but again, where is that? When I'm at Dad's, I want to be at Mom's, when I'm at Mom's, I don't want to be at Dad's, exactly, but I have this feeling like I'm supposed to be somewhere else, that I forgot something over there, maybe, or forgot that I'm supposed to be somewhere else entirely, that someone is waiting on me there.

We use Dad's address to go to this school, producing two pieces of mail bearing his name on registration day in August. An electric bill and his subscription to the *Economist* magazine. He lives with his new wife of two years. Another Filipina. And even though that's just so predictable, fucking textbook, it's embarrassing anyway. A white guy marrying a Filipina woman is one thing, but then divorcing her and marrying a second, much younger one is another, deeply mortifying, thing. On their wedding day Mom looked like she was made of glass, she dropped us off at the church with a smile on her face with so many cracks in it I wanted to run straight inside and set it all on fire.

Dad's wife's name is Sunny, and she's *so* young that Esmé's older sister went to school with her, and, worst of all, she's pregnant.

"What's going on in there?" Esmé asks, tapping against her temple with her forefinger.

"It's Wednesday, right?" I ask.

"Yup."

"Great."

Esmé studies me and I flinch. I hate to be studied, and

she knows it. She's the one who told me all about how much Scorpio is in my chart and all that. But if I'm some kind of scorpion, keeping my secrets guarded, then Esmé has managed to sneak in close to me, too close to be stung, my tail can't reach her. I have to use other defenses.

"That really *is* a pretty lip color on you. What's it called?" I ask.

"Would it be so bad?" she asks, and when I look confused, she continues. "Helping out Ali with this track thing?"

"Don't worry," I say. "She has lots and lots of friends— you know, other minors who she can ask for the free labor made necessary by the systematic defunding of public education in this great country in which we are so *blessed* to reside."

"Lucia . . ." Esmé wraps one of her stray curls around her index finger.

I don't get it—does she *really* want to waste our precious after-school hours hanging around with the sophomore Ponytails? Does she feel bad for my sister or something? Like I said, Ali has a million friends. She's over for dinner at their houses all the time. Everybody's parents love her. She's sweet, she's perfect, she's going to get a track scholarship because apparently running in a circle is something people care about, so Mom's not even worried about her college or anything. Ali is fine.

"After school we need to go see Mr. Marco at the Sunshine," I say, reminding her. "We're single-handedly keeping that shithole of his afloat."

"I just think—"

I grab Esmé by the arm and she stills. A perfect opportunity to finally change the subject has presented itself.

Jason Woods is walking across the cafeteria.

"Be still my heart," I whisper. "Hot Silent Sophomore is wearing a *new* cardigan!"

Esmé removes her glasses for the sole purpose of putting them back on.

She has a true flair for physical comedy.

Jason Woods, despite being a sophomore, is in all our senior classes. He's tall, Black, with soft brown eyes, and dresses extremely well. He's quiet in class, which only adds to the general mystique he's already established by being an apparent genius as well as the best dressed person we've ever spotted in real life.

"Where *does* he acquire these dapper threads?" Esmé asks, letting out a soft, low whistle as we watch him disappear into the crowd, until we can't see his oversize headphones or his new cardigan or his warm brown skin anymore, just the occasional pop of crisp white sneakers against sad yellow linoleum. Hands in his pockets. Head held high.

He's too cool for this school.

"Let's roll," I say, and we fall out.

We have history with Hot Silent Sophomore fourth period, and we like to lurk outside the classroom, making up a whole backstory for his life before the late bell rings. It's not like he leaves us much of a choice, being so painfully cute and so painfully silent, and all. We did the same thing last year with this gorgeous girl that Esmé had a crush on, Ashlee Ortega—we imagined that she was an aspiring tattoo artist because she always drew all over on her arms in Pre-Calc, these really interesting geometric designs that looked kind of like flowers but also kind of like dodecahedrons, we called her Hot Senior Tattoo Artist—we're not that creative with nicknames—but then she graduated, and left the position open.

And then there was Jason.

"Maybe he moved here from Australia and he's cultivating an air of mystery so as to protect his true and gentle nature," Esmé whispers as we stare at him through the tiny glass window in the door of Room 402.

"RIP Heath," I say.

We are sad momentarily as we briefly discuss asking Mr. Marco to screen *Ten Things I Hate About You* again, but then our cackling ramps back up and it must get too loud or maybe the Hot Silent Sophomore has a sixth sense that we're talking about him because he looks up and I squeak, pulling Esmé out of view while she continues to chortle like a perverted auntie.

"Yo, what did I miss?"

My muscles tense at the sound of the familiar, grating voice. Noah Bradford, annoying white guy with a man bun, *always* raises his hand when Mr. Neuser asks for questions, but it's *definitely* more of a comment than a question. Grinning his ass off for no reason, like always.

I pull my arm more tightly around Esmé's shoulders.

"Um, that day in kindergarten when we covered personal space?"

Noah laughs—but then again, he laughs easily—and pushes backwards into the classroom with his hand over his heart.

"Go ahead and drag me, then, Cruz."

"I—"

"Leave him be, Lucia." Esmé grabs my arm before I can finish forming my thought.

Damn, and I almost had something, too, something funny.

Something cutting.

Noah disappears into the classroom, shaking his head in this good-natured way that pisses me off even more. I *hate* Noah Bradford. I hate this false familiarity he forces with me and everyone else, including teachers, who he insists on basically interviewing at the beginning of each class as if we've tuned in to his podcast or something. I hate how he moves through the halls, talking loudly and clapping people on the back like he's the main character of a show called *High School*.

I'll think of it quickly enough one day—the thing I'll say that will wipe that smirk right off his face. Somebody needs to knock that guy down several pegs. And I want it to be me.

4

MY MOM AND ESMÉ'S MOM TAKE US TO CORONADO
Mall to buy clothes for Maricel's debut while Ali's at track
practice. They are so excited, it's adorable.

When we walk inside, our faces are blasted with air-
conditioning, and Esmé's mom steers us toward the boba
tea place.

"First things first, because I know you're going to ask,"
she says.

"Thank you, Mami!" Esmé says, linking arms with her.

They are cute, Esmé and her mom, Mrs. Mares, or
Linda, as we call her when she isn't there. They are exactly
the same height. I'm taller than my mom, which feels
incredibly weird, and Ali is taller than me.

Linda recently became a CPA. *Good for her*, Mom
said when she heard the news. *Good for her*, she said
again, and turned with renewed energy to her laptop,
where she was composing her latest real estate listing.
That night, as I was drifting off to sleep on the couch,
she called me over to double-check her grammar. *Baby?
Should it be "best house* on *the block" or "best house* in
the block"?

At the mall, Mom always gets taro root tea with extra
boba, Esmé gets almond tea with regular boba, and her
mom gets passion fruit tea with no boba.

"Just don't order me one with the little balls!" she says, as she and my mom leave us in line for the register to go look at some sunglasses at Sunglass Hut.

"Okay, Mami, no balls!" Esmé calls back to her, extra loud so that it reverberates against the glass and metal cavern that is the mall.

We dissolve into giggles and Esmé's mom rolls her eyes, smiling, and my mom barks out a laugh before grabbing her arm and repeating, breathlessly, "No balls!"

I love that our moms are friends because Esmé's mom always gets my mom to chill the fuck out and laugh like that. They start putting sunglasses on each other and snapping pictures on their phones and doing cringey poses.

"New profile pic!" I say, watching.

"Sunday fun day!" Esmé says. "They're so sweet, just look at them."

"I know, they grow up so fast."

The line for the boba tea kiosk moves quickly as colorful drinks appear along the counter next to a big glass jar full of large rainbow straws encased in thin, crinkly plastic. The mall is crowded today. There's always the unsettling probability of seeing someone we know from school on days like this. I've already had three Man Bun jump scares. Will I ever know peace?

"So, I got some intel from Jessa Jimenez," Esmé says, "that the Hot Silent Sophomore is going to be at the theater kids party next weekend."

I wrinkle up my nose. "So?"

Esmé crosses her arms and tilts her head toward me.

"Soooo, I was thinking we could go. And see if, you know, he's still hot and silent, in a party scenario."

"But what if he's not? What if he's really loud and annoying and therefore no longer hot in a party scenario?"

"Well, then we'd know."

"What if it's better *not* to know?"

Esmé laughs. "Philosophical."

"If the Hot Silent Sophomore is loud and annoying at a party, but we're not *there* to hear it, is he actually loud and annoying?"

"A Treatise Concerning the Principles of Hotness."

The line moves again. Our moms are buying sunglasses now at Sunglass Hut. Esmé's mom is trying to pay for them and my mom is smacking her hand away. Esmé glances at the boba tea register in front of us. Just three people between us and boba.

"But what if he's cool and not annoying at all?" Esmé presses on. "What if he's nice and funny? We already know he's smart. He's in all our AP classes."

"There are dumb people in our AP classes, too," I correct her.

"You think everyone is dumb."

I can't think of anything funny to say to that, because it's basically and fundamentally true, so I just shrug.

Only two people between us and boba.

"Jessa said," Esmé continues, "if I came I could talk to her about the costumes they're doing for the fall play. I saw a flyer she posted and they look *insane*. Do you think they somehow rented them from Off-Broadway Vintage

Clothing and Costumes? Because they look really high quality—"

"Maybe!" I say. I don't really care about Jessa Jimenez or the theater kids or where they get their costumes from. "But this weekend, Mr. Marco is screening *Clueless*. That's like your favorite movie."

One person between us and boba.

"Well, yeah," she says. "But we've seen it a million times."

"Never in the *theater*!" I say. "Never in *surround sound*."

Esmé bites her lip.

"Oh my God," I say. "We could go in costume!"

That *has* to win her over. It just has to. I can't go to some stupid party with stupid Jessa Jimenez. She sings the national anthem at assemblies with just, like, too much enthusiasm, like it's the Super Bowl or something, and all her theater friends are just *so* invested in who gets a call-back to play Peasant Number Two or whatever, like it's life or death, and I just can't.

Our turn to order boba.

"What can I get you?" the worker asks.

I give the order just as our moms are coming back over. Esmé's mom deftly places a pair of sunglasses on my face before swooping in front of me to pay before I can even get my wallet ready.

"Come on," I say to Esmé. "Let's. Do. A. Makeover."

She laughs. "Those are *really cool* sunglasses."

"You don't understand. This is an *Alaïa*. It's like a totally important designer."

My mom grabs our drinks from the counter and hands them to us.

"Cher's main thrill in life *is* a makeover," Esmé says, tapping her boba tea to mine, and by quoting *Clueless* back to me, I know she's agreeing to go to the Sunshine's screening this weekend, instead of the stupid theater kids party, and so I can finally relax.

"It gives her a sense of control . . . ," Mrs. Mares says.

". . . in a world full of chaos," my mom says.

We stare at them in disbelief.

"What?" my mom says. "That's *our* movie."

"We like, *invented* you, you know?" Esmé's mom says.

Our moms link arms and walk away from us, howling with laughter.

"I don't know how to feel," Esmé says.

I'm just relieved that the party at Jessa Jimenez's is no longer under discussion.

"So when I said we should go in costume as characters from *Clueless*," I say, "I meant as Travis and Christian."

"I know. The hair will be a challenge for me."

"Fedora?" I suggest.

"Ooh, perfect."

She links arms with me and we follow our moms into Macy's where we won't like anything they buy for us but they'll be happy *and that's what matters*, I tell myself.

"I'm not coming out."

This dress makes me feel like a sausage link in its casing.

"*Anak*," my mom whines loudly, her perfectly mani-cured toes visible from beneath the dressing room door.

"Let us see, Bombilla!" Linda says.

I peel the sausage casing from myself and shudder at the sight of the other dresses piled in the corner, a jum-ble of frills and animal print. The dressing room mirror is smudged. *Shoplifters will be prosecuted*, it warns in a cheerful font.

It's not that I don't *like* my body. Which is what Mom thinks. *Why are you hiding in those big clothes*, she always says when she sees me leaving for school. It's not that I'm hiding my specific body. It's just weird that I have a body at all. I wish I didn't have to be *perceived* as having a body.

I examine another one of the dresses that my mom has selected for me to wear to Maricel's debut. It's loud, with cutouts, so many cutouts that I'm not sure how it's sup-posed to go on. I already know it will be a sensory night-mare against my skin.

I don't want it touching me.

"Esmé," I say.

"Give it here," she says, and I toss it over into her stall.

"Anak, you have to at least try!" Mom says.

I am trying! I want to scream. I press the heels of my hands into my eye sockets and inhale deeply.

"This is cute!" Esmé says.

The dressing room structure rattles as she opens her door to model the cutout dress for our moms. I watch her sneak-ers, catwalking between them, beneath the door.

She gives a little spin.

"I love it, Esmío," Linda says.

That's what Linda calls her.

"Luz," my mom says, rapping her knuckle against my dressing room's door. "Should I go get it in another color? Then you two could match!"

"Yeah, sure, Mom, the color was the problem."

"Really?"

"No!"

My mom's phone rings.

"It's your lola," she says.

I pull on my clothes and fling open the door, grabbing my mom's phone from her hands.

"No, wait—" Mom says.

"Help, Lola," I say, answering. "She's making me try on *dresses*."

Mom clucks her tongue and Lola chuckles, her round face filling the screen. She knows me and Mom have irreconcilable fashion differences.

"Dresses? What for, apo?" Lola asks.

I freeze.

I forgot I wasn't supposed to say anything about Maricel's debut. My mom's eyes are screaming at me. Esmé and her mom look at each other.

"I . . ."

I glance at my mom. Her face is unreadable. I can't *lie* to my lola. There's no way. But Mom said I had to.

"Oh, you know how she likes to torture me," I say weakly.

Mom glares at me and snatches her phone back.

"Nanay," she says, dropping her voice low as she turns her back, walking away from us.

"What's going on, Bombilla?" Linda asks me. She glances at my mom's retreating back, knowing her friend well.

"I don't know," I say.

But something is going on, and she won't tell me, but if she won't tell me, then I can't fix it, so I really need her to. Whatever it is, it's worse not knowing.

5

ESMÉ SHUTS HER LOCKER AND TURNS TO ME.

"Maybe she's a drug kingpin."

Another school day is finally over and I'm so tired that I'm leaning against my closed locker with my full weight.

"Look alive, Cruz!" Noah Bradford says as he walks by, smiling and pointing at everyone he passes like he's auditioning for the intro reel on a nineties sitcom.

Eat my shorts, Man Bun, I'd say if we were cast as enemies in one, but I can't muster up the energy to actually reply. I just scowl at him.

He laughs.

I'm too tired for this shit. Maybe I have an iron deficiency or something. Or a brain tumor. I have to stop asking Dr. Internet about these things. Maybe when we get to the Sunshine Mr. Marco will be playing a repeat and I can take a little nap.

"Who's a drug kingpin?" I ask Esmé. "My lola?"

"No. Renalyn," she says. "Maybe the whole real estate thing is a front."

"You think my mom is Walter White?"

Esmé laughs and begins to walk down the hallway. Today she's painted fake freckles all across the bridge of her nose and her cheeks and she's wearing an interestingly sculpted, almost architectural vintage dress she found at some random resale store online for cheap. Cat Iwamoto compliments her on it as we pass her by and Esmé says *thank you* and gives her a little twirl. Esmé always looks amazing, so Cat Iwamoto isn't exactly breaking any new ground here or anything, plus she has no taste at all—she dates Libertarian Ethan and splits a warm string cheese with him every day.

I follow behind Esmé, dragging my feet, as people say hello to her and compliment her without even registering me. I can't wait to get out of here.

"I think I might have a brain tumor," I say loudly.

"You don't have a brain tumor," she says. "And I have a surprise!"

"I hate surprises."

"I know. I got us tickets from Jessa Jimenez to the play."

I stop walking and groan. "No, no, no."

The absolute last thing I want to do at the end of a long day of being around these people is to continue to be around these people.

"Yes!" She grabs me by the arm and shakes me gently from side to side. "Come on, we're young. Let's mix it up. Live a little."

"Now who's acting like a forty-something divorcée in a movie?"

"Luz," she says gravely. "It'll be fun."

It is not going to be fun.

"You didn't tell me Man Bun was in this," I say, waving

the flimsy program in the air as we file into the school auditorium, scanning for seats in the crowd. "They must have been desperate."

"Perhaps he'll disappear into the role," she says. "Due to the magic of the theater."

"I simply cannot suspend my belief that much," I say.

The crowded theater is already too loud and suffocating. I can't believe that this many people turned out for a high school production—of *Glengarry Glen Ross*, of all things. Apparently Mr. Marco is a real influencer in the arts scene.

"*This* was the production you wanted to see the costumes for?" I ask. "It's all boring suits."

"Suiting isn't boring at all," Esmé says. "Oh my God, Luz. Look who's here."

I follow her gaze.

It's Jason Woods.

He's sitting by himself to the left of the stage, studying the play program with intensity in a crisp shirt that fits him unreasonably well.

Esmé grabs my arm. Her eyes light up behind her glasses.

"Let's go sit by him," she says breathlessly.

My mouth goes dry. "No way!"

"Come on, he's all alone!"

"He's always alone. He likes being alone. Silent, and alone."

Esmé drags me down the aisle and I panic because *I can't sit next to Jason! Woods!*, so I bend my knees and dig into the ancient carpeting with my heels.

"Luz!" she says as she struggles to pull my dead weight along.

I stand up suddenly, and she stumbles forward, losing her footing at the sudden change in equilibrium. She lets go of me. At my opening, I maneuver around her and run ahead, shoving Ethan Montoya aside as I go, and I plop down in an empty seat in the row *behind* Jason Woods, not next to him.

Never next to him. That would be insane.

Esmé rolls her eyes and joins me, sinking into her seat with a huff.

I smile at her triumphantly. The lights dim and the curtain opens on the set that looks like it will fall apart if somebody looks at it sideways. In the row in front of us, Jason Woods folds down a corner of his program carefully, as if he will return to this page and read it later. What could possibly be so interesting in it, or anything else that happens in this school, is beyond me.

I complain about the stupid play the entire car ride home.

"High school theater is just so *embarrassing*," I say. "Noah Bradford can't even grow a beard and he's up there talking about putting his kids through college."

"It wasn't *that* bad."

"It was awful! A disgrace! David Mamet is a colossal asshole but even he doesn't deserve for his work to be butchered that badly."

"They *were* a little off on some of the suits," Esmé says, as she brings the car to a stop at a red light. "The time period called for slightly different lapels. I would have put them all in something with a welted breast pocket, at least."

"And why is *this* show in the zeitgeist all of a sudden? A show with a cast of *entirely white men*? Is this really, like, the urgent story of our times?"

"Jessa said she wanted to do it because she was *interested* in toxic masculinity. She was the director. She chose it."

"But Noah Bradford!" I push on. "He couldn't even just stick to the script, he just *had* to ad-lib that dumb joke and ruin the most iconic scene in the whole thing. What a flop. I can't believe it. I bet Jessa was pissed about that."

Esmé drums her fingers against the steering wheel.

"I think I'm going to sign up to do the next play," she says. "I want to do the costumes."

Shit.

"You're kidding."

"Nope," she says, staring straight ahead.

I chew on the inside of my cheek. *Shit.* Shit.

"Well, they desperately need you, I'll give you that," I say.

Esmé puts the radio on.

I don't get it. I just don't. And I'm in the passenger seat, like always, but it's nothing but dead air, and I'm falling down on my job as the in-flight entertainer, and probably more than that, and I know it. But I just don't know what to say so I don't say anything at all.

6

I ASK OUR NEIGHBOR TO FEED CROUTON WHILE WE'RE away, giving her the whole feeding protocol in a long text message with all our phone numbers and a plea to send me a picture of her every day. I'm worried Crouton won't eat while we're gone, and, irrationally, wish she could come with us. She is, after all, a tuxedo cat, always in formal wear. If I were to change her name, it would be to Janelle, like Janelle Monáe, and sometimes me and Ali call her Electric Lady, and we sing *wave your paw in the sky, just wave your paw in the sky* at her until she gets scared that we're doing some satanic ritual on her and she runs away and hides under the couch.

We have to leave before the sun even comes up because it's an eleven-hour car ride from Albuquerque to San Diego. Mom and Ali sing along to the radio in the front while Esmé and I share earbuds in the back.

Until, of course, a Selena song comes on over the car's speakers, and then Esmé violently rips them out and joins in, leaving me shaking my head and looking out the window at the Arizona desert flying by, brown and red and vast, laughing.

Mom has insisted on staying at the hotel where the debut is being held tonight even though Tita Connie told her they have plenty of room at their house for us to stay. They have two whole guest rooms, even.

"Sige na, Até," she told her over the phone. *Thank you, Sister.* "We don't want to be in your way."

When she hung up, she clicked her tongue and looked out the window of our two-bedroom apartment for a long time without saying anything.

We have lots of family in California, in places like Daly City and Hayward and Oceanside. Places that nobody in Albuquerque has really heard of, so when we make this drive west, through Death Valley, for the big family things that we can't miss, like these eighteenth birthdays, and weddings, and funerals, I'd say we're going to San Francisco or San Diego.

Expensive, Mom says wistfully whenever one of her coworkers asks her why she doesn't just move us out there. *Too expensive. And I don't want to take the girls away from their dad.*

Ha.

Mom came to the U.S. when she was twenty to work for a family as their live-in nanny. Three of her sisters were already here, working as nurses. The family Mom worked for sucked and they had all these weird rules for her, like they made her sign a contract that she wouldn't get pregnant. She lived with them for only a few years before she met Dad. When they decided to get married she moved with him, two states over, to New Mexico, where he was from and where my grandparents lived at the time. They don't even live here anymore, they moved to some place in Florida where there's not even a beach and they send us very Jesus-y birthday cards and Christmas cards, but that's about the extent of our relationship with them.

When Mom talks about the time she lived in California

with her family, about the ocean, about going out dancing with her sisters, even snotty Tita Connie, she always
sounds happy.

So it made sense that that's where she went, for a while,
just to get her bearings, when our parents divorced.

I thought about her all the time, when she was gone.
Imagining her laughing with my titas. Looking at the
ocean. While me and Ali ate cold sandwiches for breakfast, lunch, and dinner, because sandwiches are the only
food that Dad can seem to think of. All Mom's stuff was
gone. All her dresses from their closet. The wooden crosses
that used to hang on the wall next to the kitchen table. The
house was so quiet.

I was afraid she wasn't going to come back.

But then she did.

＊················＊

Mom breaks a nail pumping gas at a truck stop in the
middle of nowhere.

"Ay naku!" she cries.

"What happened, Momma?" Ali asks from the front
seat. She's wearing a track jersey and pajama pants.

"I just got my nails done!" Mom says. "Look at this, oh
no, no, no, no."

She replaces the gas pump and jumps into the driver's
seat, immediately begins searching inside her giant fake
Louis Vuitton purse, which is full of loose receipts and
half-empty sample-size lotions.

"It's okay, Tita," Esmé says.

"Noooo, it looks so *ugly*." She holds her hand up and examines it in the light. Half of the bright red nail on her index finger is gone, broken off clean. "And this was so expensive. I got gel. Tita Connie is never going to let me live this down, she's going to tell your Tita Carmen and your Tita Litang and they'll be talking-talking, laughing-laughing all night about how I can't even afford to have my nails done, *ay naku*."

"Mom, you cannot be serious," I groan. "No one is even going to notice."

She clicks her tongue.

"You don't know, that's how they are," she mutters, receipts flying everywhere as she digs in her bag.

I just *hate* the implication that she knows something that I don't. Especially this. I know all about the snotty California aunties. She complains about them constantly. They make her feel like shit all the time over dumb stuff like this.

"Where is my phone? Diyos ko, what is wrong with me?"

"What do you even need your phone for?" I snap.

Mom continues muttering in Tagalog without even answering me. Sometimes, she is so embarrassing. Scatterbrained. I glance at Esmé. I don't want her to regret coming with us if Mom is going to be acting all dramatic like this, and for no reason.

But now Esmé has her phone out, too.

"Got it, Tita," she says. "There's something called Beauty Nail at the next exit. It's open until five p.m."

"Oh thank God," Mom says, pulling the driver's side door shut with a slam. "Thank you, baby." She calls everybody baby.

Beauty Nail ends up being a lot like the salon Mom goes to in Albuquerque. It smells like chemicals. It's in an amazing strip mall with a coffee shop called El Minuto and the Law Offices of Wolski and Martinez, LLC—DUI and Criminal Defense Litigators.

The leather is cracking on the massage chairs. It's staffed by small Asian women, like Mom, in comfortable footwear and their straight black hair in ponytails. Esmé and I spin ourselves around in swivel chairs while Mom gets her nail fixed. Ali hovers over Mom's shoulder and scrolls through her phone.

My mom and her nail tech, who says she's Vietnamese, trade stories bragging about their kids, as if me and Ali aren't even here.

"My daughter won a medal on the track," Mom says.

"She's ridiculous," I mutter.

Esmé doesn't say anything.

Before we get back on the road, we sit in the parking lot and eat the rice and chicken lunch from Tupperware that Mom packed for us in a cooler. Mom, happy again now that her nail is restored, takes pictures of us to post into the family WhatsApp group—*almost there!*

We decided we didn't want to wait in line to ride the big Ferris wheel, but we're enjoying looking at it from here. All lit up. Esmé twirls in her ruffle skirt as we meander along the boardwalk at the beach across the street from the hotel.

"Okay, we are on track to be fashionably late to this

thing," I say, reading the latest text in a long string of texts from my mom.

> **MOM:** LUZ WHERE ARE U
>
> **ME:** coming back now, Esmé got into a fight with a seagull! don't worry, she won
>
> **MOM:** LUZ
>
> **ME:** oh no, another seagull!

We're all sharing a room at the hotel. Mom and Ali in one bed, me and Esmé in the other bed. She and I slipped away while they were starting to get ready earlier, their dual curling irons entangled in front of the bathroom mirror, shouting over our shoulders that Esmé just needed to put her feet in the ocean, *real quick*.

"I've never been to the ocean!" she said.

"Five minutes!" I said.

It has now been much longer than five minutes.

As I lean against the cool metal railing on the boardwalk, the vastness of the Pacific Ocean does something to still my spirit and quicken my pulse at the same time. It smells like salt. I can almost taste it.

"The ocean is fucking scary," Esmé says. "Like, why is it so big?"

"How you feel about the ocean being big is how I feel about birds not having hands."

"What about fish?"

"Same problem. But worse. So much worse."

She laughs, and leans back, holding the metal railing in front of her, like a ballet dancer at the barre.

The wave of relief that washes over me when she laughs almost knocks me over.

Things between us have been weird since the play. But maybe it's all in my head. Sometimes I think everything is in my head.

The moon is hanging low and full over the black ocean, its reflection broken in the water. We stare at it. Shoulder to shoulder.

At home in Albuquerque, I can *sense* the mountains, all the time. Like even when I'm not looking at it, I feel it. It's always there, in the east. Like a wall at my back, holding me up. Steadying me. If I'd been born here instead, maybe the ocean would be like that for me. Maybe I'd always feel the water churning in the west.

"Are you *sure* you want to go to the party dressed like this?" she asks, her black leather jacket in her hand.

I roll my eyes. If I could have convinced her to look *less* nice, I would have. "We can wear whatever we want."

She shoots me a look. She knows I'm full of shit and that my mom is going to freak out when she sees us with T-shirts tucked into black skirts and the chunky black boots she says make us look like mail carriers instead of the outfits she preapproved back in Albuquerque.

"Dare me to jump in?" Esmé asks me, mounting the railing like a balance beam.

Arms out, she places one boot in front of the other, a cat.

She's done it before. Jumped. Into a pool in her cousin's backyard. Into Santa Rosa Lake while her parents cheered her on from the shore. But I can't swim, so all I could do would be to stand there, where the water met the sand, holding my shoes in my hands, my laughter disappearing into folds of the waves she'd made with her body.

"No one ever dares you!" I say. "You only dare yourself."

When she's sure of her footing, she flicks her neon plastic lighter and raises the flame to a cigarette.

"For the millionth time," I say. "Please quit smoking."

"I know, I know, it's all very foolish of me," she says, inhaling.

"All I'm saying is—you were born way too late in the game to be in the pocket of big tobacky."

She grins at me, wiggles her dark eyebrows, then tilts her head back to exhale. A puff of smoke rises up into the darkness.

It's quiet here. I wish we could stay. No crowds. No judgmental eyes.

My phone buzzes in my pocket.

5:45 PM: LUZ WHERE R U
6:30 PM: LUZ WHERE R U
7:10 PM: LUZ!!!

"Okay," I sigh. "I've tortured her enough. Time for gendered, ceremonial hell."

"Jesus," Esmé cackles, twirling a stray black curl in her fingers as we make our way back to the hotel, down a palm tree–lined sidewalk. "It is not *that* serious. What's Maricel's deal anyway? Rich kid?"

"Yeah, and she's very mabait, which is Tagalog for, like, a good girl who does everything her parents say. Her dad does something in the tech industry, I think, and my mom is always ranting about how their family has three cars."

"Oh, I know, I've heard her. 'Luz's Tita Connie *claims* that she can't come here for Easter this year. How could that be? She has *three cars*!'"

I clear my throat and launch into my best Mom impression. "You should really study something that will help you work for the Internet. Because then you could have three cars like your Tita Connie."

Esmé is doubled over laughing.

"I really don't know if you're adequately prepared for what's about to happen," I say.

"It can't be that different from a quince."

"What's the weirdest thing you've seen happen at a quince?"

"Weird?" she asks. "What do you mean by weird?"

"I have been shuffling up and down the entire West Coast to attend the coming-out parties of newly *emerged* eighteen-year-olds for a long time. I've seen it all. The debutante who jumped down from the rafters in a rock-climbing harness. The one who made us listen to her play Bad Bunny on the violin while her sister did an interpretive dance."

Esmé laughs again. I'm really picking up steam now.

"The one who performed the karaoke version of 'What Makes You Beautiful' in its entirety while staring into a giant mirror."

"You're kidding."

"Nope. Three minutes and eighteen seconds of off-key, performance art hell. It's like they're competing for Miss America against *no one*!"

"Light bulb, you kill me," Esmé laughs. "Well. I hope Maricel wins."

The only silver lining here is that I'm not on the program. No one has invited me to participate in their Eighteen Candles ceremony since the now-infamous debut of my cousin Cecelia, where I set off a chain of vomiting children before her grand entrance when I was ten. I heard that her parents didn't even get their deposit back from the hotel because they couldn't get the smell out of the carpet. Even though my mom *said* she wasn't mad at me, and that it wasn't my fault, that car ride home was still the longest and quietest we'd had. Up until that point.

I've done *lots* to shame her since.

We walk across the hotel parking lot, which is now super full of nice, shiny cars. Mom's dusty lease, with the dented fender, is dwarfed by the two giant luxury SUVs that flank it.

When we reach the entrance, Esmé shrieks. "Wait, is that an *ice sculpture*?"

A nearby bellhop tries not to laugh as she jumps up and down in excitement.

"Are there two of them?" she asks. "Don't tell me that's *her*."

"That's her. It appears that my aunt and uncle have, indeed, commissioned two ice sculptures, in the likeness of my cousin Maricel, for this momentous occasion."

I bow to one icy version of Maricel, and then to the other one. Her arms gesture welcomingly to the doorway, like reverse gargoyles.

In the lobby, we follow the giant calligraphy signs for *Maricel's 18th* to the ballroom.

Life-size photos of her line the halls.

"Okay," Esmé says. "This is a lot."

"And if I've timed this correctly, we've missed everything," I say.

"As long as there's still food," Esmé says.

In the ballroom, there's more food than even I was prepared for.

The buffet wraps around the entire ballroom, which seats at least two hundred. Everything is white—white tablecloths, lush arrangements of white flowers bursting from the table centers, delicate white ribbons binding the silverware. Twinkling white fairy lights hang from the ceiling.

Esmé points to a pasta station with a chef, in the little white hat and everything, making pasta to order. Silver trays, overflowing with pancit and adobo, savory steam wafting and causing my stomach to clench. And lastly, a chocolate fountain with mountains upon mountains of fat California strawberries that I can smell from here.

"Holy—" Esmé breathes.

"GIRLS!" My mom's voice cuts through the crowd noise.

"Hi, Mommy," I say.

She grabs us both by the arm and drags us away from the food. She's wearing the same dress she wears to mass, a plain lavender sheath, and she's flat-ironed the hell out of her thick black hair only to curl it again at the bottom.

"Chocolate fountain," Esmé whispers mournfully as it recedes into the distance.

"Where *were* you?" she asks, hissing at me. "You almost missed everything!"

"*Almost*? What's left?" I ask, disappointed.

She shoots me a death glare.

"I mean, oh no."

"Wait—" Mom stops in her tracks, appraising our attire. "What are you wearing?!"

Esmé looks pained.

Mom is so mad she is short-circuiting and can't form sentences. "After all that—that entire day at the mall—trying on a hundred dresses—rejecting all of them—you are so—"

I give my mom some finger guns. "So you're saying you don't like it?"

My mom rubs her temples with her perfectly moisturized, manicured fingers and takes a deep breath.

"Why is *everything* a joke to you?"

Esmé winces.

"It's not," I say.

I'm being dead serious with her right now. I told her I didn't like the clothes she picked out. That I didn't want to wear them. And she didn't listen to me. She never does. I could say exactly what I think and she wouldn't listen, so most of the time I don't even bother, and that's why I have to act like this.

She doesn't give me any choice.

Mom looks me up and down one more time, mentally cuts her losses, and shoves us forward.

"Go say happy birthday to your cousin," she says. "And say thank you to Tita Connie and Tito Nelson for inviting us to this. Look at *all this*! What a blessing. They work so hard—thank God the Internet business is still booming."

"Yeah, a real sleeper hit, that Internet," I say.

We're dragged into a makeshift greenroom where Maricel and her sisters are lounging on plush white chairs in front of propped-up mirrors with Hollywood light bulbs. Ali is already there, wearing the Mom-approved outfit and giggling over something on one of my cousin's phones.

"Lucia!" Maricel says, jumping up and pulling me into a hug.

Her hair smells like coconut custard and in person, she doesn't look like Miss America. She looks like Miss Universe. If that's the better one.

"Hey cuz," I say, feeling like a little kid next to her, even though she's only six months older than I am.

I smooth out the front of my T-shirt. "You remember Esmé?"

"Of course!" she laughs, her white teeth sparkling. "You two look hella cool. Like you're in a band."

"I heard you have three cars," Esmé says.

I could hug her for that. I bark out a laugh, flooded with gratitude that Esmé is here. Because if she wasn't here, I'd feel completely insane, and I might end up screaming at my mom in front of everyone, and then she'd be obligated to disown me and exile me from the WhatsApp group permanently. So thank God she's here.

Before Maricel can respond, a photographer pops up out of nowhere and shoves a lens in our faces. Maricel arranges herself instantly into the perfect pose. Esmé and I flank her dutifully and make picture-ruining faces when the flash goes off.

"Thank you for coming all this way," Maricel says, smiling gently and taking my hand. "I can't wait for yours!"

"Oh, no, I'm not having—hey, why are you shoving me?" I say, looking incredulously at my mom.

"Let's not take up too much of the birthday girl's time," Mom says. "Happy birthday, pamangkin!"

"Thank you, Tita." Maricel kisses my mom on the cheek. "See you after the ceremonies!"

"Oh my God, they haven't even started yet?" I ask loudly as Mom shoves me through the door and back out into the ballroom.

"Shh!" Mom shushes me and pinches my arm. She gestures for Ali to follow us and she does, dutifully.

I look around the ballroom, where guests continue to flood in. This isn't adding up.

"Give me that program," I say.

Snatching the sturdy cardstock from my mom's hand, I squint to read the tiny print. I get glitter all over my hands.

Great. I'll be glittery for six to eight weeks.

"What the hell, Mom! You said it started at six."

She smirks. "Did I?"

"You tricked me," I say, narrowing my eyes. "She hasn't even done her entrance yet."

Esmé jumps up and down next to me. "Oh, thank God!"

"Traitor," I say, glaring at her.

"Can't wait to see what her talent is going to be," Esmé says, her eyes sparkling.

I can't help but laugh.

"Let's find our seats," my mom says.

The lights dim and the tasteful elegance of the white ballroom dissolves into a laser light show.

"What the—?!" Esmé says.

Mom hustles us to find our chairs as we join the room in applause. We've been seated, with name cards, at a giant round table near the back with some extended family from Maricel's dad's side, whose names I've already forgotten.

Bass-heavy music blasts as our MCs for the evening, my cousins Danilo and Shaira, enter from the back. Dan in a black suit with a white bow tie, Shy in a black sweetheart dress with a giant white bow at her waist. They grin widely for the videographer, linking arms and waving as they make their way down the red carpet to the podium at the front of the room.

"Good evening, honored guests," Dan says into the microphone with an easy charm.

"Well, you all know us," Shaira says, smiling coyly and moving a heavy pile of black curls from one shoulder to the other.

I roll my eyes, my mom smacks me.

"I'm Shy Marielena Diaz."

"And I'm Dan Bautista Diaz. And we're here tonight for the debut of . . ."

Then, in unison, "Maricel Magdelena Diaz!"

They fling their arms out as the crowd erupts into cheers.

Esmé leans over and shouts in my ear. "Impeccable timing."

"They've rehearsed," I say.

"We're so happy to be your MCs tonight as we celebrate the baby cousin in the family, Maricel," Shy says.

She holds for applause and it floods in.

"I thought Ali was the youngest cousin," Esmé whispers, clapping.

"She is," I say, feeling instantly irritated and protective of her. I look across the table past the ridiculous floral centerpiece at my sister, hoping she doesn't feel hurt by her title as baby cousin being unfairly bestowed on Maricel, who is not only older than *her* but also older than *me*, but she's focusing on the giant projector screen that has descended from the ceiling.

It displays a picture of Dan, Shy, and Maricel as pre-teens, embracing and drinking boba tea. Three sets of grins and braces.

Ali's expression is unreadable, but I feel an unwelcome pang of left-outness on her behalf. Fine, so we live all the way in New Mexico, of course we wouldn't be in most of these pictures anyway, but it still feels like we're being erased from the family narrative somehow, the same way it felt when Dad got a family portrait taken with just him and pregnant Sunny and then hung it in the entryway of their house. Like we don't even exist.

"We love you, Mari!" Dan says.

The crowd cheers and whoops, echoing them, *We love you, Mari!*

The lights dim, and a slideshow of Maricel's accomplished life begins to roll over a transcendent pop power ballad. Maricel as a little girl, blowing out birthday candles, her mom and dad resting a hand on each tiny shoulder, swelling with pride. Maricel three years ago, organizing a food drive at her church. Maricel this year, as captain of her soccer team, kneeling with a checkered ball tucked under her arm. Maricel skiing in Tahoe with Dan and Shy. Maricel playing soccer with little kids. Maricel and the huge extended family in matching pajamas at Christmas, a table overflowing with aluminum food trays and crumpled-up wrapping paper all over the floor.

The slideshow ends with a photo of Maricel and her parents, sitting with Lola in her living room in the Philippines. Maricel is holding her hand. My heart constricts at the familiar sight of that floral printed couch, a backdrop for FaceTime calls, reframed as a real place, as a real place I've never been, but Maricel has. Mom pulls out a tissue and blows her nose. Ali leans her head on Mom's shoulder and Mom rests her cheek at the crown of her head.

Lola should be here.

Or we should be there.

We should all be together, and yet somehow we never are.

I rub my arms, cold suddenly, as the room goes dark.

"And now," Shy's voice comes over the sound system. "It's our honor to present . . ."

"Maricel! Magdelena! Diaz!"

A spotlight on the door. Everyone jumps to their feet and begins to clap as a new, different, transcendent pop power ballad begins to play.

Maricel enters, now wearing a tiara, and the full power of her dress hits me. The fitted bodice, covered with gems, the skirt, miles and miles of ruffles. She smiles warmly, naturally, in spite of camera flashes and the twinkling eyes of ten dozen iPhones. Her perfect contoured makeup telegraphs her beauty, even to those of us way out here, in the cheap seats.

Mom and Ali are talking excitedly and taking pictures with their phones.

"I guess she's going for . . . Cupcake Barbie Princess?" I shout in Esmé's ear.

She shrugs, her eyebrows coming together.

Not frowning, exactly, but not laughing, either.

"She looks amazing," she says.

"I mean, yeah," I say, my hands growing tired of clapping. "Yeah, obviously."

"And now," Dan says, keeping the energy up, a natural MC. "The debutante's entourage."

The doors open again, Maricel's cotillion enters, two by two, in matching black suits with white bow ties and black sweetheart dresses with enormous white bows at the waist.

"Are there . . . ?" Esmé asks, counting them.

"Yep, eighteen of them. Just eighteen of her *closest friends*, no big deal."

The girls with identical long, dark curls and guys with the same haircut, short on the sides, long on top. Seeing double times nine.

"Well, surely some of them are your cousins," Esmé says.

"Yeah, but Maricel probably has one of those embroidered pillows that says 'cousins are the friends God chose for you' or some shit like that," I say.

Esmé snorts, but she's staring at them as they take their positions on the dance floor for the cotillion waltz.

"Imagine," I say, rambling on, desperate for a laugh. "Who would we have in our entourage?"

Esmé opens her mouth, closes it again.

A few delicate notes on the piano. The crowd whoops

and cheers. Maricel is led, gently, to the center of the floor by her escort. Each member of her entourage either bows or curtseys to her, depending on their gender assigned at birth. Her escort, a tall handsome guy who doesn't seem at all bothered by the fact he's being forced to wear a *bow tie*, holds her hand so softly, as if she will burst into a cloud of powdered sugar at the slightest bit of pressure.

"He's the valedictorian," my mom whispers. "I found him on Facebook."

"Where all the very best people in the world can be found," I say.

I cut my eyes in Esmé's direction, but she isn't even looking at me.

As the song begins in earnest, the pairs waltz across the floor in formation, gliding and twirling, exactly as upwardly mobile young people have done since colonial times. Mom pulls a small notebook from her bag. Wait. What is going on here?

Why is Esmé *smiling*?

Why is my mom taking *notes*?

Maricel's escort spins her and the crowd erupts into cheers.

"What are you doing?" I ask my mom loudly.

She closes her notebook. "Nothing," she says.

"Tell me!" I say, grabbing it from her.

"Luz—" she says, grabbing it back, her eyes wide. "What's the matter with you?"

"What's the matter with *you*?"

My mom laughs nervously at the guests who have

started looking at us curiously. I get up, almost knocking over my chair, and stomp off. I'm getting a chocolate strawberry from that damn chocolate fountain.

Mom's on my tail.

"Can we please not do this here?" she asks. "It's Maricel's birthday."

"Oh, *is it*?" I laugh maniacally. "Is it really? I hadn't noticed."

"Luz."

She looks at me, pleading, like I've exhausted her, like *please, please don't do this to me.*

It just makes me want to be *more*. More of everything she doesn't want me to be.

"Ladies and gentlemen, give it up one more time for Maricel and her cotillion!" Shy announces as the court takes a bow. "Now, please help yourselves to some delicious food, catered by Tita Rosa's, while we take some photos before the Eighteen Candles ceremony."

The lights come up and party guests begin to make their way to the food stations.

"What is in that notebook?" I ask, hissing through my teeth.

"Luz, there you are!" My Tita Connie appears. "What did you think?"

She has a short round bob that frames her face, a string of pearls and a white Filipiniana dress. Mom looks at her sister with relief, as if God himself summoned her to save her from me.

Tita Connie always calls Mom by her full name, Renalyn, even though she hates it (everyone else calls her just Rena or Ren), and my mom never calls Tita Connie by her full name, Concepción.

"It was beautiful, Tita," I say robotically, my cheeks still hot with anger.

"You look . . . *cute*," she says, wrinkling her nose. "Always so *edgy*, di ba? I can't wait to see what you wear for your debut in April."

My mom freezes.

I freeze.

"What's happening?" Esmé asks, appearing at Mom's side as Ali appears on the other.

"We *just* got the save the date in the mail," Tita Connie continues. "Good for you, being on top of that—we barely threw all of this together at the last minute!"

Tita Connie laughs musically as a bunch of white balloons fall from the ceiling onto Maricel and her friends. They jump in the air in unison as a camera flashes.

"Mom," I say, and if the word were a dagger, it would have killed her.

"Luz, let's talk about this later," Mom begs.

I look at her. Then at my tita. And back to my mom again. I *told* her I didn't want a stupid debut. I didn't *want* to put on this big performance for all of them, on demand, like a damn trick poodle. And I *know* that my mom just wants to impress her older sister, to impress everyone in the family. I know that she just wants to host, for once. To prove to them that we're just *fine*, just the three of us. Without Dad. Without three cars. Without tech industry money. But I can't. I can't be part of this stupid show anymore. It's gone too far.

"How could you do this to me?" I ask. "You are such a *liar*!"

Mom's face crumples. My tita puts her hand on her shoulder. Ali winces. Esmé puts her fingertips to her bottom lip.

And it's too much.

I spin around and search wildly for an exit sign. The room blurs as my feet carry me toward it. Then I'm pushing through the door, storming past a giant portrait of Maricel in the lobby, and out into the night.

"Lucia!" Esmé calls, out of breath, from somewhere behind me.

I'm so mad I could strangle Maricel's ice sculpture. I mime doing so and let out a scream. The bellhop slips quietly inside, possibly to call security.

"Relájate, will you?" Esmé says. "It's going to be fine."

"Are you serious?" I ask her. "Did you see that? Were we at the same party? That was a circus!"

"Again, I *did* have a quince, as you may remember."

"Of course I do, but that was when you were *fifteen*," I say. "A kid! And you didn't wear a tiara or have a pasta station."

"No, but I did dance with my dad. Kind of weird if you think about it, sure, but it made him happy. It made everybody happy."

God, that dance with her dad. Her stupid poofy dress and the way he made a funny face when he tripped on it. How they both laughed when he stepped on his own foot. How proud he looked of her. I wanted to make a joke about it, but I couldn't think of one. I wanted to hate it, but I didn't. I didn't want it to make me feel all the things that it did.

But I can't admit that, even now.

"Luz," Esmé says. "Has it ever occurred to you that you can be *correct*, but that doesn't necessarily make you *right*?"

"What are you talking about?"

"Is all of this stuff—debuts, quinceañeras—is it all some weird, colonial bullshit? Yes. Fine. But it wasn't for *me*. It was for my family."

"I don't give a shit," I say. "My family doesn't need *me* as an excuse to have a party. They have plenty of them. All the time. I am turning *eighteen*. A legal adult. She can't make me do it. She can't!"

Esmé tilts her head to one side, almost imperceptibly. "Well, I guess you'll just have to run away and join the Marines."

"Oh yeah, because they *love* five-foot-tall women who can't do a single push-up!"

I scream again. My scream echoes across the parking lot. I can't believe my mom would do this. But that look on her face when I called her a liar . . . I can't believe I did that, either.

But what did she expect?

"Lucia, come on," Esmé says. "I'll help you, it'll be fun. We can make a mood board."

"A *mood board*?" I repeat.

I squint at her. Who is this person? What's going on here? She's supposed to be affronted on my behalf. She's supposed to understand.

"Esmé, we are *not* debut types."

"And what does that mean?" She places her hands on her hips.

Her lipstick is the exact color of a plum. Or a bruise.

I sputter, pacing between the two icy Maricels.

"It means," I say, winding up, gesturing at my rich cousin's icy likeness, "that we don't go in for this corny shit. It means we're . . . we're . . ."

"Better than them?" she asks.

I stop. Cross my arms.

"I didn't say that. What's that supposed to mean?"

"It means you're being a hater, Lucia. You're being a hating-ass bitch."

"But you're a hating-ass bitch, too! It's our whole thing!"

"It's not *my* thing!" she says, her voice rising suddenly. "Or maybe, I don't want to be."

She lets out a sigh. And as she looks out over the parking lot, into the marina, I follow her gaze. The night is clear, and the white boats on the water glow in the moonlight.

"Luz, what is this really about?" she asks. "Why don't you want to have a debut? Really?"

I freeze.

"I just told you why."

I don't want a debut because they're stupid. This whole thing is stupid.

She lets out an even bigger sigh and puts her hands on her hips.

"I've been thinking," she says quietly.

Carefully.

I tense up.

"What if we're doing it all wrong?" she asks.

I blink. "Doing *what* wrong?"

"Everything. High school. If either one of us had a debut tomorrow, we'd have nothing to show for it but a slideshow of ourselves making fun of people in the cafeteria, followed by a two-person ribbon dance."

"Sounds hilarious," I said.

"Not to me," she says.

I don't have the words. I don't understand how we got here. It's all this stupid debut's fault. Everything was fine before. And when we get back to town, and put this all behind us, we'll be walking down the cracked sidewalk on our way to the Sunshine Theater, where Mr. Marco will grunt when he hands us our tickets, pretending to be mad that we paid him in quarters again.

"Luz, you never want to do *anything*," Esmé says. "You're always so *down* on everybody. And maybe . . . we've been holding each other back. It's senior year, you know? Maybe we should think about branching out. Just a little. Maybe you should join a club, too. I'm going to be busy with the costumes for the play anyway, and then you'll know more people, people you can ask to be in your cotillion. You'll need eighteen, right? What do you think?"

My throat is closing up. *Branching out.*

Just a little.

Holding each other back.

I cough to clear my throat.

"How long have you had *that* little speech prepared?" I ask.

She looks wounded. But I keep talking.

"Maybe if I've been holding you back so much, you should just go join *all* the clubs. Become *president* of joining clubs. I'll just stand there at my debut in my cotillion of one, doing a ribbon dance all by myself because I'm a selfish, hating-ass bitch."

"Lucia—"

"No, I get it. You know what? You're right. In fact, forget branching out. Let's just quit each other. Cold turkey. I hope you have a really fun, super special senior year, with all your new, super cool best friends!"

I turn around and grasp my elbows, my eyes stinging.

As I cross the cavernous hotel lobby, following the bass pulsing from the ballroom, I know that she's not following me.

Of course she's not.

I wrench open the door to the ballroom, where Maricel's debut program has progressed to the Eighteen Candles ceremony.

Maricel is seated on a literal throne. Her tiara sparkles in the light. My Tita Connie stands next to her on the stage, looking at her lovingly, a lit candle in one hand and a microphone in the other. The crowd is laughing as if she'd just told the funniest joke they've ever heard, which I highly doubt.

"But in all seriousness," Tita Connie says. "A daughter is such a blessing."

My mom stands at the fringe, her arm around Ali's shoulders, their heads bowed together as they listen.

My heart races.

I can feel the lights falling on Maricel's face as if they are on my own.

But she doesn't shake or sweat, she looks like an angel, smiling softly as her mom goes on and on about how perfect she is like she's reading from a Hallmark card reject pile for Perfect Fucking Daughter's Day.

"It feels like only yesterday," Tita Connie continues, but then she stops. She's going to cry. The crowd shouts encouragement. "It feels like only yesterday when—"

She can't continue.

Tito Nelson joins her onstage and puts his arm around her. His eyes are shining, too.

I turn around and let my feet carry me out of the room. Through the door. Past the big signs, *Maricel's 18th!*, all the way to the elevator bank.

I push the button with our floor number again and again and again.

7

UPSTAIRS INSIDE THE EMPTY HOTEL ROOM, OUR OVER-
night bags have exploded everywhere. Ali's taken over the
nightstand with sprays and serums and makeup brushes,
just like at home.

I sink onto the bed, staring at my own reflection on the
darkened TV screen.

After a moment I pull out my cell phone to FaceTime
my lola.

I don't know what's going on with Mom and her, and I
don't care, because I really, really just need to talk to *someone* sane and normal.

"Kumasta mahal," she says, picking up right away.
"What's wrong?"

Everything is right there on the tip of my tongue, my
mom being a complete and total liar, *never* listening to me,
Tita Connie calling me *cute*, the fact that Lola's *not here*,
and my mom refusing to tell me *why* isn't she here, and
how that's not fair, just all these *complaints*—all these silly,
useless, ungrateful complaints. *Hating-ass bitch* stuff.

I swipe a tear away, hoping the poor connection will
obscure my face enough to hide it.

"Nothing, po. How are you?" I ask.

"Fine, fine. How is Maricel's debut?" she asks.

I blink. "You know about it?"

"Of course, apo. I know everything," she says, cackling. "Nobody can hide from me."

"But *why* did they try to hide it from you?"

"They did not want me to feel bad about missing it because they knew I could not make it. But if nobody posts pictures to the Facebook, it would be a miracle, di ba? Do you want to make a bet about who will crack first? I think probably your Kuya Dan. He cannot resist posting a selfie."

"Why *couldn't* you come, po?" I ask, and then immediately cringe. Maybe that was rude. Mom always says me and Ali just don't get how to talk to elders because we're born in the U.S. and because Dad's culture is *so* disrespectful that he calls his parents by their first names and everything. That's why Esmé and I call our moms Linda and Renalyn as a joke. Never to their faces, of course. We're not stupid.

But even if I'm rude, Lola never yells at us and Dad always does, so who knows. Maybe I'm not good at social etiquette in any culture.

"Nothing to worry about, apo," she says. "You should enjoy the party."

"Did you have a debut, Lola?" I ask, suddenly realizing that I don't know.

She howls with laughter. "*No.* No, I didn't."

I hold my tongue with all my possibly rude questions and just wait for her to say more.

"That was something for rich people," she says. "Your mommy did not have one, either, none of my children did. Things changed a lot, especially over there, in the U.S. Seems like everyone there does this now. Maybe to seem rich, talaga!"

She laughs her gravelly laugh. I smile.

"It means something to your Tita Connie, though. She has been planning Maricel's debut since she was a baby."

I chew on the inside of my cheek, where a lump of scar tissue has begun to form. Tita Connie definitely likes to seem rich. She actually is rich, of course, compared to us anyway, and it's a huge source of drama between her and Mom. But Tita Connie had been also gazing at Maricel, sitting perfectly on her throne, Connie so emotional she was unable to get through her planned speech without choking up. Even I have to admit—that part was genuine.

But that's because Maricel does so much stuff that Tita Connie is proud of, she always has. Mom wouldn't have anything like that to say to me.

Her Eighteen Candles speech for me would go something like, *Luz, from the moment you were born, you have been disrespectful of what* should *be my unquestionable authority over you, you wear ugly old secondhand grandpa sweaters because you don't care if you make people think we are poor and you don't wear any of the pretty, expensive clothes I work so hard to be able to buy for you, you think everything is a joke and you make your dead rat face every time anything or anyone remotely nice crosses your path.*

"I miss you, Lola," I say.

"Miss you, too, ni," she says.

"Mahal kita."

"Mahal din kita."

When her face disappears from my phone screen, the room is empty again, she's on the other side of the ocean, and I'm on this one.

Later that night, Mom, Ali, and Esmé are silent as they come back upstairs to our hotel room from the party.

They all peel off their shoes in the dark.

I've turned to face the wall, pretending to be asleep.

On the long car ride home the next day, Ali and Mom and Esmé talk together about which truck stop will have the better chimichangas, as if I weren't even there.

Fine by me.

I manage to keep my mouth shut across the entire state of Arizona. Sometimes I feel like I have so much to say, but don't say it, and it builds and builds and builds until I need to just scream it all out. But then when I do that, it just gets me into trouble, and I wish I hadn't said anything at all.

I remove my sunglasses in order to read the sign again.

Here I am, back in Albuquerque, trying to wallow in misery at my happy place, my feet aching because it took forever to walk here in a city that is in no way designed for walking, and now this. I feel like a cartoon character, blinking and rubbing my eyeballs.

Because this just can't be right.

THE SUNSHINE THEATER WILL BE CLOSING

THANK YOU FOR YOUR PATRONAGE

The sign comes off the glass easily because it's only held up by two pieces of Scotch tape. Clutching the white paper in my hands, I look around the strip mall frantically—everything else looks the same. Concrete sparkling in the sunshine. A broken bottle. Cars rushing by on the street, windows down, snatches of bass floating in the warm autumn air, the radio DJ's voice blaring through an open car window passing by.

The Most Hip-Hop and R&B is my Kiss—97.3 KISS—97.3! Bosque Farms, Albuquerque.

Shoving my sunglasses into my backpack and crumpling up the stupid sign in one hand, I march through the smudged glass doors. Down the gross, stained, nineties-patterned carpet in the hallway, and right up to the ticket counter where Old Man Marco is sitting, reading a newspaper in the late afternoon sunlight.

As usual, he doesn't even look up.

"Put the sign back, Lucia," he says.

I wave the paper around. It slices through the air.

"This is horseshit, Marco!"

He looks over the top of his wire-rimmed glasses at me. Looks at me like *I'm* the pitiful one. Me. When he's the one who can't keep a damn movie theater in business. Jesus.

"How much could *popcorn* possibly cost, Marco?" I ask, gesturing with my sunglasses. The sun catches them and bounces into his crinkly brown eyes, momentarily blinding him and causing him to blink rapidly. "It's *corn*. It's our nation's most abundant crop. It's *subsidized*. Everyone hates socialism until it comes to corn."

"Lucia—"

"I mean, this is a disgrace," I go on loudly, trying to catch the attention of any random patron to back me up. But there's only one other person in here and they walk past quickly, avoiding eye contact with me.

Coward.

"Don't you buy in bulk? Haven't you heard of *markup*? Are you adjusting for inflation? You're soft, Marco, you know that? Last month it was Dollar Tuesdays. DOLLAR. TUESDAYS. You know what costs a dollar? Nothing! There's a kid in our complex who does a lemonade stand in the parking lot by the mailboxes, and *she* charges two-fifty per cup. She puts a big glass jar full of lemons out, but we all know she's serving us the frozen stuff from a can and that she didn't juice shit. Do we still buy it? Yes. That's called business acumen, Marco. Maybe we should get that little lemonade girl in here, hmm? She could show you some pointers?"

"Lucia," he says, softly now.

"You could expand, you know, build out into the back lot, so that you could show more than two titles at the same time. You could put in some carpet that *doesn't* look like the Red Hot Chili Peppers vomited out an acid trip on your floor. You could get some halfway decent queso for your nachos—my mom gets the one with the winking lady on the can. I swear to God I'd drink it with a straw if I could. Have you seen the winking lady queso? Let's see what it costs wholesale. Who is your distributor?"

Marco fills a large plastic cup with Dr Pepper, and slides it over to me. I lean my elbows on the ledge and put my head down.

"A big developer," he says, "is buying the shopping center. And the one next door."

"So what?" I ask.

"They're raising our rent. A lot."

"*Everyone's?*" I ask.

Salazar's, Famous Pho, the Supercuts, Milly's Comics, the Prickly Pear?

"It can't be."

"But it is," he says. "One ticket for *Elevator to the Gallows* at three thirty p.m.?"

All I can do is nod silently, pouting, as if I, too, am starring in a moody French film that will end in death.

"That'll be five-fifty," he says, accepting my crumpled twenty.

"Insane pricing. In this economy?" I mutter. "Insane."

He counts out my change, slowly, peering at me from the tops of his glasses. I squirm.

"No Esmé again, huh?" he asks.

I shrug and take a sip.

Esmé hasn't texted me in a week. After we got back to Albuquerque after Maricel's debut, she sent three texts.

9:00 PM: lucia, come on
10:15 PM: are you really not going to answer me?
8:30 AM: fine.

Fine, with a period.

She put a period on our friendship.

Since the period, I have avoided her at school, which means having to sit in the front row where nobody wants to sit in the *many* classes we share, because we strategically signed up for them together, and it means abandoning the best spot in the cafeteria for eating my lunch at the weird table by the door and the trash cans, which is very bad feng shui. Esmé has eaten lunch with Jessa Jimenez and the theater kids for four straight days, and I hope she's very happy being in *such* close proximity to them as they spontaneously burst into song. I hope she just loves those acoustics. I hope she finds it to be a stimulating, immersive experience. I'm fine by the door and the trash with my bad trash energy.

Marco slides over my change with a brown, softly wrinkled hand.

"Take a large popcorn. On the house."

"Oh, Marco." I shake my head. "You're incorrigible."

Inside theater number three, the lights aren't even on. When the door closes behind me, it's completely black and quiet. I check my phone. It's already 3:30.

"What, no previews?" I call up to the booth, even though I know there's nobody there.

The flashlight app on my phone illuminates a totally empty theater, the floor littered with candy wrappers and clusters of crushed popcorn, ground into the carpet. Empty cups recline in armrests.

It smells like salt and stale air.

I plop down, dead center, in the creaky seat. I throw my legs up onto the seat in front of me, feeling like one of the violin players on the deck of the *Titanic*.

The room lights up as the door opens behind me. A couple enters, tentatively, shining their own cell phone light in the dark.

"What a mess! Watch out for the rat!"

A shriek.

"What, where? Where's the rat?"

"Babe, I'm just kidding. Relax."

"Jerk."

But I can tell they don't really mean it.

I sip my drink and nestle my large popcorn into my chair next to me. Finally, the projector sputters to life. There's a rip in the screen, you can see the seam where it's been mended.

"Wow," a voice comes from somewhere behind me. "What a shithole."

I glare into the dark. That might be true, but this is *our* shithole.

I mean, my shithole.

What could I even *say* to Esmé now? She's made herself pretty clear—I've been sucking up all the valuable time she should have been using for other, more diverting pursuits. She'd rather not be sitting here, every day, making herself sick on fake butter with me, because she'd rather be making *costumes* for Noah Fucking Man Bun Bradford.

10:15 PM: are you really not going to answer me?

My thumb lingers over the reply button.

"Hey, you with the phone!"

I jump, remembering myself, and shove my phone in my pocket.

"Sorry," I mutter, but I can't believe I have to apologize to this *interloper.*

Without the movie previews, and without Esmé to laugh at this stupid couple with, the spell is broken. I can't stop thinking. I can't stop thinking about my mom's face when I called her a liar in front of everyone. About *why* my lola couldn't make Maricel's debut. Tech Money Tita Connie and Tita Nelson could pay for her flight easily. A visa problem? Something else? Something worse? If not worse, why won't anyone tell me?

When I leave the Sunshine, Marco's already printed out a fresh sign and hung it up.

THE SUNSHINE THEATER WILL BE CLOSING
THANK YOU FOR YOUR PATRONAGE

I rip it down. Crumple it into a little ball. And then an even smaller ball. And then, using all my strength, I crush it into the smallest ball that physics will allow.

The couple from inside the theater exits behind me. I watch them until they disappear around the corner, holding hands.

8

I AM GOING TO DIE IN THIS MACY'S. THIS IS HOW IT'S going to end for me. Engrave it on my tombstone: Lucia Elenamaria Cruz, she died as she lived, miserable in a Macy's with her mother.

The gowns draped over my arms have grown too heavy for me to bear while standing up, so I'm slouched in the chair by the dressing room with a mountain of tulle and sparkles in my lap.

I guess I'm having a debut.

Because that's what we do.

My mom is furiously flipping through the racks in search of more "options." Ali is trailing behind her and *ooh*ing and *ahh*ing at every. Single. Option.

I can track their location in the store by the steady scrape, scrape, scrape of the plastic hangers. Scrape, scrape, scrape. Flinch, flinch, flinch.

Mom and I have been on icy terms since we got back home from Maricel's debut. She's been leaving the apartment very early, every day this week, the only evidence that she'd been there at all was the half-empty pot of coffee she left for me to pour slowly, guiltily, into my mug.

Until this morning, Saturday, when I emerged to find her perched at the kitchen table, fully dressed with her huge, ridiculous, fake Louis Vuitton slung over her arm.

On her small feet, the pair of fuzzy slippers we got her for her last birthday.

"There is a dress sale at Macy's today," she said simply.

This was her offering me a chance to apologize to her.

"Okay," I said.

This was me apologizing.

For embarrassing her. For calling her a liar. For taking it too far.

An apology to *me* does not seem forthcoming, however. For deceiving me. For planning a spectacle that she knew I didn't want, without my consent. For going behind my back.

Mom stared straight ahead on the drive to the mall, as Ali filled the silence by talking about the track team.

"And then, Coach said something *really* funny, she said . . ."

And I just sat there, not saying anything.

And in our family, what that means is, I'm having a debut, and I'm not going to say another bad word about it.

I'll have to text Maricel later to ask her *how*, exactly, one plans a debut. And I should probably call my Tita Connie and apologize for making a scene.

Again.

Alternatively, I could fake my own death. Which would be preferable.

The chair I'm sitting in, outside the Macy's dressing rooms, is positioned for optimal viewing of the person who stands before a three-part mirror, on a little platform, like a bride in a movie, like a doll on a cake, like a ballerina in a music box, twirling pointlessly in circles. There is no one standing on that platform, and I'm sitting in the chair. In the mirror, I'm confronted with harsh reality, in triplicate: my face poking out of the pile of frills—the greasy hair piled into a small, dark, twisted knot on the top of my head. The shadows beneath my eyes. The sparkles and lace conceal my normal attire, the rattiest sweatpants I own, the faded Sailor Moon T-shirt. Mom's threatened to burn both, on several occasions, which is why I keep them on my person as often as possible.

The picked-off nail polish. The semipermanent scowl.

Portrait of the Friendless Debutante.

How, *how* am I going to pull this off? My one-person ribbon dance is really not going to be the flex that Mom thinks it is.

And why are all these dresses so heavy? Gown hoisting = Princess CrossFit? Million-dollar idea. It's the new sensation sweeping the nation. Marco should host it in the lobby of the Sunshine and charge twenty bucks a class.

Too bad he can't afford my consultation rate.

I want to punch a hole through that three-part mirror.

Mom tosses another bedazzled nightmare on top of me. I wish I knew whose fashion genes I inherited. She wears boring pious sheath dresses to church, hot pink blazers to show houses, but the casual wear situation is really where things get out of control. She buys *crop tops* that are allegedly for *me* and wears them when I won't. She's young and cute, fine, I get it, but does she really have to wear a denim romper with gold buttons to the *bank*?

I let my heavy head roll over to one side and gaze out

the exit, longingly, into the mall concourse. I go cross-eyed for a second but then—it's Esmé.

On impulse, I nearly jump out of my chair, I'm so excited to see her. But then I remember. The fight in the parking lot of the hotel, the silent car ride home across Arizona, as I pressed my forehead against cold glass. Watching her laughing with the theater kids in the cafeteria from my place by the door.

The dangling texts.

The period.

I bite the inside of my cheek. Maybe I should just go talk to her. Maybe I *have* been too hardheaded. Maybe, if I figure out the right thing to say, things could just go back to how they were before.

It's not like I can have a debut *without her*.

She's my emotional support plus-one.

I grunt as I hoist myself out of the low chair, struggling not to let the tulle drag on the floor.

Just then—stupid Jessa Jimenez walks up to her, holding two large almond milk boba teas from the boba spot.

Oh God. She's hanging out with Jessa Jimenez outside of school now? At the mall? Getting *boba tea*?

What if this isn't just some dumb fight?

What if the period is for real?

Maybe it's not too late. I could drop all these stupid dresses onto the floor. Run to her like I'm running across an airport in a rom-com.

Tell her I'm sorry. Because I am. I'm really, really sorry.

And then Jessa Jimenez and Esmé clink their boba teas together and I am instantly filled with rage.

I feel like such an idiot. I should have known how

infinitely and easily replaceable I was. Clinking boba? With stupid Jessa Jimenez? Because she's so special and interesting with her theatrical exploration of *toxic masculinity*? I can't believe I ever thought—

My mom reappears, just then, with a new armful of truly, genuinely terrible dresses.

"Is that Esmé?" she asks, lighting up, looking past me.

My eyes fill with tears.

I fling all the gowns into the chair and push past my mom to the nearest fitting room.

"Luz!" Mom calls after me.

The motion detector in the doorway beeps loudly as I blow through it. I slam the door behind me. The flimsy partition shakes.

Taking in big gulps of air, I swipe tears away with the back of my hand.

Mom's strappy sandals and perfect pedicure appear under the door.

"Luz, what's going on?" she asks.

Mom's not really the person I want to yell at right now.

But she *is* right there.

"What's going on," I say to the closed door, ". . . is that you *knew* that I didn't want to have this stupid party and you went behind my back to plan it anyway!"

So much for not saying another bad word about the debut.

I lasted for roughly one hour.

Mom heaves a sigh, leans her weight on one foot.

"Well, I knew you would never agree to it, so what was I supposed to do?" she asks.

The *audacity*.

"And then you got all upset," I say. "And froze me out, just because I had a *reaction* to what you did. Printing out and mailing save the dates to the party that I *said* I didn't want? That was not a whim, Mom, that was a premeditated betrayal."

Her feet disappear.

I hear a poof of air as she plops into the big chair covered in dresses next to the big three-part mirror, which you aren't supposed to fight with your mom in front of, you're supposed to spin around in front of it, stare at yourself from all angles, marveling at yourself, while your mom sighs wistfully and tells you that you're a beautiful blessed angel baby from heaven.

"It's not a *party*," she mutters, her words verging on bitter.

I snort.

"Okay, it's not *just* a party," she says.

I cross my arms across my chest and suck my teeth. She is technically right, though. It's not just a party. It's a grotesque theatrical production. It's a sick celebration of feminine purity and piety and beauty. A display of the illusion of wealth, which we don't have. It's—

"Lucia, your lola is coming for it."

"What?" I ask, breathless, flinging open the fitting room door.

She nods. Slumped in that dressing room chair, hugging her purse to her chest. She's wearing a floral baby doll dress today and suddenly, *she* looks like she's the one whose mom forced her to go to Macy's.

"So Lola's okay?" I ask.

Mom sits up in the chair.

"What do you mean?" she asks, on edge suddenly. "Of course she's okay."

"Well . . . it just kind of seemed weird, when she didn't come out for Maricel's, because she always comes, and then you said—"

"Don't worry about what I said."

She stands up and makes her hands busy reorganizing all the dresses I abandoned on the back of the chair.

Ali walks in, and shoots me a look like *what's going on in here*, and I shoot her a look like *the hell if I know*, and Mom just keeps stabbing the plastic hangers back through the dress sleeves until she straightens up and points a naked hanger at me, and then at Ali.

"Listen to your mother. I know what you girls think about me. Silly Mommy can't do this. Silly Mommy needs our help. But *I'm* the adult. I can handle things."

"Okaaaay," I say.

"Of course you can, Mommy," Ali says. She means it. Or she sounds like she means it, anyway. Maybe Ali is a better actor than I give her credit for. Someone get Jessa Jimenez on the horn, a star is born!

Because of course Mom needs our help, and that's fine, she's all by herself out here and that's how it's always been. Even when she was with Dad, she felt alone, because he was useless. Just because I think she's a little in over her head sometimes doesn't mean I think she's *silly*. Just because she's embarrassing sometimes doesn't mean I think she's *incapable* of things. The whole reason why I get so pissed at the California family is because they make her feel like garbage whenever they talk to her. She has always done more than enough, been more than I need, especially because *I don't need this stupid party.*

"All I want is for you not to worry about *anything*, except school," Mom says. "And track," she adds, pointing the plastic hanger at Ali. "And Luz, all I need from you now is to accept this party without making your dead rat face in all the pictures. That is *it*. I just want a nice picture of you to put on the fridge, and a nice picture of the three of us to frame and to put in my office, when I have an office, one day. Tapos! Finished, done! Okay?"

"Okay," we say simultaneously, baffled.

I guess, if my lola is going to come, to go through all the trouble of getting a visa and buying the expensive ticket and making the journey with three layovers and leaving the coconut farm and the sari-sari store, all to stay with us in our crowded little apartment, then it makes sense my mom would want to make the most of it.

And if we did that, and we did everything right, maybe she'd stay for a while.

Maybe she'd stay forever.

Maybe now that we're older, she'd have more fun here. I can show her that I can make adobo now and Ali will just have to suck it up and eat one shrimp with the head on, at least, and then Lola will have a better time here, and she'd stay. I could take her to the Sunshine, and show her the butter popcorn technique, she could meet Mr. Marco, and they'd get on like gangbusters, *God*, as long as it stays open long enough for her to get here.

It has to be. It just has to be.

"No dead rat face," I promise. "I can do that."

My mom nods, relaxing her shoulders. "Good. And I need a list of your friends for the program."

"What friends?" I ask.

"Ay naku." She throws her hands up in the air. "You know how a debut works. You need eighteen friends for your cotillion waltz. You can worry about who will be in your roses and candles ceremonies later, but you need to start practicing your choreography for the waltz ASAP."

"But Mommy, I don't have—"

"Ano na naman? This is all I'm asking of you, Luz, just make a list of your friends and text it to me, what is the problem? I'll use the Canva or something, just like for my real estate flyers, I'm sure there is a nice template for a debut program on there, and don't worry, I won't use glitter since you're more concerned about Mother Earth than your own mother."

"But—"

"Anak," Mom snaps. "I don't care *who* you bring. Just bring eighteen. Ewan ko sa 'yo."

Ewan ko sa 'yo could be polite, as in *it's up to you* whether we do pork or chicken adobo for dinner tonight, but here, it's not. Here it's, *ewan ko sa 'yo*, dismissive—it's your call, it's your responsibility, just like everything, just like everything that I'm responsible for, and everything I already handle, on a daily basis, *for her*, without complaint, and yet she still wants more from me, she wants more than I can give her, and it's not that I don't *want* to, it's that I *can't*, because I just don't have *eighteen friends*.

My blood is at a boiling point.

It's radioactive.

But then Ali puts her hand on my arm.

"Seventeen," she says. "You just need seventeen."

She squeezes.

I fill my lungs and bite my tongue.

I put my hand over hers and squeeze back.

"No," Mom says. "You're not supposed to be in it, baby, you're too young, you aren't out in society yet."

"What does that even mean, Mommy?" I ask.

She shrugs. "You know, like, *out*. In society."

"Okay, yeah, so it means nothing. Ali is doing it," I say.

"Eee!" she says, jumping up and down, and she's so happy that I have to laugh, and Mom does, too, and she's officially overruled whenever the baby is happy. And right now she is genuinely, gleefully happy.

Ali will be there. Ali will take the heat off me. Ali will be sweet and defuse the tension. Like always. And now my stomach twists with guilt, because her blood must boil sometimes, too.

But she never shows it.

"Okay, fine," I say. "I'll send you a list. But I'm not wearing that."

I point to the short little number Mom has in her hand with the low neckline.

A smile breaks across Mom's face.

She hustles past me into the empty fitting room.

"Well, I'll just try it on then," she says, closing the door. "Since we're here."

God, give me strength.

Sitting alone at lunch, without Esmé, I think of lots of funny things to say, but I have no one to *tell* them to. If I say something snarky in the cafeteria, but Esmé isn't there to hear it, does my snark even make a sound? A Treatise Concerning the Principles of Being a Loser with No Friends.

For example, from my new vantage point at the table by the door and the trash cans, I can see this one dude who brings, among other things, a single hot dog in a Ziploc bag to lunch every day. He does not bring a bun—and the hot dog itself, smooth and pinkish gray, does not appear to be cooked.

Today, however, in a shocking new development, he's brought *two* hot dogs, neither of which appear to be cooked, in two *separate* Ziploc bags.

This astounds me.

Why is it, I ask myself, that his disgusting uncooked hot dogs can't touch each other? *Why?* And then I think, in a weird 1920s radio announcer voice to myself: *Well, hot dog!* And I start laughing and laughing and he looks at me from across the table like I'm coming unhinged. Me! The one eating a normal lunch, Spam and rice.

You don't know everyone's story, Esmé would say if she were sitting here next to me. *What if all he has at home are hot dogs? What if he's gluten-intolerant? What if he's neurodivergent and hot dogs are his current food hyperfixation?*

She's a much better person than I am. Always thinking of

stuff like that before I do. I feel like she's somehow used her witchy powers to psychically reprimand me, even though she's *not* sitting here, she's sitting over there, with the theater kids, at their usual table, acting like they invented black clothing. Our former spot, the headquarters for our now defunct Pinay/Chicana coalition of two, has been overtaken by the Asian Club, half of their membership white guys who are way too into Japan because of anime.

Uncooked Hot Dog Dude gathers his stuff and leaves, giving me a clear view of the next table over. Sitting there, a whole bunch of people I don't know, maybe they're sophomores or first-years or something, and I *desperately* want to ask one of them if they saw the guy with the two hot dogs today, suddenly, I feel I will die if I don't tell them, *two uncooked hot dogs in their own individual, separate Ziploc bags*, it's unbearable, please, *please* tell me that you saw that, too, please, please. Tell me that I'm not wrong.

I pick up my backpack. I can make friends. I could, if I wanted to. I need to. I have to. No big deal. Just seventeen friends. Just seventeen friends who will dress up in matching outfits and submit to dance rehearsal for hours after school, for several months. Sure. Must start somewhere. *Start here*, a little voice inside whispers. *The hot dog thing is funny. The hot dog thing is great.*

Oh God, I'm walking over to them.

One's putting makeup on another one, one is reading alone, there's a couple sharing headphones, and someone who appears to be playing Pokémon GO on their phone, either that or recording content for an extremely niche A Day in the Life of a Sophomore or First-Year in Albuquerque, New Mexico, video.

They point their phone camera at me. I'm staring down its lens.

Jesus Christ, this is pathetic.

I twirl around and head for the door.

I can't. I can't even initiate a simple conversation.

How am I supposed to go from zero friends to eighteen friends? That is *so* unreasonable. That is not a S.M.A.R.T. goal. That is a D.U.M.B. goal. Depressing, unachievable, maddening, something-else-that-starts-with-a-*B* goal.

I dump my trash into one of the open cans by the cafeteria exit. Above them, the bulletin board for "Student Activities" screams out with socialization opportunities.

At the center of the cheerily decorated metal frame, lined with our school colors, there's a flyer for the drama club, COSTUME CREW NEEDED! *Stupid, Judas flyer.* That's the source of all my problems right there. I grab the flyer, tear it in half, and toss it into the trash. Costume crew for high school theater productions. What a ridiculous waste of time.

I cannot believe that when Esmé said we were doing high school all wrong, she actually suggested I should *join a club*. One of these things—School-Sponsored Student Activities. By suggesting that, she made it painfully obvious that she doesn't really know me at all, and that she never knew me, not really. She can't have. *Just look at this sad-ass bulletin board.*

Mock Trial, nope, Yearbook, *hell* no, *Anime club*? What a joke.

And then—

ARE YOU FUNNY?

This is a really shitty flyer, even compared to the others, handwritten in Sharpie, like a serial killer would. That's all it says. *ARE YOU FUNNY?* Simple. Confrontational, almost. Beneath the serial killer scrawl, a QR code, centered neatly against the white page.

I look around, at the cafeteria, at all these dummies, talking and laughing and talking and laughing. Esmé in particular is laughing her ass off, right now, at something Jessa Jimenez is saying.

What could possibly be so funny?

I stare at that QR code again.

ARE YOU FUNNY?

I take out my cell phone and open the camera app to scan it.

Because *I'm* funny, damnit.

If Esmé doesn't appreciate it, maybe somebody else will.

9

AFTER I FOLLOWED THE QR CODE AND LEARNED THAT this was a stand-up comedy club, I got like, marginally excited. It's a solo activity, really. No silly team building or anything like that. But now that I'm actually here, in the school auditorium, and there's more than one man bun in the room, I'm less so.

Multiple man buns in one place is never good.

My chair creaks as I attempt to look around, covertly. According to my cursory count, there are maybe twenty dudes in here? Mostly avoiding eye contact with one another, so at least I'm not the only friendless loser, even if I'm the only girl.

I recognize a few guys from my classes—Danny Wong from Physics, Russell Bernstein from Statistics, and Rahul Mathur from Contemporary Issues. I'd file all three of them under Generally Harmless/Nondescript. Everybody signed in on a piece of notebook paper by the door, but no one has emerged yet as our fearless leader. Who will it be?

The auditorium door opens, and in walks Noah Bradford.

No. No way.

I sling my backpack over my shoulder and march for the exit.

This is why you don't join clubs.

"Oh, Cruz, don't leave on my account!" he says.

I don't have time to reply because to my shock, walking in right behind Noah, is the Hot Silent Sophomore.

Jason Woods.

He sees me standing there with my backpack on.

"Looking for the comedy club?" he asks me. "You're in the right place."

And I'm so speechless, because that's what Jason Woods sounds like, and his voice is so deep and warm and *resonant* that all I can do is nod and drift back to my seat.

Noah Bradford throws his backpack on the floor, because he's an animal, and my shock deepens to new levels as Jason Woods strides onto the auditorium stage. He rolls up the sleeves on his loose-fitting flannel button-down and clears his throat.

Is he going to speak, because if he's going to speak, again—?!

"Hey, good to see you guys here," he says.

I'm screaming internally.

"Welcome to Open Mic Club. I'm Jason," he says.

I'm losing it.

"We're going to be working on jokes and going to open mics," he continues. "I've got a list. They're usually free to participate in. I'm thinking we can meet Tuesday/Thursdays after school. Right here. We'll need to do community service projects, too, in order for the school to sponsor us. Got one lined up at a retirement home already, but we'll need some more ideas on that."

Damn, in spite of everything, I'm dying to text Esmé about this. She would never believe it. Jason Woods is a stand-up comedian, captain of the man bun jokesters. Who knew.

"So, that's it," Jason says, holding one hand to his forehead, blocking the glare of the spotlight. "Anybody want to tell any jokes?"

Crickets. The most crickets you have *ever* heard.

A brief rustling of paper.

The shifting of bodies in the creaky auditorium chairs.

I'm getting that feeling, just like in class, of adrenaline punching through my veins like *don't call on me!* When your heart feels like it's going to jump out of you but you're trying to keep your face looking as casual as possible, like you've *intentionally* chosen this moment to read the poster on the wall behind your teacher's head but then also, maybe, *just maybe*, this tiny voice inside whispers— that if the teacher *did* call on you, you just might come up with something great.

"I'll go," a voice from behind me says.

Aha. Noah Bradford, of course.

"Great, let's give him a hand." Jason claps awkwardly and we all follow suit.

Noah steps up to the microphone. He's dressed like a youth pastor at a megachurch.

"Hey, so," Noah says. "My girlfriend asked me to take her to this cat café for lunch."

His hand goes to the back of his neck, bashful, like he didn't just start right out of the gate with *no big deal, I have a girlfriend* energy.

"And I was just like, I didn't know you were Asian."

My blood turns to ice.

There's a smattering of laughter from somewhere behind me. I turn around to see who it was, but everyone has already stopped. Onstage, Noah smiles to himself and turns the page in his notebook, like he's about to move on, like he's going to just turn the page on that tired old racist joke—hilarious, groundbreaking, never-before-seen humor, Asian people eat cats, *wow*.

And Danny Wong is sitting right there but he just looks at his hands, shaking his head. Sure, it's dumb. Sure, we've heard it before. But damn. Do we really just let him do it?

That little whisper in my heart that tells me that I might come up with something, something great—it turns into a bullhorn.

"Boo," I say softly. Then, I sit up, and say it with my whole chest. "Boo!"

Two full rows of dudes in seats twist back to look at me. Noah spreads his palms wide, his Moleskine notebook falling open.

"Excuse me?" he asks, laughing a little, laughing *at* me, like something might be wrong with me.

"You heard me, I said *boo*," I say.

I turn into absolute steel and give him a big thumbs-down.

"There's no *booing* in Open Mic Club," Noah says.

I look at Jason. "That was never established."

Jason's mouth opens and closes several times before he leans forward, propping his elbows onto the seat in front of him. "I would say it's generally considered poor form to 'boo' one's colleagues."

Despite saying this, he looks like he might be suppressing a laugh, and I feel a surge of hope that I might be able to win him over to my side.

"Even when they're making *bad* jokes?" I barrel forward, incredulous. "How will he ever grow as an artist without any honest feedback?"

Jason smiles.

"Um, may I continue?" Noah asks from the stage.

"That depends, do you have anything *original* in that little diary?" I spit.

"Whoa," Danny Wong says. "This is a lot for a Tuesday."

"If you're so much better than I am," Noah says, beckoning me, "then why won't you get up here?"

I blink slowly, crossing my arms.

"Well," I say, stalling. "I don't happen to have anything prepared."

"No worries, Cruz," he says. "Some people are artists. And some people are critics. It's a healthy ecosystem. We need each other."

I turn to Jason, the Formerly Silent Sophomore. "Is there fighting in Open Mic Club? Because I'm *going* to fight him."

"Nice reference," he says knowingly. "But no."

I blush.

"Okay, here's how we're gonna settle this one," Jason says.

He stands up, claps his hands, and points to Noah onstage, who looks extremely put out, like he's never been so insulted in all his life, like he's about to speak with Jason's manager.

"Noah, you're going to bring five minutes of material to the fundraiser at the retirement home on Saturday. And— sorry, what's your name?"

He gestures to me with an open palm, like he's asking me to dance in an old-timey movie.

I gulp, staring at his hand. "Lucia."

"And Lucia will also bring five minutes of material to the fundraiser as well. Whoever's material gets the bigger laughs will be deemed a true artist. May the best jokes win. Fair?"

He looks between both of us. The rest of the room is completely still.

Noah snaps his Moleskine notebook closed. "Fine."

"Lucia?" Jason asks.

Everyone turns to look at me, but it's Esmé's face I see, the boats in the marina, the bass from the ballroom at Maricel's debut pulsing in the background. *Maybe we've been holding each other back.*

Well, how's this for branching the fuck out? Maybe she was the one holding *me* back.

"Yes," I say, leaning back and crossing my arms. "Great."

I think I'm doing something called a Power Pose, but with Noah being up on the stage, and all the extra height from the man bun, I just can't lean back far enough to compensate for how utterly terrified and small I feel on the inside.

"Splendid," Man Bun says, glaring at me.

This is going *very* well.

I have not made one friend, but rather, further entrenched myself with one enemy.

Five-Minute Set
Draft IV
Some Actual Funny Jokes About Cats!

Do you ever get the feeling that people only like you because you don't need anything from them?

My sister wanted a dog when we were little but our dad said no. He told us he prefers cats because they take care of themselves.

Very Dad energy, right? "Being good" equals not bothering me with your pesky needs!

Maybe just my dad? Cool, cool.

Also, it's just not true. The thing about cats. Cats think they can take care of themselves but they are delusional. Mom got us a cat when she and my dad got divorced. They wouldn't allow dogs in our apartment. The cat came with the name Crouton from the shelter, which is a horrible name but it felt wrong to change it.

Crouton is a runner. She tries to bolt out the door when we come inside with our arms full of groceries. She's always plotting her escape, always, like Shawshank Redemption style. She's, like, tacking up a giant poster of Taylor Swift from the movie Cats in her room. My sister and I think it's our room but it's really hers, the whole apartment is Crouton's world and we're just living in it.

The thing is, Crouton would not survive five minutes in the streets. She won't even eat unless you warm her wet food up for ten seconds in the microwave. Twenty seconds is too hot. Five is not enough. She'd rather starve. And her food must be served in this special square dish. She's afraid of dishes that are round. I'm serious.

So, if she were to get free, what is her plan? There won't be any warm Gravy Lovers Seafood Medley in the alley behind the Super Walmart. And all the dishes are round! It's a nightmare!

But sure, Dad, cats take care of themselves.

When my parents divorced, Mom left me and my sister with Dad for a while. She went out to California and stayed with her sisters.

During that time my dad got mad because my sister's teacher called him to ask if everything was okay at home because her hair wasn't brushed.

Mom used to do our hair before school. Brushing it and parting it and putting it into little pigtails or braids. This was also when she cleaned the wax out of our ears with a bobby pin. The metal was cold. When she helped us into our tights, she pinched our legs in her hurry to get us on the bus looking presentable. It felt a little like a good girl assembly line. I knew she was tired coming off her night shift when she did this but she did it, dutifully, every day. And because she'd be asleep when we got home from school until it was time for her to get ready for work again, this was sometimes the most time we got to spend with her all day, and I didn't mind her cold fingers or their accidental pinches, at all.

Dad was mad about the teacher calling and asked Ali why she couldn't brush her hair herself like I did.

The next morning, I laid out both of our clothes on the bed before school. And I brushed Ali's hair and smoothed down her cowlicks into butterfly clips. I thought about cleaning out her ears with a bobby pin, too, but I was scared, thinking about a diagram of the inner ear I saw in my science textbook, that I would rupture her eardrum by accident. But I didn't know how long Mom would be in California, either, so then I thought about both of our ears just filling up and filling up with more and more wax until we couldn't hear anything anymore and when the teacher called on me I wouldn't answer and then she'd call home to my dad and he'd be mad again.

When Dad saw me doing Ali's hair, he said that's my big girl.

He looked so relieved. So I didn't say anything about the earwax.

But I couldn't stop thinking about it all day.

At school, after lunch, I threw up.

He had to come get me. When he saw me sitting there in the nurse's office, wearing a too-big T-shirt the nurse had given me from a plastic bin because my other one smelled like bile, he looked mad because he had to leave work and like why can't you just take care of yourself?

Anyone else?

Jesus this isn't funny at all. How did we wind up here?? We were talking about cats. Revise.

According to YouTube, I might need something called a button here.

I've been scribbling in a notebook I bought.

It was ninety-nine cents. Those damned Moleskine notebooks that Noah uses are like ten dollars. Madness. Are they made of real moles? Actually, what is a mole? *No—don't google now. Too much work to do.*

Unfortunately just having a notebook has not magically solved all of my problems, though it felt like a strong possibility when I was standing in the aisle at the pharmacy, where they were all lined up in neat stacks with their crisp white pages, next to all the shiny pens and planners, everything seemed easy to fix, I just needed to buy these things and everything would sort itself out.

But no.

Standing in front of my full-length bedroom mirror, I count the pile of crumpled-up pages at my feet. At least thirty cents' worth. I'm cocooned in my gray sweatpants and my Sailor Moon T-shirt because I need maximum comfort. The messy bun has been creeping higher and higher on my head as this night has worn on—it's almost as ratty as my new nemesis Noah's.

"The thing about man buns is—" I say, giving myself finger guns in the mirror.

What the hell am I doing? I have no idea whatsoever.

"What was I thinking about the other day that was so

goddamn funny in the cafeteria?" I mutter, pacing back and forth across the carpet. "A kid that eats hot dogs for lunch every day? What's so funny about that?"

And now I'm talking to myself.

"Lucia!" my mom calls from down the hall.

"Yes! Oh my God, Mom!"

I run to the kitchen where my mom is spooning pancit into a big plastic Tupperware for her lunch tomorrow.

"What's something funny that I said recently?" I ask.

She straightens up and stares at me, dead in the eye.

"Can't think of anything."

"I'm serious!" I say, crumpling into a chair at the kitchen table. "I really need to know . . . for a project."

I barely catch myself. I'd almost spilled the beans, and I am *not* telling her about Open Mic Club. She *did* say that I think everything is a big joke. This is just more fuel for that fire.

"What project?"

"It's community service," I say, which is true. "For a school club."

"Not falling for that again," she says.

"Why is that so hard to believe? I have interests!"

"Interests in what? Cosplaying as a vagrant?" she asks, gesturing at my threadbare pants and stretched-out T-shirt.

"Wow, Mom, that was really messed up. And funny!"

I stand up and run back to my room to write that down, but then I turn on my heel when I remember.

"Wait, why did you call me over here?"

Wordlessly, she hands me a pearly white envelope,

massaging the back of her neck. She looks tired. She showed houses yesterday and then pulled a graveyard shift last night.

"What is this?" I ask.

Inside the envelope, I find a simple card with a message written in delicate cursive:

Tita Renalyn, Lucia, and Ali:

*Salamat sa coming to my debut
and for the perfect gift.
xoxo, Maricel*

"Through God, all things are possible"

I wince. I still haven't called my tita or texted Maricel. I'd tell myself that by now it's all blown over, but I know better. It absolutely has not. In fact, I wouldn't be surprised if Tita Connie sent this envelope with overnight express shipping, just to make a point.

They're classy, we're not.

"What gift?" I ask, waving the thank-you note in the air. "Wasn't the gift of our presence enough?"

My mom leans on the kitchen counter and closes her eyes as if she hopes she'll have a new daughter when she opens them.

"We gave her a gift card. For microblading. Whatever that is."

"Who is 'we'?" I ask.

"It was on the registry," she says, pinching the bridge of her nose. "I signed your name to the card. You're welcome."

"There was a *gift registry*? What the *hell*?"

"Luz, please."

Sucking on my teeth, I glare at her. She raises her hands to her temples and presses her fingertips to them, gently.

I'm sorry, but I cannot believe that she shelled out a hundred bucks, at least, for perfect, rich-ass Maricel's eyebrows? Why?

"You make a list of all the things you want for your gift registry," Mom says.

No, *no*, not another thing for the debut to-do list. I didn't know I'd have to make a gift registry, *where is my notebook*—?

"Microblading wouldn't be a bad idea, anak," she says, looking pointedly at me.

I cover my eyebrows with both hands.

"You stay away from them!" I say.

"And I need to book your venue," she says, sighing.

She opens upon her laptop, the grooves beneath her eyes darkening as the glow of the laptop screen hits her face at its high points. She's probably staring down a list of more things she says I don't have to worry about, but that she'll ask me to do eventually, so I may as well just learn what they are all now.

"But my birthday is still like, six months away," I say.

"Yes, and we should have booked it six months *ago*," she says. "Ay naku, it's just, you know, I was still studying for my real estate license exam, and I wasn't sure how much I would be able to afford . . ."

She taps away at the keyboard, her brow furrowed with worry.

The unsaid words building up inside me have reached critical mass.

"See," I say. "*This* is why I can't stand this debut shit. It's such a waste of money."

"Lucia."

Her use of my full name freezes me in place. She presses her palms together and looks me in the eye.

I swallow.

"It is worth it," she says. "You are worth it."

Is that why this matters so much to her? Like getting my picture taken in front of a big cake with my face on it will prove she loves me or something?

To who?

"I'm worrying about the debut," she says firmly. "And you are worrying about school. That's it. Okay?"

I suck on my teeth.

"School, Luz. Will you at least talk to the guidance counselor like you said you would? You know I can't help you with this college paperwork. I don't know enough about it to help you. Mommy is uneducated."

My throat begins to close.

I hate that she beats herself up over stuff like that. It's not *her* fault they make the applications so confusing and the scholarships so hard to get. It's not her fault I got kind of a shitty score on the ACT in June and she cried because she couldn't figure out the math problems I got wrong, either. I'm retaking it and she's stressing out about it, even though it really doesn't matter that much.

"Okay, okay, I will!" I say, clutching my elbows. "I'll go on Monday."

Her face looks pained.

She doesn't believe me.

She really doesn't believe that I will do this simple thing and, worse, she believes that it's her fault. I remember the way she looked at Tita Connie when I called her a liar. Like she'd failed. Like she was a bad mom. Because I was a bad daughter.

I'm such an asshole.

"And—" I say before I can stop myself, the words are tumbling out of me, anything to make this feeling go away, anything to make that look on her face stop. "I will look at venues. For the debut. I'll make a list and compare prices and we can look it over together. Okay?"

She blinks, and straightens up. "Really? You're going to do it?"

Suddenly I feel like I'm wearing my old church dress at Cecelia's debut again. I feel like I'm eleven years old. The itchy collar is growing tighter and tighter around my throat. The lights are getting hotter and hotter.

I blink that all away.

"Sure. Fine. I will."

She narrows her eyes at me like she's going to try to make me sign a contract or something, but then, they drift over to the couch where surely she is imagining her feet propped up with a good movie playing in the background while she falls asleep.

"I got this," I say, giving a big thumbs-up. "No problem."

But the moment I get back inside our bedroom, confronted by the pile of failed jokes adorning the floor, I deflate. The night is quiet, Ali is out with friends. I open our bedroom window to let in the cool night air. A siren wails in the distance.

I plop down at my desk/Ali's getting ready station, I open my laptop but I have no idea where to start. With hotels, like Maricel's debut? Hold the ice sculptures, of course.

But my heart drops when I see the prices for renting a ballroom.

That can't be right. There's no way.

My cell phone is in my palm before I know it, my thumb hovering over Esmé's contact. She'll know how to fix this. She always does.

She'll have the perfect pep talk.

But then, my heart twinges. The corkboard behind our desk is lined with photo booth pictures of me and Esmé.

Her beautifully done winged eyeliner and my plain, boring T-shirt.

Her arm slung around my shoulders. My hand over my face, hiding from the camera.

How long *was* she planning her "branching out" speech? Was she thinking about it when we took this picture, on my birthday last year? When we got burritos from our favorite food truck and went to Cosmic Bowling with our moms?

Did she tell Mrs. Mares what I said?

Does *she* think I'm an asshole, too?

Goddamnit. I wipe away the accumulating wetness from my eyes.

Forget it. I will do it myself. I will turn to the place where I learn how to do everything: the Internet.

How to plan a debut, I type into the search bar.

Oh my God. A gold mine.

Of course, why didn't I think of it sooner? My cousin Cecelia's debut disaster went viral years ago. There are tons of videos just like that, on YouTube, and articles and blog posts from girls planning their own debuts and documenting their whole experience.

I won't even *need* to text perfect Maricel and concede that I don't know what I'm doing.

I can do it all on my own. It's perfect. *Ewan ko sa 'yo.*

Check out my TikTok videos for more, one of the articles says. And duh, of course, why didn't I think to search TikTok?

I open the app on my phone and type in: *18th birthday debut.*

Get ready with me for a day of scoping out venues for my debut!

A day in the life of a girl planning her debut!

My debut aesthetic!

Flashes of ball gowns, twirling skirts, pink, pink, pink, all blurring together.

Cake towers and corsages and camera flashes.

An actual red carpet.

A car with a big dumb red bow on it, like on TV.

I scroll and scroll.

I've chewed my nails down to complete and total destruction at this point.

Then, finally, a video titled *Planning your Debut on a Shoestring Budget* by a user named DanielaLove appears. She's got more than a thousand followers and this video has tons of comments:

thank u so much Daniela. i don't have much of a budget and my mom never had a debut so i really want to make mine special 4 her

Thank God for DanielaLove.

That's my girl. I can feel it.

"Hi, everyone!" she says, her beautiful round face smiling in the middle of the screen.

She's wearing brown lipstick and gold cross earrings. Her brown skin is simply *glowing*. Her bedroom behind her is like a brighter, tidier version of mine, complete with photo booth pictures with her and her friends tacked onto a bulletin board above her bed. Eerie. Of course, *she* has tons of friends, and there is a clip from her debut intercut with her introduction to prove it—this girl is working with a full court.

"So glad to be here on hashtag DebutTok," she says, flashing a peace sign.

DebutTok. Wow. Of course there's a whole Internet infrastructure around these things, mirroring the real-life infrastructure. Catering services and photography studios with quinceañera packages, a whole store in the mall just for quince dresses, and apparently, there's a whole debut hashtag.

It's the coming-of-age industrial complex.

"I'm going to talk about planning a debut on a budget, and a short time line."

Thank you, DanielaLove.

I run to grab my ninety-nine-cent notebook, leaving my crumpled-up jokes forgotten on the floor.

10

THE FUNDRAISER AT THE RETIREMENT HOME IS ALREADY here and I'm on the bus, furiously scribbling jokes into my notebook, on the opposite pages from all my notes on *How to Plan Your Debut on a Shoestring Budget*.

"San Mateo," the automated announcement comes on, and I jerk up, almost having missed my stop.

"Shit!" I say, snapping my notebook closed and scrambling to collect my things.

An older Filipina lady nearby glares at me over her giant overstuffed tote bags.

"Pasensya na po, Tita," I say.

She blinks rapidly in surprise.

The doors open at the bus stop and I fly out into the street. My backpack bounces against me as I jog past a strip mall with a gas station and a liquor store and a karaoke bar, to the retirement home, St. Lucia Independent Living, which offers the finest care to every resident, according to their website.

I laughed when Jason emailed out the address for the event and I saw the place has the same name as me.

See, I'm a saint, I replied to his email. I will win, for it is divinely ordained.

See you Saturday, Saint.-J

My heart raced a little at his reply, which is stupid. Stupid crush on Hot Silent Sophomore. But I couldn't help it. *He has a nickname for me.* I'm dying to tell Esmé, which just makes me sad all over again, and sadness is not funny, so I put her out of my mind.

A super bored-looking front desk person in a suit buzzes me through the glass doors.

"Hey, I'm here for the show," I say, panting.

They point down the hallway, and my sneakers squeak against the linoleum as I pass by cheerily decorated bulletin boards with inspirational quotes.

Inside St. Lucia Independent Living, there's an open door into a large, high-ceilinged room, filled with rows of folding chairs and a small sound system playing oldies in the corner. In front, a stage, like the kind that would appear in our school gymnasium for holiday concerts, with a single mic standing at the center. Clusters of balloons are tied to the chairs at the aisles.

Throughout the room, young professional types mingle with the elderly residents of the home, their parents, or their grandparents, I suppose.

The guys from the comedy club, including Man Bun Nemesis, congregate around a table with bowls of snacks.

Giving Noah a wide berth, I sidle up next to Jason. He's wearing an amazing cowboy shirt today with intricate threading at the pockets.

"Hey," I say, trying to sound breezy and casual.

"Hello, your holiness," he says, bowing.

"That would be the pope."

"Oh, wait, you're *not* the pope?" he asks. "This is awkward. That's why we were invited here today."

"Shoot, that makes sense," I say, nodding.

"So, do you think you could pretend? To be the pope?"

"I do it all the time. Wait, why *were* we invited here?" I ask.

"They hold community events now and then, like this one, and charge a small entry fee, to increase their budget so that they can do more special things for all the residents. I offer our services at a very reasonable price. Free."

Just then, Alyssa Vasquez and some other girls from the school dance team appear in the doorway, wearing their school color T-shirts, joggers, and white sneakers. It's a uniform I would be fine with wearing; unfortunately, dance team isn't a viable option for me to recruit potential friends from, given that I'm extremely uncoordinated.

"Hey!" Alyssa waves at Jason, her car keys with a million keychains on a lanyard dangling from her hand.

They hug and I look at the ground. The carpet in here is hideous.

"Ready to reprise our classic routine from last year?" she asks him.

She completely ignores me even though I'm standing right here and we have gym class together. But maybe she doesn't recognize me, she typically only sees me from behind when she's lapping me on the track. I "run" a fifteen-minute mile, which is the time required for a passing grade. She holds the school record at a 6.25-minute mile.

"I've been practicing," he says. Then, as an aside to me, "The dance team is also a regular on the St. Lucia Independent Living circuit."

"Jason's like our manager for all the over-sixty clubs," she says. "I'm Alyssa."

I know, I think.

"Lucia," I say.

"Okay," she says. "We're gonna go stretch."

The girls all follow her. Noah Bradford makes a beeline over to join them, his dopey man bun bouncing.

"Okay, they need to *stretch*?" I ask. "Like they're going to do *Swan Lake* or something?"

"Stretching is very important when you're doing any physical activity," Jason says. "To prevent injury. There's actually a mobility class in here right before this. I'm all warmed up."

"You're joking."

"No. My grandma lives here," he clarifies. "So I come and take it with her. It's a pretty nice place."

"Oh my God, where is your grandma?" I say. "I love grandmas. Is she a fat grandma or a skinny grandma?"

"Excuse me?" He laughs.

"Both equally lovely. And there is no in-between. Tell me I'm wrong."

"She's a skinny grandma," he says. "Her doctor prescribed her bacon."

"That seems . . . wrong."

"What kind of grandma do you have?" he asks.

Suddenly, the thought of my lola, coming here to see us, like actually being here, makes my mouth go dry. What if we can't pull off the debut? What if she and my mom have a huge blowup again? What if, when she sees me in real life, outside of a FaceTime frame, she's disappointed in me, too?

"Jason!"

Topping out at ninety pounds soaking wet, a string of

pearls, a puff of soft gray waves, and clear brown eyes, a skinny grandma approaches us.

"This is going to be a blast," she says. "I just told everyone they had to come."

When Jason hugs her, she almost disappears into his arms.

"Grandma D, this is my friend Lucia."

My friend? My cheeks burn.

"Hello, dear," Grandma D says.

I'm doubly surprised, because this skinny grandma is white, but I have a white grandma, too, don't I? She takes my hand when I offer it. It's soft and warm. Her face is all freckles and laugh lines.

"I love a funny woman," she says.

"Me too," I say, but then when I realize she means me, I swallow nervously, mentally scanning all my stupid jokes. I hadn't thought about grandmas listening to them. I was only thinking about stupid Noah Bradford and how much I wanted to destroy him.

"Hey, man."

Noah reappears, the devil himself, clapping Jason on the back. He wedges himself in, with his back to Grandma D.

She wrinkles her nose at the back of his head.

"What order are we going in?" Noah asks.

"Let's go sort that out. Excuse us, Grandma D," Jason says, leading Noah away from her, then looks over his shoulder at me. "Lucia, you ready?"

"Born ready," I say, glaring at Man Bun. "Nice to meet you, Grandma D."

"Knock 'em dead," she says, and winks.

My heart begins to knock at my ribs as I follow Noah and Jason over to the makeshift stage. It's way too bright in here for comedy, really. It's the middle of the afternoon. And there are way more people here than I thought there would be. My insides are churning. Shit.

"Jason, you have a white grandma," I say, to distract myself.

He laughs. "She's actually not my grandma. I just call her my grandma. She and my grandma were best friends."

I look at Grandma D, perched like a little bird in the front row of the folding chairs arranged neatly facing us. She waves. She's sitting by herself.

So does that mean . . . ?

"My grandma passed away," he says.

My heart constricts.

Russell Bernstein, Danny Wong, and Rahul Mathur appear, their arms full of bags of Takis.

"Those are for the residents," Jason says, gesturing to the Takis.

"I need brain fuel," Russell says.

"Does your brain run on palm oil and monosodium glutamate?" Rahul asks.

The guys all start jostling one another but I'm still thinking about Jason Woods's grandma and her best friend, Grandma D, and how nice it is that Jason still comes to see her, and wondering *when* Jason's grandma passed away, and seeing Grandma D sitting there, all by herself, the little paper program in her hands, smiling, and she has no family around her or anything, and my face is getting hot, because oh God, what if Lola *isn't* okay, what if Mom is *lying*?

She's always lying. What if Lola is *sick*, and she had, like, appointments or something and *that's* why she couldn't make Maricel's debut, and she's only coming now to mine because she might not have much time left and she wants to see everyone before she goes? That would explain why Mom is pushing it so hard and she wants it to be perfect—

"Hey, Saint," Jason asks.

I shake my head. "Yeah?"

"You okay with that show order?" he asks.

Not having heard a word they said, I blink away tears before they have a chance to form.

"Having second thoughts, Cruz?" Noah asks. "Not too late to back out."

No. I will not concede to this Man Bun. I will worry about Lola later.

"Let's do this," I say.

"Welcome everyone," Jason says, holding a microphone at the front of the room. "We have a very special program for you tonight, and we're starting off strong with a talented group you may remember from last year, everybody jump out of your seats and put your hands together for the Del Norte High Dance Team!"

The music booms from the loudspeakers as Alyssa Vasquez and the dance team girls jump up—Alyssa actually does a *backflip*—and proceed to lead the seniors and their families, step-by-step, through the choreo to "Crank That (Soulja Boy)" by Soulja Boy.

Jason is doing the moves right along with them, and pointing at Grandma D, who is getting really into it in the crowd.

At the side of the "stage," Rahul and Danny are going off script, doing the worm, and Noah and Russell are intermingling with the audience, encouraging everybody to do the dance and participate.

It's so overwhelmingly *goofy*.

Though some might call it wholesome. I suppose.

And now Noah is standing next to Grandma D and doing the dance moves along with her, slapping his knee and then slapping his foot, and she's laughing, and having a great time, and everyone is, and I had no idea that the dance team even did stuff like this.

Russell Bernstein comes up to me, moving his arms from side to side.

"I can't help but notice," he says, out of breath, "that you aren't cranking or rolling over here."

"You're very astute."

"Here, watch me," he says.

"Oh, I am. And you look very, very cool."

"It's not about looking cool," he says, hitting each move with a little extra pizzazz. "It's about feeling good."

I stick my arms out in front of myself in a half-hearted Superman pose.

"There you go," he says, and bounces away, to an elderly man in a wheelchair, who is waving his arms from side to side.

After the song ends, the dance team performs another routine they've been working on. It's not bad. I've never seen them perform before. Esmé and I usually hide in her car during assemblies, where she smokes and I complain and we listen to the radio. I always imagined that

131

the dance team would suck, but they don't, and realizing that is accompanied by a sinking feeling, the source of which I can't quite pinpoint.

"Thank you again, Del Norte High Dance Team!" Jason says, on the mic again, as the crowd cheers and the dance team waves and exits.

It's time.

As Jason, continuing to act as the host and MC, warms up the crowd, Noah and I stand off to the side, in the darkness, waiting to go on. He's going first, I guess. He seems to have gone into some kind of stand-up warrior mode. His jaw tense and his fists balled up, his dumb little notebook tucked under his arm. He bounces lightly on the balls of his feet. Does he really care about beating me *that* much? It's kind of . . . sad.

"Hey," I whisper.

His eyes dart around, like this is a trap. "What?"

"Listen. I want to tell you why I hate that joke you told."

"Are you trying to sabotage me or something?" he asks.

"No, dude, I'm trying to tell you the truth," I say, hissing. "Which is that people make that stupid joke about Asian people eating cats and dogs *all the time*, and it's tired, old, and racist."

He looks at the ceiling and sighs. "Here we go. Now I'm a racist."

"The *joke* is."

"That joke is my go-to opener. It always gets laughs. Danny Wong's never said anything about it. It's not that serious."

"Noah. You remember from History last year? 'Yellow

132

Peril' propaganda? Scaring Americans into thinking Chinese and Filipino people shouldn't be allowed in this country because they're taking people's jobs?"

"Yeah . . ."

"That's funny to you? What is the joke exactly? That we're *so* low, so dirty, so beneath you, that we'll steal your pets and eat them? So we don't even deserve to be here, right? Because we're practically not even human?"

I can't believe I said all that. It's all spilling out of me. It didn't even bother me that much, hearing that stupid joke everywhere. Hearing him repeat it. It's tired. It's transparent. It's everywhere. I didn't think it bothered me.

And I won't cry. Not in front of this Man Bun. I *won't.*

"Do you know many times . . . ," I say, sucking in a deep breath, ". . . I've heard that damn *stale*, thousand-year-old joke?"

Noah is quiet under the lights.

Jason is saying something onstage that kills with the retirees and their families.

"Wait, you're Chinese?" he asks. "No, you're Filipino?"

"Yeah."

Onstage, Jason wraps up his last joke. The room fills with applause.

"But like, not *full*, right?" he asks. "You're mixed with something."

I roll my eyes.

Why did I bother? Waste of breath.

"Okay, everyone," Jason says over the sound system. "Please welcome to the stage, a founding member of the Open Mic Club, Noah Bradford!"

The crowd claps and cheers as Noah looks at me, his face unreadable. I cross my arms and look at my sneakers, feeling him pull away and climb up onto the risers.

He takes the microphone, looks out into the crowd.

"Hey, hey, everyone," he says. "Does anybody have F7?"

A chuckle from the audience. Okay, so Noah thought about his audience. This time. Maybe he just wasn't thinking about *why* he was saying the things he was saying. Or maybe he was, and just didn't care. He just wants a laugh and he knows he'll get it no matter what. It doesn't matter to him if what he's saying fucking sucks. He's so shallow and entitled. Because everything in life is easy for him like that. He can just go through, every day, never worrying about anybody else and everyone will just laugh and clap him on the back. His whole life.

"Oh wait, bingo night's *tomorrow*," he continues, opening up his ten-dollar Moleskine notebook to the page where his stupid *go-to opener* must be written.

He gazes out into the faces of those seated in the crowd and those of us standing on the side of the stage—at Jason's Grandma D, at all the guys from the club. At Danny Wong. Then me. He clears his throat.

And turns the page.

"Every time I pour myself a glass of water, my mom asks me if I'm thirsty. And I'm like, oh, is that what this is for?"

I'm too surprised to laugh, but everyone else does.

"I just like how it tastes," he says.

I suck on my teeth. Whatever. So he skipped it. He's probably going to want a ticker tape parade for it, too.

"Hey," Jason whispers, a shiver tingling at the back of my neck. "You're on next."

Looking at all the faces in the crowd, laughing at stupid Man Bun, my guts liquefy.

My armpits dampen. I try to remember what I had planned to say. I can't remember anything. I clutch my notebook to my chest.

When it's my turn to get up to the mic, the spotlight feels ten times hotter than it should. The crowd is huge, twice as huge as I thought it had been, three times as huge.

After a smattering of clapping, the room falls deadly silent.

My palms are somehow cold and sweaty at the same time. My fingertips tremble at the pages of my notebook.

"Hey," I say, and it comes out dry, like there's nothing real behind it.

I clear my throat and to my horror my mouth fills with bile.

No, no, no.

"So," I say, swallowing hard. "There is this guy at school who brings an uncooked hot dog to lunch every day."

Grandma D leans forward.

I want very much to run through the propped-open door, past the bored-looking receptionist, and not stop running until I cross the threshold into my bedroom, and dive into my bed, never to leave again.

"So, one uncooked hot dog," I say, stammering.

I can't even read what I wrote down, so I'm trying to pull the words from the air, from that deep place inside the grooves of my brain where they had previously seemed so clear, so sure.

"Gross."

I try not to look at them, the faces in the crowd, but I can't help it.

Jason is nodding, his eyebrows raised high, as if to say: *And?*

Someone coughs.

Grandma D sinks against the back of her chair.

And with that small movement, I know I've plummeted in her esteem as quickly as I was raised in it—not a funny woman, after all.

Not a Funny Girl. Not a Fanny Brice. Not going to prove anyone wrong, after all.

And it crushes me. Absolutely crushes me.

Because I think I'm so fucking funny, don't I? I think I'm so much smarter than all these assholes. I think I'm so much better than Jessa Jimenez with her directorial debut and Noah Bradford interjecting into every class about who was at the Prickly Pear last night and possessing the absolute audacity to write in his Moleskine notebook about his girlfriend and the cat café and repeat it onstage, believing wholeheartedly that what he's doing is *actually* comedy— and now it's my turn. I'm the one up here.

I have the microphone. It's my chance.

And I'm blowing it.

But I can't let it die here. That tiny voice in my heart, that one that whispers, despite everything, despite every single person telling me otherwise, that *maybe, maybe you'll come up with something great.*

"But then," I choke out. "The other day he brought *two* of them, so at least he's doubling down."

To my intense relief, and probably to everyone else's as well, laughter ripples gently throughout the room.

Not big, but not insignificant.

A ripple of laughter that seems to say, *at least you made a joke. We were worried about you for a second there.*

"Whew, told a joke," I say. "Check."

More laughter.

"I'll work on that one," I say, folding down the corner of my notebook page, and something quiets in my heart.

For now.

Jason Woods smiles.

"So. Any cat people in the house tonight?" I ask.

Later, as we're cleaning up after the show, and all the residents have left, I'm neatly folding up a tablecloth, as I learned from the Internet, when Man Bun comes over to me.

Russell Bernstein and Rahul Mathur are gleefully stomping on balloons and popping them while Danny Wong records them on his phone. The dance team and Jason are stacking the folding chairs and leaning them up against the far wall.

"Hey," Noah says, his hands in his pockets.

So, he's come to gloat. His jokes got the bigger laughs, therefore he is officially deemed un-shitty, hooray.

He wins, and I'm the loser.

I squint at him and say nothing, placing the tablecloth into a basket. He jumps to remove the next one, folding it sloppily.

"What do you want?" I snap.

"*Nothing*, Jesus," he says. "I just wanted to say I liked your hot dog kid joke."

"But?" I ask, and snatch the crumpled tablecloth from him so I can refold it into a neat square.

"But, nothing," he says. "Like you said onstage, you'll work on it. You'll figure it out."

What is this? I eye him suspiciously.

"Do you want to talk it through?" he asks.

"What do you mean?"

"It helps to talk it out sometimes. Jason and I debrief after every set we do. You know, this worked, that didn't work. And then we try again."

I flinch. That sounds horrific. Every part of it.

"I know," he says. "But this is just one of those things where, unfortunately, you have to fail publicly, a lot, in order to get better."

"I don't remember signing up for this MasterClass," I say.

"Whatever," he says, turning away.

I bite my tongue.

"Wait," I say, with a sigh. I look up at the ceiling tiles. "Thank you."

"For?" he says, some of that familiar Man Bun swagger returning.

"For skipping the joke," I say.

Noah crams his hands into his pockets again.

Smirks.

"Oh, I didn't do that for *you*, Cruz," he laughs. "Something better just came to me."

My hands wrench the tablecloth as he shakes his head and turns his back on me, walking away.

I want to throw it at his head, but then he'd know he got to me. Why would I even *thank* him for that? What was I thinking?

Then he turns around.

"What's the joke exactly?" he asks.

I blink. "Huh?"

"Your question, from before. I'm asking you now, about your hot dog guy. What's the joke exactly?"

I don't know. The hot dog guy brings an uncooked hot dog to lunch every day. It's disgusting. The joke is that *he's* disgusting? No. It's that he looks very normal, but he does this one really weird thing? Then it gets *weirder*, and I can't explain it.

"It just drives me crazy," I say.

"Why?"

"Because I can't imagine what could possibly be going through his head."

"But you don't ask him."

"No."

"So, you sit across from this dude in the cafeteria every day, observing him, obsessing over his thought process, and you could just say 'hey man, what's the deal with the hot dogs,' but you don't?"

"No," I say. "So, what?"

"So, is this joke about him or you?"

Obviously, it's about *him*. He's the one with the hot dogs.

"How could this joke be about me?" I ask.

"They're all about you, Cruz," he says. "You're the one telling them. Who else would they be about?"

A chorus of cheers erupts from across the room. Russell and Rahul are in a handstand contest with Alyssa Vasquez by the folding chairs.

"I think you did your man bun too tight today," I say.

He laughs. "So you're saying you like my hair better when it's down, flowing over my shoulders, blowing in the wind?"

"*Bro*," I say. "Relax."

Russell drops to his feet, followed by Rahul. Alyssa, having held out for the longest, wins. Noah, seeing this, cheers and everybody claps. She does a graceful dismount.

Jason crosses the room to us.

"Great set, Saint," he says. "You too, man."

"*Saint*?" Noah asks.

"Is that your official ruling?" I ask Jason pointedly.

Let's just get this over with.

"Well, unfortunately I left the applause-o-meter in my car during the show," Jason says. "But based on my obser-vations, I do think that—"

"It's fine, dude," Noah says. "I forfeit."

"Well, it's settled then," he says, takes my wrist, and lifts my hand over my head like I've won a boxing match. "You win."

"Wait, but—" I'm flustered, both by Jason's fingertips

around my wrist and by Man Bun's sudden pivot, and it's all really confusing.

"Hey!" Rahul calls out from across the room. "We're all going to Taco Cabana for two-for-one Cabana bowls. You guys want to come?"

"Always down for Taco Cab!" Noah says.

Jason looks at me.

The dance team and the comedy club are all laughing and grabbing their bags as they file out of the room.

"Lucia!" Alyssa calls out. "Come!"

But it's not like she actually wants me to come. Or that it would be such a great time. Taco Cabana isn't even a top five burrito in town for me. Maybe not even top ten. And what am I supposed to talk about? They already heard about the hot dog guy so I have nothing left to say. And they're all friends already. They already have their own thing going on, their own jokes probably, and I won't know what they're talking about or what to say.

"No, no," I say. "You guys go ahead."

"Suit yourself," Noah says as he puts his arm around Jason and steers him to the door. "I wanted to run something by you."

Jason looks over his shoulder at me. "See you at the next meeting?"

The next meeting.

I chew the inside of my cheek.

"Yeah, maybe," I say. "We'll see."

Jason waves as he and Noah disappear through the doorway.

The room is unrecognizable from when we walked

in, all the tables and chairs tucked away to the side, the stage gone. Just ugly carpet. No windows. No applause, no laughter.

And it all comes flooding back. The silence.

The lights click off. Apparently they were on a motion sensor. And because I've stopped moving I'm standing there alone in the dark.

11

OKAY, FINE, SO I DIDN'T WANT TO GO TO TACO CABANA for two-for-one Cabana bowls with Noah Bradford and Alyssa Vasquez, but I don't want to go home, either, to my mom, to see her with her stress face on, poring over party-planning stuff, asking me whether I did this or that, and another FaceTime call with my lola, who may or may not be sick, when I'd have to just pretend like everything is fine when it's potentially very not fine, not just to Lola but to Ali, who is always watching me as if I know what to do. Which is a mistake.

The sunset in the west is a brilliant, fiery orange, striped with golden wisps of clouds and airplane contrails. The air smells crisp, like fall. Like time passing. Like change.

I hate it.

There's only one movie on the marquee above the entrance to the Sunshine Theater tonight. It's a horror movie, which I hate. Whenever Mr. Marco was showing one, I'd cover my eyes the entire time while Esmé laughed with glee at the blood gushing and the bones crunching and all the stupid people wandering into darkened basements.

Marco has replaced the paper sign on the front door about the theater closing and I dutifully rip it down again as I walk inside.

"Lucia, please stop doing that," Mr. Marco says, startling me.

He's not at his usual post behind the ticket counter, but rather, he's taping up more paper signs onto all the framed movie posters that line the walls. *$10, $20 . . .*

"You are *not* selling your movie poster collection," I say.

"No Esmé again?" he asks.

Instantly, I'm furious. Who cares about Esmé? No, there's no Esmé anymore and there never will be again. Because she found someone better and left me in the dust. Everyone always does. So. Joke's on me for thinking I could change it, everybody laugh and point at Lucia, ha, ha, ha.

"You *can't* sell these," I say.

"Well, I may not be able to. I already put them on eBay. Nobody seems interested."

"That's because people are stupid and they have no taste."

He shakes his head, in his old man sweater and his old man glasses, and goes back to carefully taping up price tags.

But these posters can't come down.

They've always been here.

They're supposed to always be here.

"You're really just going let this happen?" I ask, my voice rising. "You're not even going to try?"

"I did try," he says gently.

"Well, try harder! This is an important place to people!"

"What people?" he chuckles. "There's no one here."

He gestures to the empty lobby, lined with his vintage movie posters and the stained carpeting, crushed from our footsteps, Esmé's and mine, and yes, other people's, too, before, in some time before, when the numbers lined up somehow and there was enough to pay the rent. Why can't we get back there?

There must be someplace along the way where things went wrong and if I could just figure that out, I could fix it. I know I could.

"I'll think of something," I say, slapping a ten-dollar bill onto the ticket counter. "Keep the change."

Inside the theater, I prop my ninety-nine-cent notebook open on my knees.

I start scribbling about how nobody on eBay has any taste in movies or movie posters and how everyone is stupid and this is why we can't have nice things like special movie theaters that take the time to curate interesting stuff and not just show the same soulless robot car superhero movie over and over.

But then I scratch it all out.

I already tried writing jokes about other people, like the hot dog guy at lunch. And that wasn't very funny. And I tried writing about myself, about my dad, and Mom, and Ali, and that definitely wasn't funny at all.

But there has to be a way. There must be.

So, in the light of the movie screen, which I do my best to ignore, because it's a horror movie, I write.

Blocking out all the sound. I write manically. Until my hand cramps. Until the muscles in my neck scream. Until I can't even read my handwriting anymore. And I keep writing on the bus on the way home, in the flickering streetlamps that we pass beneath, rhythmically, and when I get home, I write, cross-legged on my bed by the lamp on my nightstand, ignoring a call from Lola, flipping my phone over when her face appears on the screen, *no*, I can't talk to her, not yet, I just have to keep writing, to find a way to say what I mean so that *someone* will finally, finally understand. That someone, if not Esmé, if not Mom, *someone* will laugh out loud because I'll find a way to make them understand it so fully and completely that they'll not only say they agree with me, but also that it's perfectly reasonable to be a hating-ass bitch under these circumstances. When they hear how I've captured perfectly how absurd everything is, they'll see that it's all very funny, actually, and because it's funny, it's going to be okay.

———

There's this guy who brings a single uncooked hot dog to lunch every day in a Ziploc bag. And I've never talked to him. And he has no idea that I think this much about him.

He probably has no idea who I am.

He's just minding his own business, he's usually reading a book for most of the lunch period or scrolling through his phone, and then he eats his single hot dog right before the bell rings and for some reason I'm very fixated on this.

I'm very fixated on other people.

Especially what I find annoying about them.

Why is that? What is the joke here, exactly?

I find a lot of things annoying about other people. Got a rave review from my best friend recently. She called me a hating-ass bitch.

And she was really right.

I saw this movie, Funny Girl. *And Fanny Brice was this comedian who made fun of herself. She said basically that people were going to laugh at her anyway, and by turning herself into a joke, on her own terms, she was taking control. She was taking control of the narrative.*

But if the joke is about me, what is it about, exactly?

I'm Filipina, right?

And I'm turning eighteen next year.

And I don't want to have a debut.

—————

Unless you happen to be one of the fifty or so active members of the Rio Grande chapter of the Filipino-American Association, you probably don't know what a debut is. *Insert explanation here—it's like a Filipino quinceañera, but it's when you're eighteen, not fifteen, etc.* So, you might be asking yourself, or, for the purposes of this joke anyway, just pretend you're asking yourself: Why wouldn't I want to have one?

How could this radiant young woman before you, in sweatpants and a crusty Sailor Moon T-shirt, the very picture of grace and poise, *not want* to be the focal point of an elaborate, choreographed waltz?

I happen to have the perfect video all queued up to show anyone who asks me this question. That framing might suggest that people ask me this question all the time. They do not. The only person who has ever asked me is my best friend, and, again, she's not talking to me anymore because—*punch line, callback, something else here?*

I like to call this video, Exhibit A.

There will be no further exhibits. None will be necessary. Content warnings in effect for late-stage capitalist colonial class cosplay, rose gold, and vomit.

When you click on the link you'll see this video is titled: DEBUT GOES HORRIBLY WRONG—UNDER THE SEA THEME. Hashtag eighteenth birthday, hashtag Filipina debut.

If you know, you know, but if you don't, buckle up.

It starts, like all home movies do, with an establishing drone shot. Of a hotel. And it's just a hotel in San Diego but we're meant to understand it's a big deal.

Cut to: the hotel ballroom. Here, we're treated to time-lapse footage rolling over a gentle piano track—the camera pans across a set of rose gold balloon letters inflating to form the words HAPPY BIRTHDAY CECELIA.

This is *cinematography*.

Cut to: a hotel room. The camera closes in, tight, on my cousin, because this is a video of my cousin's debut from almost eight years ago, by the way.

Cecelia Cruz Santos, a stunning eighteen-year-old Pinay morena, dedicated to her ten-step skin care regimen, is perched in a plush white chair and wrapped in a seafoam robe. The camera lens seems to cradle her face in a gauzy, gentle light. As the piano track comes to a crescendo, a disembodied hand dusts her cheeks, gently, with rose gold highlight. Her eyelashes cast demurely downward.

Is this person famous? you might ask. The answer is, absolutely not.

It's literally just her birthday.

Cut to: the ballroom, where the beat drops. A fog machine gushes as the party guests flood in.

Next, Patty the Party Planner, forty-five, dedicated to her ten-step skin care regimen, takes the spotlight: a clipboard under her arm and a rose gold professional grade Lavalier microphone hooked gently behind her ear. She speaks with the velocity of a morning radio DJ and the authority of the auntie who doesn't let you eat food over the carpet.

"Ladies and gentlemen, how are we doing tonight?" she asks. "Welcome to the beautiful ballroom, here at the Marriott Marquis San Diego! I'm your host, Patricia Celebrado Almajose Bigayan. We have *such* an exciting program ahead, in honor of our debutante: Cecelia! Cruz! Santos!"

Applause.

Patty raises her palms to the heavens as her voice booms from the loudspeakers. She is standing in between two giant layer cakes with seafoam green mermaid cake toppers and shellacked with, you guessed it, rose gold fondant—which is inedible, did you know that?

"Tonight, we celebrate Cecelia, who has blossomed into an amazing, beautiful, GOD-LOVING young woman."

Belated content warning for the word *blossomed*.

"Let's begin by acknowledging God's presence here tonight," Patty continues.

Cecelia's family—two hundred of them, anyway, including those from overseas, plus fifty of her nearest and dearest friends from high school and various extracurricular activities that I'd never be caught dead doing—bow their heads.

The room stills as Patty begins the blessing.

"Lord God," Patty says. "Giver of life and constant companion . . ."

Suddenly, the camera swipes over to eleven-year-old Lucia Cruz, also known as me, because yes, I was there, soy yo, c'est moi, the true star of this viral video. I'm simply *Luz* to my mom, who is about to be mortified. Stay tuned!

The image comes into focus: Young Luz, stumbling across the dance floor. Sweaty, with frizzy black hairs at her crown, tugging at the itchy collar of the church dress that she has worn against her will because, as her mom always says, children do not have rights. With her other hand, Luz clutches a stack of notecards up against an upset stomach.

"Lord," Patty continues. "We offer you praise on this very special day . . ."

There are three important ceremonies in any Filipina debut. There's the cotillion waltz, in which the debutante and her court, eighteen friends, present a choreographed dance to the guests. The Eighteen Roses, in which the debutante is presented with a single rose from the eighteen closest men in her life, including younger relatives. And the Eighteen Candles, in which the eighteen closest women and girls in her life share a kind word about what she means to her, while holding a candle.

In preparation for her cousin Cecelia's Eighteen Candles ceremony, young Luz has carefully written out a nice memory about the time Cecelia took her to the open-air mall in Mission Valley. It was the first time Luz had ever been to California. The first time she'd ever seen a palm tree. The first time she'd ever had halo-halo. That day, when Cecelia handed Luz a long plastic spoon to share the dessert with one hand and gave her shoulder a gentle little squeeze with the other, for a moment, just for a moment, she felt okay.

About all of it. Her dad saying that nothing would change when he left. That they'd still see each other all the time. A lie. About her mom's car, running out of gas on the side of the highway, because she said she could stretch out what was left in the tank until payday. She couldn't. About her little sister's face, confused and scared in the back seat, because she didn't know what was going on, and she kept looking at me, I mean at Luz, as if she knew.

About her lola's suitcases, all packed, in the entryway, because even after she'd come to help out her mom after the divorce, she was leaving, too.

When Luz was with Cecelia that day, beneath the palm trees, she realized how much she wished she could be like her. Somebody pretty, and gentle, and always doing and saying the right things.

Cecelia wasn't someone that you could just leave like that.

Luz, of course, did not write any of that on the note-cards for the Eighteen Candles ceremony. And I don't know why I'm writing it now, because I'm not going to say any of this onstage, because none of this is funny. But there's a joke in here somewhere. There has to be.

Luz wrote an Eighteen Candles speech about halo-halo, purple and sweet and crunchy. About palm trees. Because that's the only way she knew how to say what she meant.

But she would never make this speech.

Seeing all these party guests who were going to be listening to her, looking at her, imagining the weight of the microphone in her palms, and everyone's face trained on her, and the sensation of sweaty bodies crushed closely together, has compelled her to push through the crowd in search of air.

Oh no, you might be thinking. *Is she going to—?*

Yup. Luz projectile vomits. Half-digested lumpia mingled with lumps of rose gold fondant, which is apparently inedible, now coats the dance floor, glistening.

"OH—" Patty the Party Planner gasps.

"OH—" the party guests gasp collectively.

This event sets off a chain reaction of vomiting amongst all of the children present. Totally classic birthday party stuff! Right? Confused, Cecelia peeks out from behind the blue velvet curtain where she has been waiting for her entrance cue from Patty. The curtain had been red originally, but her father arranged for the hotel to swap it out in order to match the Under the Sea theme.

Spotting this movement, the expert cameraman manages to capture the *exact moment* when Cecelia's face dissolves from puzzlement to abject horror at the sight of her titas and titos, in their church outfits, scrambling to scoop up her baby cousins, slip-and-sliding around on the dance floor, now impossibly slick with puke.

Straightening up, Luz grimaces when she spots the beautiful debutante. Cecelia's tears sparkle under the blue light, matching the jewels in her tiara perfectly. Not relevant to the story but what does a tiara have to do with Under the Sea? It keeps me up at night.

When Luz locates her mom's face in the crowd—eyes wide, her hands covering her mouth—she hugs herself tightly. Luz's younger sister, Ali, hides behind their mother's legs, but she's still watching.

The worst thing about being an older sister is being watched like that, all the time. The pit of Luz's empty stomach fills up with shame because it was my fault—her fault.

Don't you just hate it when you throw up in front of a huge crowd of your bougie family members at your cousin's debutante ball, setting off a chain reaction of vomiting children so heinous and grotesque that the footage goes viral, and then every time those family members see you for *the rest of your life* they not-so-subtly remind you that they were unable to recoup the security deposit from the hotel, and all the carpeting had to be replaced, because of you?

There are 101,978 views and 587 comments. This one haunts me:

EmmaGee03 says, *Poor thing! Beautiful dress though. Does anybody have a contact for the MC? My 18th b-day is two years out . . . time to start planning!*

12

"YOU CAME BACK!" JASON SAYS WHEN I ENTER THE auditorium on Tuesday for the next meeting of the Open Mic Club.

The crowd has thinned out considerably since last week. The twenty dudes from the first meeting whittled down to only Jason, Noah, Rahul, Russell, and Danny. Five.

Plus me.

I came back. Because, this morning, my mind wiped clean of debuts and dresses and candles and roses and vomiting, having dumped it all into my notebook, I woke up with an epiphany.

"Hey, I was thinking," I say. "How much money did we make for the old folks' activity fund?"

"About a hundred dollars and some gum," Jason says. "Why?"

Rahul and Russell bump chests.

"Do you guys know the Sunshine Theater?" I ask.

"Yeah, of course." Jason nods. "That place is awesome. Heard it was closing, though."

"But it *can't* close. It's an *institution*," I say. "There's nowhere else like it here. What if we held a fundraiser to save the movie theater? Like, as the club?"

"So, you are staying in the club, then?" Jason asks.

I feel my face get hot. "I mean, yeah, I guess."

"Wow, now we *definitely* need to apply for the diversity grant," Danny says.

"We can get twice as much funding if we've got a girl!" Russell says.

I do a double take at Russell, long limbed, and nondescript, in his dorky fleece and ill-fitting jeans. Did he just quote *Mean Girls*?

Noah looks skeptical. "A fundraiser sounds like a lot of work, Cruz. It would take more than a hundred bucks and some gum to save that place."

I wave my ninety-nine-cent notebook in the air.

"It's no sweat. I'm kind of a budding event planner right now. And I think the idea would just be to get them over the hump, pay their debt down a little—revitalize interest in the place. Maybe we can get some eccentric billionaire to swoop in if we do a comedy show, maybe get somebody to headline? Get a local band or something?"

Danny Wong raises his hand and says, "My cousin is the drummer in that band Burly Boba."

"No way!" Noah says. "Nice."

Okay, if he likes Burly Boba, maybe that means he'll actually help out.

I push forward. I have to get them all on board. I just have to.

"And if it works, I can get Mr. Marco, he owns it, to agree to let us do our shows there, to raise money for the club and you know, work on new material and stuff," I say. "We could have a regular place to perform."

"I think it's a great idea," Jason says.

The guys start chattering about the Burly Boba band and who we could potentially get as a headliner.

Good. Things are happening. I'm making things happen.

I am in control. Of the narrative.

I hug my ninety-nine-cent notebook to my chest, a lifeline.

Later, Mr. Marco leans on his elbows and reads his newspaper at the ticket counter at the Sunshine.

"Marco, this is happening. Just accept it," I say.

And yet he continues to ignore me.

Maybe he just needs a jump start.

"Wow," I say. "Thank you for offering to save my livelihood, Lucia, you're a hero, Lucia, you're like Catwoman but for small business owners, Lucia? These are just some examples of the many things you could be saying right now to express your gratitude."

"Wasn't Catwoman the bad guy?" he asks, folding his newspaper inside out to read the travel section.

"If looking as good as Eartha Kitt is wrong, I don't want to be right."

Marco stares at me over the rim of his glasses and does not even crack a smile, not even a twitch. I'm looking *extra* ratty today. I refuse to believe the irony failed to land.

I'll get him one day. He's my white whale.

My phone lights up. It's my mom.

Today is Sunday, her one day off, and she's been running around town looking at caterers for the debut. We're supposed to meet up at a venue this afternoon and of course, I've totally lost track of time and will be late.

"Hi, Mommy." I pick up, pulling on my backpack and

hustling to the door. "You'll thank me later, sir!" I call over my shoulder to Marco as I run out into the bright afternoon.

"We don't have a motif!" she practically screams.

I pull the phone away from my ear, wincing. A gust of wind attacks me on the sidewalk, blowing all my hair into my mouth.

"A what?" I sputter.

Well, at least we're both running late. I can tell that she's driving because I hear her broken turn signal ticking away in the background. It's been that way for about three years. It drives me nuts. It's one of the reasons why I always preferred driving with Esmé.

"I was trying to reserve the lechon and I got to talking with the butcher and he started asking all these questions like which party planner we're working with, and also which florist, and what's our motif? We don't have any of those things!"

"Mommy," I say, trying to model a calm demeanor, before she crashes into a mailbox or something. "We have a party planner. The party planner is me."

As I knew she would, she has slowly, but surely, delegated the majority of the debut planning tasks to me, either directly, or indirectly by making a big show of being unable to handle them thereby forcing me to just do them myself. It is an infuriating yet familiar cycle of frustration, guilt, and acceptance made more infuriating by the fact she pretends it isn't happening or, worse, doesn't realize it.

"Did you secure the pig?" I ask.

"Yes, of course I secured the pig!" she shouts. "The pig is the only thing I know how to secure!"

The bus rounds the corner and I take off running to catch it.

"The pig is the most important part," I say, trying to catch my breath. "The pig is the lynchpin. Everything will fall into place *around* the pig."

"But what about your eighteen roses?" she says.

I squeeze myself onto the crowded bus, desperately trying to follow the thread of this conversation.

"What about it?" I ask. "You said I had time for that one!"

"You know what I mean. Your eighteenth rose."

I mentally run through the debut program again—*your eighteenth rose*, the Eighteen Roses ceremony, where the debutante dances with "important men" in her life, each of them giving her a long-stemmed red rose. This could be grandfathers, uncles, brothers, cousins, friends, and—right.

The dad. The whole thing usually ends with a longer dance with the dad. Because he's so important.

Or whatever.

"Come on, Mom," I say. "Can't we just omit that part?"

I angle my body so that I'm not nose-deep in somebody's armpit. I know that Mom doesn't want to see Dad or even talk to him.

"Omit?" she says. "We can't omit!"

"Can't you and I just dance?" I ask, laughing. "We can do the chicken dance. I know that one."

"Hindi nakakatuwa!" she snaps. "No chicken dance."

"Who cares if Dad's there or not?"

"Well that's how it's *supposed* to be. That's what everybody *expects*."

She clicks her tongue.

I bite mine. It doesn't really matter if that's how it's supposed to be because that's not how it is, is it?

"Just because we are no longer together," she says, refusing to use the word *divorce*. "He is still your father. So, that's what we're going to do. It's just . . ."

The bus comes to an abrupt stop at a red light and I almost lose my footing.

"What, Mom? *What?*"

She needs to say something but she won't just spit it out.

"I haven't told your lola that he remarried," she says.

There's silence on the other end. Silence, except for the broken turn signal clicker. I can't believe she wouldn't have told her own mom about something that big. Something that hurt her that much. But then again. Yes, I can.

"Why not?" I ask.

"I don't know," she says. "It's embarrassing. And it's all so very final now."

"What, your divorce?"

"Naku, yes, okay? I feel like I failed," she says. "And what's everybody going to say? She's so young."

"A fetus," I concur. "With a fetus. Babies having babies."

"Luz, *please*."

"You're the one who brought it up. So, you're saying you want Dad to come but not bring Sunny because Lola doesn't know Sunny exists?"

Lola coming back is making things complicated. There are all these things I'm supposed to pretend not to know and I can't keep it all straight, just like I can't keep straight which version of Mom I'm dealing with. I never know if she's going to be confiding in me like a friend or telling me what to do like a mom. I don't know what she wants from me, or how to fix this. I want to. But I don't know how.

"No, no," she says. "Well, I don't know. Do *you* want Sunny there?"

I want to scream.

No, I don't want Sunny there. I don't want *anyone* there. I don't *want* this party.

"Whatever you want, Mom," I say. "Just tell me what you want and I'll do it."

"I don't know what I want," she says.

My neck and shoulder are cramping so I move my phone from one ear to the other. I take a deep breath.

"If *you* talk to Lola about Sunny," I say, "I'll talk to Dad and invite him to do the roses thing, okay? I'll invite him. I'll do the whole thing."

"I don't know . . . ," she says.

"Mommy, she's not going to care. I promise."

"Maybe you could talk to her," she says.

Christ, is she crying?

"Fine, fine, I'll talk to Dad and I'll also talk to Lola. Okay?"

"Thank you, anak."

At least maybe she'll relax now and—

"But you still need to think of a motif!" she screams, dialed back up to ten immediately.

"Can't the motif just be 'Pig'?"

"Luz!" she says.

"No? Okay, motif has moved to the top of the list. On it."

"Okay. And your friends? For the cotillion?"

"Yeah, yeah. Don't worry. I'll see you soon."

I hang up, and contort myself so that I can pull my notebook out of my backpack.

The pages are a mess of debut planning notes, half-baked jokes, and ideas for the Sunshine fundraiser, and whatever the hell it was that I wrote last night that started off about hot dogs and ended up at chain-reaction-vomiting at Cecelia's debut when I was ten.

I clutch the unwieldy to-do list in front of my face.

"On it," I whisper, willing it to be true.

All the venues we looked at were out of our price range.

We are back to square one.

The only thing standing between my mom and a full meltdown is the fact that I told her I'd pick a "motif" by tomorrow and make a list of decorations we needed, per *How to Plan Your Debut on a Shoestring Budget*.

I click on DanielaLove's video again. I've watched it about ten times already.

"Remember," she says, flipping her long black hair. "There are lots of things you can do to make the space look nice without spending too much money, as long as you have a cohesive *theme*!"

She claps her hands.

I slump over my desk, in a very un-debutante posture.

Cohesive theme. Cohesive theme.

DanielaLove doesn't list any examples of themes, which I am praying is the same thing as a motif, so I try to find another video that does by scrolling through the DebutTok hashtag.

My head grows heavy, so I rest it in the crook of my elbow.

What was Maricel's theme? The ice sculptures, the pasta station . . . maybe her theme was: *We're Rich*?

I should call her to ask, but turning my cell phone over and over again in my palm, all I can think of is the horrified look on her mom's face when I called *my* mom a liar in front of her. She literally clutched her pearls.

Perfect Maricel probably thinks I'm feral, too.

Oh, well. How much of a help would she really be, anyway? There's a very low probability of finding any ice sculptures that fit in our budget.

Perhaps a tasteful ice cube?

A video entitled EIGHTEEN ROSES CEREMONY: CATARINA'S DEBUT!! scrolls into view.

But what about your eighteenth rose? Mom asked.

In the thumbnail image, Catarina's wearing a stunningly puffy white ball gown; it's almost as wide as she is tall, with traditional bell sleeves. Something about her is cool, though—a flower crown that tilts jauntily to the side, in one ear a delicate gold chain dangles, and in the other ear, a stud catches the light. Black nail polish.

In the still image, she grins from ear to ear, her hand hovering in front of her face as if she's about to cover it because she's cracking up too hard. Portrait of a Fun Debutante.

I click play.

What Catarina is laughing at is her dad.

Her dad, in a bow tie, doing a goofy dance.

Laughing faces crowd around the tables lining the small dance floor, craning to see. It's not a hotel ballroom, maybe a restaurant, and it's packed with family, empty plates and crumpled napkins piled high, empty bottles, candles twinkling, and one auntie at the corner of the frame who has taken her shoes off her aching feet. She is clapping along to the beat.

Her dad hands Catarina a red rose.

Find out how much roses cost, I scribble in my notebook.

Suddenly, the song changes to "Dahil Sa Iyo," 1964, sung by Cora and Santos Beloy, a song that my mom and Lola used to sing on the karaoke machine in our living room.

Catarina and her dad don't do some big choreographed dance, waltzing and sweeping around the room with their feet in sync, because it's a tiny little dance floor, in a tiny little restaurant, with their family pressing close around them, and a little baby asleep in a tita's arms already.

Her dad just hugs her. And they sway side to side.

Until the song switches. And she holds on to her dad until on cue, a little boy runs onto the dance floor, holding out one long, red rose to Catarina.

Seeing him, Catarina releases her dad, who looks at her with so much feeling that I want to look away, and begins to waltz with the little boy, probably her brother, or baby cousin, the stem of the red rose resting in their adjoining palms.

The little boy says something to her and she leans down to hear better.

Catarina smiles at him, so tenderly, and he's looking up at her like she's the best person in the entire world, and her dad, off to the side now, is looking at her, too, everyone's looking at her, but she's just looking at that little boy and listening to him carefully, really listening.

I click the video off.

Swiping tears from my cheeks, I pick up my pen again.

There's no point in wanting the things that are supposed to be but aren't.

I have work to do.

"Saint Luz has the floor," Jason says. "For the remainder of the meeting."

"Okay," I say, slamming my fraying notebook down onto the podium in the auditorium. "Let's save the Sunshine."

I'm already in a bad mood, because nothing is happening fast enough, and I still don't have a debut venue, and I have to go my *dad's* house tonight and stay with him and Sunny for a couple of days because Mom picked up some extra shifts to cover for someone, so she isn't going to be home really at all. I said *why does that matter?*, and she got mad at me, and made me call Dad, and reminded me that I promised to talk to him about being my eighteenth rose, and I'm supposed to talk to Lola about Sunny, which I still haven't done, and so I said *fine* and I called him.

I did everything she asked. Like I always do. She acts like I don't, but I do.

Jason, Danny, Russell, and Rahul have their notes in front of them. Noah is off to the side, doing sit-ups.

"*Must* you do that now?" I ask.

"Gotta get my reps in, Cruz," he says, his head appearing over his knees at three second intervals. "Comedy is very physical. Not everyone realizes that."

And not everyone realizes that you are a. Fucking. Dumbass.

I massage the back of my neck.

Best to ignore him.

"Where are we with folding chairs?" I ask the group.

"Grandma D says the retirement home will donate them for the evening," Jason says. I give an appreciative nod and make a satisfying *check* on my list with my pen. Thank God *someone* here is on top of things.

Jason takes a gulp from his shiny metal water bottle, which reminds me that my blood is entirely made of coffee at this point. I make a small note in my notebook's margin.

Hydrate!

"And the headliner?" I ask, turning to Danny, who was supposed to talk to his cousin about the band.

"Well," he says, trailing off.

"What? Well what?"

"My mom and my aunt are kind of in a feud right now. Something about a baby shower and an air fryer. I don't know exactly, but the tension is thick."

"And? So?"

Danny winces a little and I feel a twinge of guilt, but I really don't have time for this. Anyway, whose aunts *aren't* locked in a constant, ever-shifting and ever-deepening feud?

I keep my gaze steady.

He blinks his dark eyes first.

"I'll text him right now," he says.

"Thank you," I say, harsher than I mean to.

But Jesus, how hard is it to send a text?

On my list, next to *Headliner*, I try to write the word *pending* but it's so illegible that tomorrow I may not be able to read it, so I scribble it out.

Try again.

But my hand is shaking. Damnit, coffee, you Judas. I scratch out the whole thing and move on.

"Uh, okay, what else?" I ask.

"Food?" Russell says. He sits up straighter in his chair, opening his notebook. "I had an idea. What if we work with Mr. Marco to create a little menu: a twist on movie theater food. Like fancy popcorn balls, nachos? My sister is a caterer and at her wedding she had these amazing little—"

"Fancy?" I cut him off. "No. The Sunshine Theater isn't fancy. That's the whole point."

The fake butter that coats your insides. The queso that you have to scarf quickly, while it's still molten hot, before it turns to solid plastic. The grocery store white bread hot dog buns, the plastic mustard and ketchup dispensers.

Esmé and I had a contest once to see how much relish and onions you could pile on before the whole thing collapsed when you lifted it to your mouth. It was like Jenga but for condiments. That's what I said, anyway, and when I said it, she laughed.

"Fancy just for the fundraiser," Russell says, twirling a pencil around his index finger. "To make it special."

"It's already special," I say, trying to twirl my pen but my hands are still shaking from the caffeine so I send it sailing across the room.

The guys follow the pen with their eyes as it skitters across the floor.

I clear my throat.

"And the flyers?"

Noah has switched to doing squats. This is supposed to be his job. Graphics to post across social media platforms. But, instead of telling me he's done it, like he said he would, he's staring intently at a spot on the wall, with his hands behind his head.

"Noah?" I ask, hating that I have to say his name.

"Oh, yeah, no problem. It'll take five minutes."

My eye twitches.

"But it shouldn't only take five minutes. We said we wanted to come up with some ideas for a hashtag. And pick a color scheme. And get some nice pics of the theater."

"Yeah, yeah," he says. "I will."

"You know what, it's okay," I say, pulling my backup pen from my bag. "I'm going there later anyway. I'll just do it."

I scribble out Noah's name next to the words *Social Media Campaign.*

"You'll do what?" he asks. "Take the pictures?"

"I can do the whole thing, it's fine," I say. "I'll have ten hashtags to run by you guys before the next meeting."

"You're the boss," Noah says.

Ignoring the looks that the guys are giving one another, I flip to a fresh page in my notebook.

There. The clean lines are calming. Start again.

It'll be fine.

"Okay, that's it," I say, pulling my bag over my shoulder, expecting them to walk out with me, but they hang back.

"Great," Jason says. "Thank you."

I give a weird thumbs-up and leave the auditorium, worry twisting in my stomach as they begin talking quietly behind me.

Great, now they think I'm a bitch. They want to kick me out of the club and give up on the Sunshine just like everybody else. If that's the case, so be it, I'm already doing it all by myself anyway.

I don't need them.

I'm gathering more and more steam as I stomp all the way to the bus stop on the corner. The sun is so bright it's blotting out everything, leaving nothing except a vision of Noah Bradford's stupid smirk, haunting me, *you're the boss!* Well maybe I wouldn't have to act like one if everybody else would just get with the program.

All I want is to go to Mom's apartment and put on pajamas and go to bed absurdly early watching a movie and cuddling Crouton, but I can't, because I have to go my stupid *dad's* house tonight.

There's a crushed-up beer can underneath the bus stop bench, and I kick it, hard, letting out a frustrated scream.

A brown, yeasty sludge spills from it as it skitters across the concrete.

"Hey."

I whirl around, and Danny Wong is standing there, with a yoga mat slung over his shoulder. His hands are tucked into his pockets.

Danny Wong and I have never really talked before, and I don't know why he would have followed me, if that's what he did. Today he's dressed simply, but well, he doesn't have a stylistic flair like Jason does, but he obviously takes care in his appearance, nice skin and nice hair, and most important, properly fitting jeans.

He doesn't comment on my outburst or my kicking of the beer can. He looks past me, at the approaching city bus.

"You want to come to yoga with me?" he asks.

The bus grinds to a stop in front of us, spilling passengers from its doors.

"I don't do yoga," I say flatly.

Almost imperceptibly, he raises an eyebrow at me. Looks me up and down.

"Maybe you should."

If he's trying to say that I seem tense or inflexible, like, metaphorically, then, well, maybe he has a point.

"I don't have any extra clothes," I say in protest.

He looks at me sideways again, at my baggy sweatpants and oversize T-shirt, with that little eyebrow raise and the barest hint of a smile. "Luckily, your carefully selected school attire transitions well from day to evening."

"What exactly am I supposed to wear to school, Danny? Would casual suiting meet your standards?"

When he steps onto the bus, he looks over his shoulder at me.

"Come on," he says.

I open my mouth to protest. I really don't have time for this, and anyway, my failed foray into the realm of after-school activities with the comedy club seems to prove everything that I'd always insisted on with Esmé—I officially do not play well with others. Right?

I let an elderly passenger with a lot of bags get on in front of me. I look helplessly at the bus driver, who doesn't care what I do, one hand on the wheel.

Would it be so bad? Esmé had asked, that day when Ali wanted us to help out at the track team fundraiser.

"In or out?" the driver asks.

I get in.

On the bus ride over, Danny explains that the yoga studio is pay-what-you-can. The teachers are volunteers or in training for their yoga teaching certification. I'd never noticed it before, even though it's located in the strip mall with the used bookstore, a boba tea shop, and a store that Esmé likes that sells crystals and herbs, which we always called the Witch Store even though that's not what it's called. There's a Blake's Lotaburger standing on its own in the parking lot. I suggest we pound some premium angus beef with green chile before class but Danny tells me that's not a good idea.

My heart aches as we pass by the Witch Store, and I

can't help but scan the parking lot, hoping to see Esmé's car tucked neatly between the fading painted lines on the black asphalt. I steal glances through the glass doors, hoping to see Esmé there, her wing-tipped eyes carefully selecting the perfect new stone. She isn't there, but it still feels like she is, it feels like she's in there right now and so am I, and I'm making fun of her penchant for magic rocks and she's telling me I'm acting like a real Bitch Ascendant, and that we'll buy some incense for Mr. Marco that's supposed to bring abundance and he'll roll his eyes as he accepts it but he'll place it right behind the counter, next to the devotional candle we got him that has the alien from *Alien* instead of any of the saints.

Following Danny's lead, I drop a few crumpled bills into the shoebox at the front desk at the yoga studio and fill out a waiver on a broken clipboard. I don't know how I could possibly hurt myself by yoga-ing too hard. Isn't it just a lot of lying on the floor and stretching?

Inside, I cringe when Danny rolls out his mat near the front of the room, right in front of what I presume is the teacher's mat, and right next to the floor-to-ceiling windows that face the sidewalk, and the parking lot beyond it.

"Can't we go in the back?" I whisper. "Preferably in the corner?"

"Sorry, I am not a *back row* student," he scoffs.

"But anybody walking by can . . . *see* us."

"Now you're some kind of shrinking violet? What's the difference between this and being onstage?" he asks.

I clutch my borrowed mat to my chest. "I don't know. But it is."

Onstage, I'd started to feel some semblance of control. Onstage, I was in charge of what people saw. What they knew about me. What I wanted them to know. It's not at all like someone observing me from a window, so clearly trying and failing at something new, in the bright light of day.

"You want to be near the teacher if it's your first time," Danny says. "So you can see them and so they can see you. Don't worry, it's my favorite teacher today. She's amazing."

He steps onto his mat and casually dives over his toes, bending in half.

I can't believe it.

"Damn Daniel," I say. "You're all bendy. I can*not* do that. Wait. Do I need to be able to do that?"

"They'll offer modifications to all the poses if you need them."

"I feel like you're speaking some kind of yoga language."

He rolls his eyes at me.

"The different yoga positions are called poses," he says. "And if you can't fully do them for any reason, there's a modification, like a different version of the same thing, so you're still using the same muscles."

The studio around us is already filling up with bendy-looking people and their mats, unfurling onto the cold, glossy floor, twisting themselves into unholy pretzels. Wearing the proper attire, spandex, tight and sleek, some have matching sets even. What if I don't *want* the teacher to *see* me? What if I'm the only one who needs *modifications*? Everyone will see. And I look so stupid and out of place in my clothes. Maybe this is a bad idea.

I stare longingly at my shoes, tucked into a cubby by the door.

Just then the teacher sweeps in, flicks off the lights, and closes the door. She's extremely pregnant, and I relax a little. Because Dad's shiny new wife is also pregnant, and she can no longer tie her shoes. How much could this instructor-in-training really put us through, when she can barely do the poses herself? I roll out my mat. Surely, even I can do better yoga than a pregnant lady.

"Hello, beauties," Danny Wong's favorite yoga teacher says.

Danny gives her a conspiratorial little smile and she winks at him.

And then, this tiny little pregnant woman proceeds to completely wreck me—mind, body, and soul.

I quickly learn that yoga is not lying on the floor and stretching.

Yoga is, in fact, hard.

The teacher, whose name is Celeste, is bending and holding and balancing just as well as all the spandex-clad students around me, including Danny.

I'm sweating profusely and almost cry out in agony when I find the clock on the wall and discover only five minutes have passed. And it feels like I'm the only one who is screaming internally. Everyone else's movements are fluid, whereas my muscles are shaking. Celeste's voice is a litany of instructions laden with unfamiliar vocabulary and grammatical curiosities that my mind processes at half speed. What did she say? Left leg or right? Side body? What is a *side body*? Shine my heart at what?

"And now, time to fly."

Suddenly, everyone in the mirror is tucking themselves like they're ready to go upside down. I tuck my T-shirt into the front of my pants, panicking.

Celeste is still crouched in a squat, with her forearms in front of her. She leans forward, shifting her weight onto them.

Then I hear the magic word: *modification*.

"A modification: Grab a block for support. You can also stay on your forearms, especially if you have sensitive wrists."

The bendy person on my right grabs one of the foam blocks they've stacked at the top of their mat, and places it beneath their feet. I didn't bring a block with me, but the person on my right sees me looking at theirs.

"Take one," they whisper.

I'm embarrassed to have been noticed watching them. I deeply wish to be invisible here and I feel the opposite. I whisper a quick thanks and snatch a block, placing it beneath my feet the way they did.

I crouch, every muscle in my arms lighting up as I lean forward. I feel all the connections activating, ones that must always be there but I hardly notice usually, from the muscles that wrap around my rib cage to the ones that cradle my shoulder blades.

"If this is where you need to be, good," Celeste says. "I'll be staying here, doctor's orders. If you're ready for the next step, maybe you can take the full arm balance. If you take the arm balance, then maybe you can take the handstand."

I laugh out loud. The idea of doing a handstand, in theory, seems like a possibility, sure. Faced with the reality of all it means in order to make a handstand happen, however, it's just so absurd. Just crouched and leaning slightly forward, every muscle in my upper body is hot, and shaking, and my heels are still planted so firmly on the mat. They'll never leave the earth. It's not possible.

Celeste smiles at me.

"Play with it," she says.

I glance at Danny on my left, who is crouched, like me. And then, miraculously, slowly, he lifts his lower body. His toes are pointed, his body a little ball, his arms become a shelf for his knees and then his legs lift, higher and higher. His breathing is steady. Concentrating hard.

"Good, Danny," Celeste says.

He falters, almost recovers, and then falls backward, to the earth.

"Good, Danny," Celeste says again, just as warmly as the first time.

I turn my gaze to my own hands. Eyes on my own paper now. My body is alive. Something clicks inside of me. Something that seemed impossible.

If this is where you need to be, good, Celeste had said.

This is the first step, getting in position. Connecting the dots. Building strength. But it's the suggestion of the next step, the one that made me laugh, light up with fear, it's an invitation and a question. Maybe you can balance. Maybe you can take the handstand. Maybe not, not yet, but I can imagine it now. I'm in position. I can imagine leaning forward, I can imagine lifting, slowly, from my center of gravity, my mind and body moving together, and lifting, and flying.

I lift a toe off my foam block. Just one toe.

And I fall over, collapsing in a heap.

"Good," Celeste says.

And Danny smiles at me, that little knowing smile of his, before going back into position, and trying again.

And there's something forming in my mind here, about all of this, with my body warm, and the jumble of my usually furious thoughts, quieted.

Something about doing things imperfectly, falling over.

About this place, which is Danny's holy place, like the Sunshine is for me, a place where people know him, where he tries to fly.

After class, when we drop into our seats on the bus, and all the adrenaline subsides, my muscles feel pleasantly achy.

"You loved that," says Danny Wong.

"*Love* is a strong word," I say. "I *love* Flamin' Hot Cheetos."

"You loved that," he says again, hugging his yoga mat across his chest.

He looks out the window at the city rolling by, little brown houses and the yellowing trees lining the streets.

I don't know why I can't admit it, necessarily, but I also don't correct him a second time.

"Maybe I've been a secret jock all along," I say.

"Let's not go that far," he says. "But if you want to come again, just let me know."

"Oh," I say.

Again? Like, more than once? To yoga, with Danny Wong? Like, Danny Wong, my yoga friend? I swallow.

"Okay," I say. "I'll let you know."

13

WE EACH HAVE OUR OWN ROOM AT DAD'S HOUSE, BUT when I wake up in the morning there, Ali is asleep on the floor next to my bed.

The sky is a pale pink, the sun hasn't appeared over the mountain's crest yet.

Last night, Sunny came to Mom's apartment to pick us up. When we saw Sunny's car pull into the parking lot, Mom retreated into her bedroom. I sighed, hoisting my overnight bag onto my shoulder.

"Mommy, you know she's not going to come up!" I called out to her. "You don't have to hide!"

Ali zipped up her duffel bag after checking for the millionth time that she had all of her little potions.

Sunny's car idled outside, at the bottom of the stairs.

"Love you, Mommy!" Ali called out.

But she didn't appear.

I roll over on my side, peering at Ali's sleeping form on the floor, wrapped in the floral comforter that she never would have picked for herself. There's a similar one on my bed. When we showed up to Dad's house for the first time, our rooms were just there, done up already, like he ordered them from a catalog, like showrooms, two bedrooms for two girls who we didn't know.

I crawl out of bed with my pillow and settle in next to her on the floor.

Dad takes us all out to dinner at the Cheesecake Factory.

He said he wanted to celebrate a major milestone in Sunny's pregnancy with all of us, "as a family." According to an app they are both using to track the development of the baby, it is now the size of a can of soup.

When he said that, I suggested that we go to three different restaurants that Sunny has mentioned liking before: Los Cuates, Sadie's, and El Modelo.

And he picked the Cheesecake Factory. In the mall.

I'm so mad and I wish I could text Esmé. She'd instantly understand.

When Mom and Dad were married, we never, not once, not one single time, ate dinner at a restaurant. He said it was a waste of money, even though he can't cook at all, and that meant Mom spent a *lot* of time cooking. Before and after her shifts, even when she worked a double, she was always boiling, searing, baking all these foods that she didn't know how to make because Dad wanted to eat potatoes au gratin and pork chops, even though no matter how hard she seemed to be trying, everything always came out overcooked and under salted and even though Ali wouldn't eat them, because she's so picky, and Dad said she'll have to learn, let her be hungry, so I showed her how to make instant noodles if she got hungry in the middle of the night because she does eat noodles.

After they divorced, Mom took me and Ali to this all-you-can-eat Chinese buffet restaurant, and we clinked our plastic cups full of soda from the soda fountain, and we piled our plates with noodles and rice and created a distraction while Mom slid crab Rangoon into her purse and we ran to the car laughing so hard that Mom was crying and my lungs ached and it was the best day.

Dad holds Sunny's hand delicately as she sinks into the booth at the Cheesecake Factory.

This kid is not even born yet, and Dad is taking them out to dinner.

There is a pitcher of water on the table, and Ali pours from it into our empty pint glasses, handing the first one to Dad. I already want to flip this table over and they haven't even brought us bread.

But I promised Mom that I would talk to Dad about the debut. And that I'd ask him to be in my Eighteen Roses ceremony. So that's what I'm going to do.

I take a deep breath.

"Rosali," Dad says. "When's your next meet again?"

Ali places the water pitcher down gently.

"You were planning to come?" she asks.

She's not giving an attitude. She's genuinely surprised.

"Of course I'm going to come," he says.

He's not. He just says stuff like this in front of Sunny to make it seem like he's a good dad. I suck on my teeth.

"It's in two weeks," she says. "At Sandia."

"Great," he says. "I'll be there."

Sunny rests her hands on her belly. "Can I schedule you

guys for a cleaning?" she asks. "Should be about time for another one."

Sunny is a dental assistant. At our family dentist. Which is how she met Dad. Which is horrible.

I'd rather let my teeth rot out of my head than sit in that chair with her. But Mom will probably make me. Now, Mom takes little road trips across the border with her friends to get dental work done, but me and Ali are still on Dad's insurance.

Please be nice to him so that it stays that way, anak, she always says.

And as the old adage goes, if you can't say anything nice, shut the fuck up and stuff your face full of bread so you can stay on your dad's dental insurance, so that's what I do as soon as it appears in front of me.

"Can I get any apps started for you guys?" our server asks, cheerfully clicking a pen.

"No thanks—" I start, because I can already hear Dad saying that "apps" are a waste of money, too, but he cuts me off.

"Yeah, let's do the avocado egg rolls for the table," he says. "I know you guys love Asian food."

What is "Asian" about an avocado roll at the Cheesecake Factory?

"You got it, boss!" the server says.

I want to tell the server to relax because there's no way in hell Dad is going to leave a decent tip, but they probably already know that.

"So, Lucia," Dad says, leaning forward, his arm around Sunny.

My hands ball into fists in my lap.

"Are those college applications all in?" he asks.

I can't believe it. *Are those college applications all in?* Such an interesting choice of words, all passive language—all in where? Filed by whom? Completed by whom? As if they just get magically submitted by fairies. *Are those college applications all in?* As if he knew where I was applying, as if he ever asked, as if he'd offered to help with them. As if he offered to pay for college, which he could, but he hasn't. The only thing he's said about my college application process, at all, was that when I was filling out any financial aid forms, I should put my parents' contribution as zero. *It's basically true*, he said, *your mom doesn't have any money.*

Be nice to him, anak, Mom's voice pleads in my head.

"Just about," I say, and take a big gulp of water. It's freezing, and as it makes contact with my teeth, a sharp pain shoots from one of my molars down into my jaw.

God*damnit*. Goddamn Judas tooth.

"You okay?" Sunny asks.

"Yeah," I say. "Brain freeze."

Ali fiddles with her gold cross necklace. She's put on a dress and heels for some reason. I guess she read the words *upscale, casual dining* on the Cheesecake Factory website. Well, she can be upscale and I can be casual. I'm wearing what I always wear.

As if Dad is reading my thoughts, he squints at me from over the top of his menu.

"Is that a *men's* shirt, Lucia?" he asks.

Well, what was I *supposed* to wear to Sunny's my-baby-is-now-the-size-of-a-can-of-soup party? No attire was specified on the formal invitation.

"Yes," I say.

"You know, you can leave some clothes at my house," he says. "Some nice clothes for when we go out together."

By *nice clothes*, he means girly clothes. For when we go out together. So, this is going to become a regular thing now? Maybe if I stab myself in the eye with a fork I can be excused from this and all future "family" outings.

"And you, too, Rosali."

I feel Ali flinch next to me. He's the only one who calls her that.

Dad leans back in his chair.

"You each have a *whole* closet at my place," he continues. "I know the one you share at your mom's must be really cramped."

Now I want to stab *him* with a fork. Our cramped closet at Mom's, stuffed with all of Ali's track uniforms and her many, many, many pairs of jeans and little dresses that slide off the hangers and onto the floor is *just fine*.

I flip open my menu and it smacks the table loudly.

"Lucia," Dad says warningly.

"Sorry," I mutter.

Sunny rubs her belly anxiously.

They don't have rice at the Cheesecake Factory, apparently, but at least they have pasta so I can still tuck into a big bowl of something.

I would like to submerge myself in a sea of Alfredo sauce.

The server reappears with the avocado eggrolls.

"Can I get some entrées started for you folks?"

"Sure can," Dad says.

I've never seen Dad banter with a server. The folksy act tonight is extremely off-putting. Dad is a very serious person. He has strict routines. He has a strict fitness routine, he has a strict social routine, and he has strict eating habits, not meaning that he eats super healthy or anything—but rather that he only eats specific things at specific times and he doesn't like to try new foods. And he doesn't banter with people.

But I guess Dad is different now.

"Normally, she likes to get fish," he says, chuckling and patting Sunny's pregnant belly. "But that's against the doctor's orders, for now, so she'll have the steak Diane. I'll have the filet mignon, well-done."

I want to claw my face off, because it's so embarrassing that Dad is one of those order-for-my-wife types, and also because he's just politely requested that his steak be burnt to a crisp, but whatever, it's his life, and it's his dime.

I open my mouth to order my pasta when—

"And the girls," Dad continues, "will each have a club sandwich, with fries."

Ali puts her hand on my arm. She correctly senses that I have almost blacked out from rage.

He didn't just order for Sunny. He ordered for *us*.

And he ordered sandwiches.

Sandwiches.

Cold. Sandwiches.

"I'll get that started for you!" the server says. "Anything to drink?"

Cyanide.

"We're good with water," Dad says.

Well, there's the Dad I know. Still cheap.

"Lucia," Sunny ventures delicately, once the server removes our menus. "You're turning eighteen in the spring, right?"

I take a deep breath to steady myself, because poor Sunny, I know she's trying, and I don't *want* to hate her, it's more that I hate the situation, but she's right there in the middle of the situation, isn't she?

"Yup," I say flatly.

Ali sips her water.

"Are you planning to have a debut?" Sunny asks.

"A what?" Dad chuckles.

I freeze. I had not accounted for Sunny bringing it up before I did. And now I'm all mad at Dad for ordering for us and for being, well, himself, and I'm thrown off and I can't remember my carefully planned speech about how it would be cool if he would show up and do this thing with a rose and a little dance, it doesn't have to be a big deal, it could be thirty seconds, and I could pick the song, something not corny, and he doesn't even have to stay the whole time if he doesn't want to.

"A debut," Sunny says. "When a girl turns eighteen and gets presented to society."

"I see," Dad chuckles. "It's pronounced *debut.*"

"No, it's not," I snap. "She said it right."

"If you say so," he says, but he doesn't believe me. "And what does this 'debut' entail?"

"It's a beautiful tradition," Sunny says. "The debutante gets all dressed up, with all her friends, and they all say nice things about her, and there's dancing—"

"Ha!" Dad says. "Doesn't sound like Lucia's thing."

My blood runs cold.

Because that's what *I* said.

What does it mean that me and my dad said the same thing? When he doesn't know about what's my thing and what isn't? He just ordered me a cold sandwich.

"Well, I bet your mom would like to throw one for you," Sunny says.

"Ha," Dad says. "I'm sure she would. So, she'll be asking for money soon, is what you're saying."

"Kevin," Sunny says gently.

"What? It's true. She's terrible with money. And this sounds expensive."

Is she terrible with money or is it expensive having two kids and an ex who doesn't help even though he could and even though he's definitely *supposed* to but she's too afraid to push it? Is she terrible with money or is she paid like shit even though she literally stops people dying every night?

Is she terrible with money or are you just the worst person who's ever lived?

I want to scream.

"It's a big deal in a girl's life," Sunny presses on. "Lucia's becoming a woman."

"Well, she doesn't care about girly stuff like that, do you, Lucia?" Dad asks. "You just *had* to wear your dirty sneakers and ruin all our wedding pictures."

"I told her she could wear whatever—" Sunny says.

"And she's doing the same thing tonight," he interrupts her, gesturing at my shirt. "She doesn't care about anybody but herself, she wore whatever she felt like even though I told her it was a special dinner."

That's it.

"*What* exactly is so special about this dinner, Dad?" I snap. "Sunny's baby is as big as a can of soup? So the fuck what?"

The server, who has just arrived with our food balancing on his forearms, winces.

The air is sucked out of the room.

Dad is slowly, but steadily, turning red in the face.

Ali holds her breath.

Sunny's eyes well up.

She reaches into her purse and pulls out a square envelope. She reaches across the table and hands it to me.

I don't know what else to do, so I open it. Inside is a square piece of cardstock. Like the kind that you can get printed out online for special occasions. The kind that covers our fridge at Mom's. The Christmas cards, the debut invitations.

When I pull it out, blue glitter falls into my lap.

I don't even have time to fully react to the nightmare of glitter, glitter stuck to me, *glitter stuck to me forever*, because of what's inside the card. It's an ultrasound photo, with a blue border, with a little speech bubble coming out of the baby's mouth.

I'm your baby brother, the speech bubble says. *And I can't wait to meet you!*

I stare at it and stare at it.

Ali looks over my shoulder.

And we stare at it together.

Our baby brother.

14

DAD YELLS AT ME THE WHOLE DRIVE BACK TO HIS AND Sunny's house from the Cheesecake Factory Can of Soup Party That Was Secretly a "Gender Reveal" Party.

After my "outburst" he had barked at the server for to-go boxes and basically threw his credit card at the poor guy.

"Here's Sunny, wanting to do something nice," Dad says, blowing through a yellow light. "And you have to crap all over it."

I am seriously considering jumping out of the car at the next intersection.

I can't do this with him anymore. I just can't.

I feel bad enough *without* him yelling at me, is the thing.

I feel bad all the time. Whether he's there to point out what I messed up, or, as is most often the case, when he's not. I feel bad anyway.

Why did I have to say *Sunny's* baby? Of course I wish I hadn't said that. I wasn't trying to make her cry. Of course I said what I said because I was trying to say it in the meanest way possible, but I meant to be mean to *him*, to inflict some kind of pain on *him*, like he was doing to me. That's *his* baby, I meant to say, so why should I care? If he's going to go changing now, finally, for this baby, then good for that baby, I guess, but why do *I* have to act excited about that?

The problem is, of course, that I do care. And I'm still clutching the dumb little ultrasound photo. *I'm your brother.*

I *know* she was just trying to be nice.

But now Dad's just ranting and ranting about her like she's not even sitting right there, with her fingertips pressed to her temples, in the passenger seat, not saying anything. And neither am I.

I focus on the signs of the strip malls flying by. High Desert Photography Studio. Sprouts Organic Grocery. Burrito Town.

Maybe Dad's right. Maybe I am selfish. Maybe I *don't* care about anybody but myself.

"So disappointing," he says, again, but what else is new?

Later that night, I lie on top of my stupid floral bedspread, staring at my debut to-do list in my notebook. I don't have a motif. I don't have eighteen roses, I don't have any roses. I don't have a cotillion. I don't have a venue.

I've already tried all of my typical self-soothing techniques. I watched half of a movie I've already seen. Then I watched a video of somebody watching that same movie and reacting to it. Then I watched a video of somebody explaining how to fold a fitted sheet. Then I finished watching the movie.

And I'm still full of dread. Because what I really want to do is to call my lola.

To see her face. To see her couch. Still there. *Still there.*

But I'm scared.

Somehow I just know, deep down in my gut, that I'm right.

That something is wrong. I don't know what, but something, something bad, and when I talk to her it'll show on my face and then she'll see that I know.

And then it'll be real.

I can't accept that. Because I need her to still be there. Nothing is how it's supposed to be.

She was supposed to come back eventually.

She was supposed to fix everything. And take *care* of stuff.

The way she did when Dad left and she showed up with her big suitcase and her gravelly voice and her big booming laugh. She was going to fix everything, I knew it.

My vision blurs as the items on my to-do list merge together, a big mess.

I have to get out of here. This stupid floral room from a box.

So before I can talk myself out of it, I pull out my phone and text Jason Woods.

I've never snuck out before. Ironically, Mom is always so scared that I'll sneak out when she works nights that she sometimes calls me at 2:00 a.m. "just to check in" and when I only answer the audio she makes me turn the video on to prove to her I'm *actually* in my bed, and so one time I went to sleep with that day's newspaper on my nightstand so I could hold it up next to my face like a hostage when she called, as a gag.

Of course I was always actually in my bed.

It's not like I've ever had anywhere to go before.

Jason texted me back and said that he and some of the guys are going to try to get some stage time at an open mic tonight and that I should come, if I want.

From my window, I can see that there's a halo around the moon, which is either good luck or bad luck, I can't remember which one Esmé said.

Maybe if I just texted her a question like that, she'd respond. What if I just said, *I know you put a period on our friendship but I have a very important question about the moon*? And also, I have Jason Woods's phone number. And I texted him. And he texted me back. And I'm sneaking out to meet him at an open mic night.

And I miss you.

That's it, I am going.

I pull on my big ugly grandpa sweater from Savers, grab my notebook, and tiptoe as quietly as I can across the darkened living area, eyeing the hallway that leads to Dad and Sunny's room.

Next to the TV, Dad's DVD collection, alphabetized and categorized by genre, takes up nearly half a wall. He still buys them, if it's a movie he really likes. He says he likes having a physical thing. Once, he took them all down and let me help him reorganize them by the film's director, and I tried to memorize them all, and when we sat together, watching movies, he pointed out how the camera lingered here and cut away there, and what the lighting meant and the score, how the director is in control of all of that, and I tried to memorize everything he said about each one of them, what was important about them, what they contributed to the film canon, and I still remember, even though we never talk about movies anymore.

"Até?"

"JESUS—" I start, and almost collapse from the adrenaline that surges through my veins.

Ali is standing in the kitchen, with a glass of water, in the glow of the microwave. She's wearing pajamas and slippers that she brought over from Mom's.

"What are you doing?" she whispers. "Oh my God, are you sneaking out? Can I come?"

The last thing I need when we're trying to sneak into a bar is my little sister with her giant Disney princess eyeballs and baby deer energy ruining everything.

"No, you can't!"

"Please, please," she says. "I won't be weird, I promise."

"Ali, *no*!" I whisper.

She follows me anyway as I make my way to the front door. She watches me as I kneel down to lace up my shoes.

"Crazy night," she says.

"Yeah, one for the books." I grab my jacket from the hook by the door where Sunny has adhered a wall decal that reads *Welcome to Our Home* in cursive over the framed portrait of her and Dad.

"Super weird about this whole . . . *brother* thing," she says.

I sigh, straightening up and pulling my jacket on.

"It makes it seem more . . . real," she says, and hugs herself.

And I remember how I found her this morning, curled on the floor next to my bed. *Why?* Why is she always *watching* me like I know what I'm doing, when I don't, I just don't. Can't she see that I can't fix any of this? That I'm letting Mom down, that I was shitty to Sunny and she didn't deserve it, that the debut is going to be a total bust?

She should not look to me for the answers. I don't have any.

"Yeah, super weird," I say. "I'll see you later."

I can't look her in the eye as I slip away into the night, leaving her there, feeling relief, guilt, relief, guilt, twisting in my gut, always.

So, the city bus this late at night is definitely, well, different. I try to look like I know where I'm going and I know what I'm doing so that nobody messes with me.

I follow the route to the address Jason texted me, to one of those fake Irish pub–type places in a strip mall with a nail salon and a hardware store. But something stops me outside the door. I lean my weight on one foot, then the other.

Should I just go inside? A *bar*?

"Hey!" Jason says, popping out of his car, and my heart jumps a little.

"Hey," I say. "So, are they even going to let us in here? It's like a *bar* bar."

"We've been here for the open mic night before," he says. "We've got an in. Just be cool. It's Tuesday."

"I'm cool," I sputter. "Super cool. Tuesday Cool. Super Tuesday Cool."

"Right," he says, laughing.

He opens the door to the place and gestures for me to go in ahead of him. Such manners.

Inside the bar, the floor is sticky. Low ceilings, dark wood paneling. Sparsely populated. The bartender is an old white man who looks like the ghost in one of those stories that ends like, "but Hank hasn't worked here in over ten years!"

He's wearing suspenders and strokes a snowy white beard as he listens intently to a customer's order.

I've never been inside a bar before. I fold my arms protectively around myself.

"You look uncomfortable."

A voice comes from so close behind me that I jump and yelp.

Noah Bradford Man Bun Nemesis, laughing like he's in on some joke that nobody else heard, as usual.

"I'm *fine*," I say, trying to drop my shoulders down away from my ears. Every muscle in my body feels tightly coiled, tense.

"Have you cracked that hot dog kid joke yet?" he asks.

I feel the weight of my notebook in my backpack with all those weird "jokes" that poured out of me as I sat there, in the light of the movie screen, at the Sunshine. A weird, formless mass of scribbling and nonsense that started being about the hot dog kid and then somehow became about Cecelia's debut when I was ten.

"Not yet," I said.

"You'll get 'em, Cruz," he says, punching me lightly in the arm. "Keep it up."

I flinch.

"Mr. Woods," the ancient bartender says to Jason, tossing three paper coasters onto the bar top.

"Sir," Jason says, tilting his head. "Three seltzers?"

"You got it," he responds, tossing a rag over his shoulder.

He has spectacular mutton chops.

"That man's not real," I whisper to Jason. "He's straight out of central casting."

"Oh, he's genuine. The rag's in SAG, though," he says, winking.

A shiver runs through me as I avert my gaze from his laughing brown eyes.

I clear my throat.

Once we have our seltzers in hand, Noah leads the way deeper into the pub, to where Rahul is waiting in a booth near the stage in the corner—well, less of a stage and more of a short, raised platform wedged in between two booths with cracked leather seats. An old TV hangs above it, an error message flashing over the blue screen of death. He waves us over. He's wearing a red bomber jacket I've never seen him wear to school.

"Hey, Rahul," I say. "Nice jacket."

"Oh, thanks," he says. He adjusts it against his narrow

shoulders. He must have carefully selected this red bomber jacket to wear tonight, because he's still wearing it, even though we're inside and it isn't cold. Maybe this is his lucky open mic jacket.

"Have you done this before, too?" I ask him.

He nods. "First time for you?"

My mouth is dry. "Yeah."

"Don't worry," he says. "Builds character."

"What does that mean?"

"You'll see."

When Danny and Russell show up, they cram into the booth with us.

As the appointed open mic start time approaches, I start to see what Rahul may have been alluding to as the bar begins to fill up with single dudes clutching Moleskine notebooks. Most of them white, in their early twenties. Tattoos. Beards. Drinking beer.

Slightly different crowd than my first venture.

Jason and Rahul lean forward to talk to each other as I, sandwiched between them, sink deeper and deeper into the seat.

"Hey guys, sign-up sheet is down here in front," a dude in a plaid button-down shirt says, waving a pen. He must be the host.

The guys all jump up, jostling to sign their names to the sheet. Jason twists around, points at me.

"Lucia, want me to put your name down?" he asks.

I swallow.

"Oh, sure," I say, trying to look grateful. "Thanks."

Dude after dude steps up to the microphone. We only

get three minutes each, which I know, now, feels like an eternity when you're up there.

Danny Wong gets up onstage next.

"So I started watching that reality show, *Love Is Blind*, with my grandma," Danny says. "I was enjoying this sweet bonding time with her until she turned to me and was like, 'It's too bad your personality sucks, too.'"

After him, Russell Bernstein.

"I was doing homework the other day and I was on my third hour in a row of staring at my computer screen. So I was like, I've earned a break to look at my phone screen now."

A generous chuckle.

"Okay, thanks, man," the host says, patting him on the back as he hands the mic over.

A smattering of applause.

The host scans the sign-up sheet, balancing the legal pad against a bony hip. "Looks like we have a young lady comic in the house tonight."

Seriously?

Noah whoops loudly.

Not helpful.

"Come on up, Lucia Cruz," he says.

Rahul and Danny have to slide out of the booth to let me out. My sweaty palms stick to the gross leather seat as I claw myself forward.

My stomach twists.

Those fifteen feet to the stage comprise the longest walk of my life. The weight of the eyes on me. All of them. All these guys. Men. Looking at me. The *lady* comic.

I might throw up.

"Thanks," I say into the microphone as I pull it down to my height.

My voice reverberates, impossibly loud, and suddenly, it's the quietest room in the world.

Out in the crowd, heads turn away, or gaze down at their phones. Arms cross. Their body language instantly telegraphing their feelings. Their regard for me. *Unimpressed*.

But why should *I* have to impress *them*? Aside from Danny's and Russell's material, it's been ten different versions of the same joke about tuning out their girlfriend when she talks. From ten different versions of the same stupid V-neck T-shirt.

I shouldn't be nervous. I should be *bored*.

I tuck my unopened notebook under my arm.

"Hey," I say. "If you guys are all *here*, then who's manning the comment section?"

Jason snorts into his seltzer.

A rush of adrenaline surges through me.

"Seriously, did you at least *appoint* someone to stay behind on 'Well, actually' duty? I'm worried that a journalist with a PhD will have to go one night without your vital input on how she can improve her piece on the topic she's studied for ten years and you just heard about yesterday. Geniuses."

Smirks. Chuckles. Eyebrows raised. Dead stares.

But whatever their reaction is, they *have* to listen to me. They don't have a choice. I have the mic.

It's the most powerful I've ever felt in my entire life.

I pull the microphone off the stand.

"Listen, it's not like—"

Just then, Esmé walks into the pub.

Our eyes meet.

She freezes. I freeze.

Her palm rests on the glass of the open door. Jessa Jimenez is right behind her. Wearing a truly silly red beret.

"I-I really . . . ," I stammer, gazing over all their heads, at her. ". . . uh . . . yeah, cool jokes, guys. Your girlfriends talk too much and they like lipstick. Groundbreaking. Hilarious."

"Have you considered wearing some?" someone yells out.

Sweat forms on my top lip as I scan the room to figure out who the hell said that. A couple dudes to my left are chuckling, their arms crossed, but when I look at them they drop their eyes to the floor.

"Come on, man, give her a break. She's like in high school or something," another voice rises from the darkness.

All the power I felt just a moment ago, gone.

I feel so small. Smaller than I have ever felt.

Exposed.

And Esmé's eyes are full. I can see it, even from all the way up here.

They're full of pity. For me.

"Whatever," I say. "Fuck this."

Quiet.

I replace the mic in the stand. A thud echoes and reverberates through the room and a storm gathers in my heart, *I don't care, I don't care*, I tell that storm, my feet moving one in front of the other, rushing past the booth where the Open Mic Club guys all sit, puzzled, past the round table where a single dude claps slowly, past the mutton chop bartender and his gross rag.

"Luz—" Esmé says.

I push past her, and stupid Jessa Jimenez, through the door and out into the night.

Esmé follows me outside. The temperature has dropped precipitously. The streets are empty.

"Dude!" she says. "Are you okay?"

I ignore her question, because *obviously* I'm not, and I'm trying to remember which way to the bus stop, but then—I left my backpack and my wallet inside. I run my hands across my scalp and close my eyes and take deep breaths.

"You're in the Open Mic Club?" Esmé asks.

I turn around to face her.

"I guess," I say. I kick at the sidewalk with the toe of my shoe. "I know, it's embarrassing."

"What's embarrassing about it?" she asks. "I think it's cool. Perfect for you, actually."

My throat begins to close up around all the things I want to tell her.

"Yeah, you know," I say. "I just really wanted to find a way to spend more time with Noah Bradford."

Esmé snorts.

Then she tucks her hair behind her ear.

"Do you mean Jason Woods?" she asks, looking at her shoes.

"What?" I ask. "No, no. I didn't even know he was in it. I swear."

My face is getting hot. I had wanted to tell her about Jason. There was so much I've wanted to tell her, about so many things. My lola. The debut. Mr. Marco putting price tags on his movie poster collection. And it's all on the tip of my tongue now.

But what if she doesn't care anymore?

"Those guys were jerks in there," she says, after a moment. "Don't let them get to you."

My shoulders tense. Does she really think I can't handle those jerks talking a little shit to me? That was nothing.

"They weren't getting to me," I snap.

Esmé sucks on her teeth. "*Okay.*"

No, *no*, why did I have to say it like that? I chew on the inside of my cheek. I'm just so, so caught off guard to see her.

"What are you *doing* here?" I ask.

Esmé shrugs, crosses her arms. "Jason invited Jessa."

"Really?" I ask. "I didn't know they were friends."

"What, you don't think Jessa is cool enough to be friends with Jason Woods or something?"

"I didn't say that—"

"Jessa and the theater kids are really cool, okay? And I like hanging out with them because they're people who *like stuff* and they're not embarrassed to be excited about it."

"Are you saying that *I* don't *like* stuff?" I ask, disbelieving.

Because I do. I like stuff. A lot. I like movies. I like driving around and talking about movies. I like strip malls. I like talking about all the weird stuff people do and say at school. With her. I like *her*. I miss her.

"If you want to do the costumes and hang out with the theater kids, that's fine!" I say.

"Thanks so much for granting your permission."

"Jesus, okay, you don't need my permission, but how was I supposed to know that's what you wanted to do?"

"Because I tried to tell you a million times!"

"Well, I get it, now," I say. "Okay? I get it. You like costumes. Can we just go back to being friends now?"

There. I said it.

It just hangs out there. Because she's not saying anything. She's not saying anything.

Please say something.

And my throat is closing up again and my face is getting hot because she's still not saying anything.

"You don't get it, Luz," she says, and her dark eyebrows are knit together, and her lip is quivering. "You don't get it all."

She shakes her head and marches away from me, pulling open the door to the bar.

Jason Woods is standing there on the other side, holding my backpack with the duct-taped straps.

She looks down at my backpack, and then up at him.

"Excuse me," she mutters, and then slides past him.

He opens his mouth to say something and then closes it, moving out of her way.

I swipe away the tears spilling out of the corners of my eyes as he lets the door close behind him.

"Are you okay?" he asks.

"Why does everybody keep asking me that?" I ask, through tears. "I'm *fine*."

"Yeah, you seem fine," he says, not unkindly. "Do you need a ride home?"

"No, no, I'm just gonna take the bus."

"Come on," he says, slinging my backpack over his shoulder. "I'll drive you."

15

I'VE NEVER BEEN IN A GUY'S CAR BEFORE. I'VE NEVER been in any of my classmates' cars besides Esmé's.

Jason's car is really clean. It doesn't smell like stale cigars like Esmé's car, and the clock on the dashboard displays the correct time. The car smells like Jason Woods. Which is very good.

I open up the center console and the only thing inside it is a phone charger; there aren't even any drive-through napkins or loose pens or quarters.

"Well, sure," he says. "Make yourself at home."

I open the glove compartment. All the car manuals and insurance papers are stacked neatly.

"This car is immaculate."

"It's my pride and joy," he says, as he pulls out of the parking lot.

The city lights are a sparkling grid in the valley.

"Here," he says, handing me his phone, connected to the sound system by cable. "You control the tunes."

It feels so weird to be handed someone else's phone. It's like looking at someone else's brain.

"I control the *tunes*?" I ask, and scroll through his music library.

"Yeah, Saint," he says. "Tunes."

"Um, do you even listen to tunes, though?" I ask. "It's all comedy albums."

"Well, you know. Student of the craft and all that."

He takes this seriously. I must seem so silly to him, barging into the first club meeting like that with no preparation, no comedy albums in my phone, not a single joke written.

I chew on my thumbnail, my leg bouncing up and down with nervous energy. This has been a *weird* night. Jason Woods saw me bomb onstage, and then he saw me have a tantrum and storm offstage, and then he saw me *cry*, so where do we go from here, exactly?

"Have you always liked comedy?" I ask, because maybe focusing on him is best. And he's still so mysterious. In fact, the more I learn about him, the more mysterious he becomes.

"My parents are really into it," he says.

"*Really?*"

"Yeah. We all went to see Amani Johnson last year at the Kiva Auditorium together. Amazing night."

"Wow," I say, fighting back an unwanted pang of jealousy that I experience every time I hear somebody talk about their parents like that, using words like *amazing* and *together*. "Your parents sound cool."

"What about you?"

He's just being nice. Obviously I've never done this before.

"I'm new to it, I guess."

I finally locate a music playlist on his phone.

"Oh my God," I say. "You have a playlist called 'Karaoke Tunes'?"

"It's more of a setlist."

"*You* like karaoke?"

"I love karaoke. Me and Noah go to the one they do on Wednesday nights at Leisure Bowl."

"Okay," I say, sitting up straighter in my seat. "Before I ask what your go-to karaoke song is, because I need to know, first I have to ask: How, *how* are you friends with that guy?"

He laughs. "He's a little clueless about some things, sure, but isn't everybody?"

I wrinkle up my nose. "Seems like kind of an understatement."

"He's open, though. To learning stuff."

"But he's just so . . . Man Bun! And you're . . ." I clear my throat.

Really great. Funny. *You keep an immaculate car in perfect alignment with your immaculate dress.* Easy to talk to. And I was so afraid he wouldn't be, before. I was so afraid that after all those ridiculous, fantastical stories Esmé and I made up about him, that he'd be just like everybody else at school—awful. And yet.

"You're cool," I say.

"Well, thanks, Saint," he says. "But you know Noah likes you, right?"

Noah. Noah Bradford?

"Excuse me?" I ask.

"You heard me correctly."

He has this twinkle in his eye like this supposed to be fun information. It isn't. I grip the door handle. Grind my teeth. Noah Man Bun Bradford.

"You're joking."

"It's plain as day to me, and everyone," he says. "You gotta open your eyes more."

What is he talking about? I'm constantly observing everyone all of the time. Jason Woods has no idea that there's nobody more watchful, frankly, more paranoid, more defensively observant, than I am. That guy hates me.

"My eyes are open. They are wide-open, believe me. You're messing with me."

He shakes his head, *nope.*

There *is* something kind of unsettling about *how* Man Bun hates me, it's true. Like he enjoys it a little too much. Like he's openly laughing at me and I'm supposed to like that he finds me amusing.

"He doesn't *act* like he likes me," I say.

"Is there really just one, particular way to act, in that situation?"

Yes, you pine from a distance, silently, like a normal person, stuffing it down deep inside until it either goes away or you take it to the grave. But Jason knows that Noah Man Bun likes me and that must mean the other guys do, too, and that is so awkward, and now it's going to be a whole thing. What if he tries to ask me out or something? Then I'm going to have to figure out a way to tell him no without him pivoting instantly from liking me to hating me, which is what happened with my lab partner in eighth grade science. One day we're feeding the hamsters and laughing and the next day he's putting hamster shit in my pencil case because I said I didn't want to "be his girlfriend" because what does that even mean when you're in eighth grade?

I swallow that down because Jason seems to be a Man Bun Apologist, and anyway it's too much to explain about the hamster pellets and everything, a story that sounds funny, sort of, but is actually not funny, not at all.

"I don't know how to feel," I say. "I'm going to need roughly three to five business days to process this information."

He laughs.

It worked. Saying something quippy like that usually gets people to stop asking questions about stuff I don't want to talk about. Which is what I wanted. But I can't help feeling a little pang in my chest when he does.

"Okay," he says. "New topic. How come you're not friends with Esmé Mares anymore?"

I eye him suspiciously. "How do you know about that?"

"I mean, you guys sat together in all our classes. And at lunch. And you don't anymore."

It's a little unnerving, this thought that I may have been observed in the same way that I've been observing everybody else. I really did not think that anybody noticed me, really. Esmé, yes, of course, but not me.

Oh.

"Wait. Do *you* like *Esmé*?" I ask.

He clears his throat. "She's cool."

But that's exactly what you say when you like someone.

"You do," I say, pointing at him. "You like Esmé Mares."

He looks straight ahead, focusing on the road, but he's got this little flustered smile on his face, and shrugs this weird little shrug, so he definitely, definitely, does.

Of course he likes Esmé. And not me.

That's not really surprising. That's how everybody feels. So, it's not like I can blame him. And it's not as if I *liked*

him, for real. It was more a crush for entertainment purposes only, to get through the day with a little intrigue, it
was more like a shared delusion that I'd build with Esmé,
like fan fiction, based on a real person, sure, but spun off
into a version of him that didn't actually exist, so it's not
like this could really, actually hurt me.

"Well, you have really good taste," I say. "She's amazing."

"So how come you guys aren't friends?" he asks. "If
you don't mind my asking."

I look out the window, at the red lights blinking at the
top of the Sandia Mountains, radio transmitting antennas
reaching up into the night sky.

"She's amazing," I say. "I'm a piece of shit."

"Hey," he says. "Don't talk about my friend that way."

I hug my backpack to my chest and study him.

He's serious.

"Fair enough," I say.

"So," he says "Circling back to go-to karaoke songs . . ."

And it makes me smile.

I made a friend. *Hey, look at that.*

I really did.

And in spite of everything, Esmé is the one person I
really want to tell.

The next day, Sunny drives us to school and I let Ali sit in
the front where she asks her all these questions about the
baby that I would never think to ask, like are they already
discussing baby names, and what's the next milestone after

the soup can phase, dumb stuff like that, and I decide as soon as she pulls up to the drop-off lane that I'm not going back to Dad's house after school today. That's not happening, I really don't care if Mom's at her apartment or not.

"Thanks for the ride," Ali says.

"Sure," Sunny says.

Ali hops out, and seeing her friends, she waves goodbye to us and runs to meet them, ponytail bouncing.

"Hey, Lucia?"

I wince. I'd almost fully slid out of the back seat without a *hey, Lucia*.

"Yeah?"

Sunny twists around to look at me, her arm on the back of the passenger seat. She has a simple manicure, not like Mom, who always goes for the reddest red.

"If you do have a debut," she says, "I know your dad would like to be included."

I can't help but snort. "Are you serious?"

She tilts her head to the side. "I know he's . . . tough, sometimes. But that's the only way he knows how to be. How to show he cares."

"Well, he should learn a different way," I snap.

Sunny studies me. "You know how men are," she says. "Hardheaded."

It's something my mom says, too. About "men." And I hate it so much, as if what they're saying is, *oh well*, nothing they can do about it, that's just how they are. Mom says *I'm* hardheaded, too. Spelling out the idiom in the heat of an argument—*your head is so hard*. And I hate that so much. To be compared to him.

What does Sunny even *see* in my dad? What did Mom see in him? Why is he like this? It's an infuriating mystery. Why my parents are the way they are. Why they do the things they do. I don't understand. My mom deserves so much more, in so many ways, than what she got, and so does Sunny, but it's not like they ever listen to me, it's not like anyone ever listens to me, it's not as if pointing out the obvious makes any difference whatsoever, they just come up with excuses.

That's just how men are.

That's just how it is.

"See you tonight," Sunny says.

"Yeah," I say, lying.

Because she will not.

And I slide out of the back seat, close the door, and I don't look back, but I feel like she's watching me anyway.

When I show up at Mom's apartment after school, she's there. And she's sitting at the kitchen table.

And she's crying.

"Mommy?" I ask.

She has her laptop open, and all these papers strewn out in front of her. Crouton is on the table, watching her, in a crouch, her tail curled around herself.

Mom pretends that she only got Crouton because me and Ali wanted her, and that she's not allowed on the table or the countertop, but whenever she thinks we aren't looking, she lets her, and once, when Crouton got an eye

211

infection, Mom let her sleep with her in the same bed, so that she could "flush out her eye with saline" every hour until it was cleared up.

"What are you doing here?" she asks, wiping her eyes with the back of her hand.

I drop my backpack to the floor and slip off my shoes.

"What's wrong?"

"Are you hungry?" she asks, getting up and turning away from me, to the kitchen, where the rice maker is already blinking red.

She opens the refrigerator.

"Are we just going to keep asking each other questions until somebody blinks?" I ask.

She shoots me a death glare.

"There's fish," she says. "And eggplant."

"Okay," I say.

I lean against the counter while she makes me a plate, her slippers smacking against the kitchen tiles as she shuffles this way and that way to warm up the leftovers.

When she opens the lid of the rice maker, steam billows, a little cloud, and I wasn't actually hungry until I smelled the rice.

She places my plate down on the table and I sit in front of it. She shuffles back into the kitchen to grab me a spoon and a fork and she sets that down in front of me, too, and whisks Crouton off the table and onto the floor before grabbing two mugs of coffee and filling them from the coffee maker that's on its last leg, still limping along, though, day by day. We go to sleep every night hoping for coffee in the morning and so far, it still works.

Mom sets a mug of coffee down in front of me and then one in front of herself. She rests her elbows on the table and dabs the corners of her eyes with her fingertips.

"Baby," she says.

And my eyes fill with tears.

Before she even says anything.

Because she never calls me that.

And she looks up at the ceiling, her eyes shining.

"What?" I ask.

"Your lola," she says. "She has cancer."

My throat is thick and my face is hot, and the rice is still steaming on my plate.

I knew it. And even though I knew she was going to say it, I thought I still had time before she did. Before her saying it made it real. I thought I still had time to figure more stuff out. I thought we all had more time. I thought Mom had more time to sell a house, and then another one. I thought Ali had more time to eat a shrimp with the head on. I thought we'd finally be able to visit Lola, if not this year, maybe next year, or the year after that. That we'd finally get to pack the big suitcases I've seen in my cousin Maricel's pictures when she goes over there. Fill them with things Lola would want, with gifts for my titos and titas and cousins who I haven't even gotten to meet yet. Candy and stuff that's hard to get there. I thought I'd have time, to figure out all the forms we need for customs and find a map of the airport in Japan so that Mom wouldn't have a meltdown because she's always lost, because she's always stressed out by forms, I thought I'd have to dump out all of Ali's stupid beauty potions and serums before we get to security because they're too much liquid for the plane.

I thought that we'd get off the plane at Ninoy Aquino and they'd all be there.

And Lola would say, *welcome home*, and it would feel like it.

It really would. And everything would be fixed.

"I'm sorry, Mommy," I say.

And she's crying again, and I hold her, because there's never enough time, and it isn't fair.

I don't know what questions I'm supposed to ask. I don't know what I'm supposed to do or what needs to happen now, so I just hold her until her sobs subside.

Mom blows her nose.

"She's been in treatments for two months already," she says. "And she's responding well. It's early stage, and they think, maybe, she'll be okay. It's just that everything is so expensive, and the bills—I just wish I could help more."

Her face looks too pained to continue. I squeeze her hand and wish she wouldn't do that. Make herself sick with guilt.

"But she's set on coming for your debut," she says. "She thinks by then, she'll be strong enough. And I think it's good for her to have something like that. To look forward to."

She doesn't say, *so that's why it has to be perfect*.

But I hear it.

And so, that's what it will be. It will be perfect.

Somehow.

I pull her laptop toward me.

"So, let's look for flights to book for her. Okay?"

Mom nods, blows her nose again.

"Okay," she says, letting me help her.

Because I'm the only one she lets help her.

Later that night, after Mom leaves for her shift, after we've assembled a list of potential flights for Lola—all with at least two layovers, not ideal, but unavoidable, the ABQ airport is just *so* small—and after we've sent them to her and my Tito Nando, after we've reviewed current B-2 visa requirements, and after I add the visa processing fee to the debut budget, one hundred and eighty dollars, for a maximum stay of one hundred and eighty days, and make a note that Lola must prove that she can "self-fund" her stay, and she must also prove that she has no intent of remaining in the United States or "abandoning" a residence outside of the United States, and after we used the State Department's official "appointment tracker" to calculate the current wait time for a B-2 visa appointment at the U.S. Embassy in Manila, one hundred and forty-four calendar days, after we've done all that, I throw my backpack onto the floor in my bedroom.

And the strap that's been held together with duct tape comes loose.

"No!"

I kneel down and hold the broken leather in my hand.

It just feels a little too metaphorical, like a bad omen. Everything that is hanging by a thread will soon fall apart.

When Dad saw my duct-taped backpack the other day, he offered to buy me a new one, but I keep insisting this one is fine. And it is fine.

I bought this backpack with Esmé last summer at the consignment store across the street from the Sunshine.

It was the day that Mr. Marco was screening a *Mystery Science Theater 3000* marathon. Esmé's mom had made tamales for us to take with us to the movies, but we didn't want to offend Mr. Marco by being all blatant with our feast, so we pooled our cash to buy the backpack.

And we were going to buy popcorn, too, *obviously*.

It's not a movie without popcorn.

"Esmé, check it out! This backpack looks like the lost member of ABBA," I said.

I held it up for her to see as she squeezed through the cramped aisles, lined with loud print dresses and denim men's shirts to reach me.

Black leather, lined with fringe at every seam.

Esmé's eyes went all starry as she gently held it aloft, then pulled it to her chest. She twirled around with it, as if it were her dance partner.

"You are the dancing queen," she sang loudly, as if no one else was in the crowded store but us.

Because she was never afraid of being herself. Of having fun. Of letting people see her.

And now the strap is broken.

I press my fingertips to the tape that's lost all its stick.

I can't anymore. I just can't do any more things. But there are so many more things to do before I go to sleep. And I just want to put on sweatpants. And the most giant sweater possible. I don't want any fabric constricting me. But Mom snatched all my "smelly" cozy outfits from my bedroom floor before leaving for her shift and put them in the laundry room on her way out.

there's adobo in the fridge, she texts me, with the emoji of a computer mouse because she thinks it's a refrigerator.

Pulling open the door to her closet, I'm struck with the particular scent of her—a uniquely Mom blend of perfume, shampoo, and moisturizer. Her closet reminds me of being a little girl, watching her get ready to go out to dinner with Dad, when they were still married. But in the full-length mirror propped up against the wall, my reflection looks nothing like she did then. I don't know whose scowl I wear on my face, but it isn't hers.

After searching and searching, I come upon the perfect sweater for this moment. I call it Mom's Depression Sweater. Shaped like a large box, it's a soft, girlish pink that I never wear. Wasting no time, I pull it over my head, marching into the kitchen to claim the Tupperware of yesterday's rice and chicken adobo, along with a fork from the drying rack where several Ziploc bags are tented upside down after being washed for reuse because they are expensive.

After I stomp back into my room, I open my laptop. The glow of the screen dulls the sharp edges of my discomfort as I scroll passively through debut planning articles.

But the anxious feeling just won't go away, no matter how many of these articles I read or how many items I add to the to-do list in my notebook.

I close my laptop, grab the leftovers Mom texted me about, flop onto my bed, and open my phone to scroll through debut planning videos on TikTok instead.

This does not feel any *more* productive, necessarily, but it also doesn't feel any less so.

All of the "getting ready" videos blur together, always the same, girls laughing and curling one another's long dark hair.

At bottom of the screen, there's an icon shaped like a video camera. I've never clicked on it before. I've only ever scrolled.

I click on it.

My face appears in front of me, flipped, huge, filling the screen. Jump scare.

I hold the phone as far away from my face as possible.

In the frame, Ali's side of the room is a mess behind me, her bed unmade and covered in crumpled clean laundry she hasn't bothered to put away. I try to angle myself to hide it, but there's no point.

My stained Tupperware, sitting on my nightstand, full of clumpy rice and greasy chicken, is also prominent.

Oh well.

RECORD.

"Hi," I say, and my voice sounds very desperate and very uncool.

But that's how I feel. Desperate to get these words out of me.

"This is my first video. Maybe my only video. I don't know."

My gaze wanders all around, unsure of where to look.

"I don't know anything," I admit.

Searching my own face for answers, I find none. The lighting is off-balance, half of my face is in shadow from my Sailor Moon desk lamp. Eyes cupped in dark circles. Nevertheless, I keep talking, the bar at the bottom of the screen marking the passage of time.

"So, I've been watching a ton of the videos on here, and you've been really helpful to me. Especially DanielaLove, hopefully I can figure out how to tag you. Shout out to you and your Shoestring Budget because, *wow*. These things are expensive. This is going to cost more money than I've ever . . . yeah. Anyway, confession time."

I clear my throat.

"I'm turning eighteen very, very soon, and basically *nothing* is planned for my debut."

Rubbing my forehead, I expose my chewed-down nails and chipped polish. Quickly, I retract my hand and curl it into a fist in my lap.

"I can't even come up with a *motif*."

I laugh a bitter laugh.

"Unless lechon is a motif. Maybe I'll just waltz around with the pig? Put it in a barong? Print off program cards with information about cholesterol?"

I swallow.

"My lola is coming in from the Philippines for this . . ."

My throat begins to ache.

". . . and so it *has* to come together . . . but I just feel like I'm *not* going to be able to pull it off. I don't know what to do. I'm . . . scared."

I stare into my own face. Release a steadying breath.

"You guys all really look like you know what you're doing. Did you always?"

I take a big bite of cold rice and chicken.

"Anyway, bye forever probably," I say, covering my full mouth. "Oh my God, don't look at my nails, I know they're hideous, my mom already yelled at me about them today!"

When I click "upload," I make sure to tag my video with #18THBDAYDEBUT and #debuttok.

Sinking back against my pillows, I tuck my knees into my chest and rest my chin on them.

On second thought, I reclaim the Tupperware and cradle it, the smell of the savory velvety sauce sending comforting signals to my brain.

My phone begins to ring. Dad's number appears on my screen.

I silence it.

Crouton jumps into my lap, warm, purring. The apartment is quiet.

In the morning, I wake up to a bunch of notifications on my phone. But they're not missed calls from Dad, beyond the one, and a text from him that says he heard from Mom where I was and that he was glad I was safe but it was so irresponsible to come here and that Sunny was worried and blah, blah, blah—I don't even read the whole thing.

All these notifications are from TikTok. A bunch of them.

From a user called babylyn02:

omg you are *everything*. the adobo meltdown is hilarious. been there. I definitely did not feel like I knew what was I doing when I was planning mine either, as a fil-am i was really stressing the details too. u got this, girl xo

I shake my head, confused, wiping the sleep from my eyes, and read it again.

The next comment under my video is from somebody called angelinalinaaa:

You will be ok, bb. Check out my vid on cheap decorations. will link below. Also you don't have to have your party in an expensive venue. You can do it in your church's basement or in somebody's backyard. Your lola will love it no matter what!

What the *hell*?

My eyes fill up with tears, which is surprising, because I thought I didn't have any tears left at this point.

Why is everybody being so *nice*? Maybe they wouldn't be, if they knew that I'm a hating-ass bitch who makes fun of other people from the corner of the cafeteria and therefore has no friends.

But. They don't know that, all they know is what I said in my video, which is that I'm scared to host a debut. In that way, it's all they need to know, and it's the truest thing I've ever said, to anyone, and I said it to a bunch of strangers, and now here they are, their little hearts floating in my phone.

Another one:

my mom yelled at me today for my nails too lol

Then:

to be honest my motif was "blue & gold", LMAO, i'm not creative enough to do, like, "under the sea in the 1940s" or whatever. Why not have yours be "pink and gold"? That pink looks so perfect on you. Post more vids, we wanna know how it comes together.

Pink looks *perfect* on me? Okay, Mom's Depression Sweater is one thing and a pink debut is another. But honestly it's a good tip.

I pull my notebook off my nightstand and thumb through the pages to find my debut checklist. I put a check next to "Pick a Motif," and scrawl in the words *A MOTIF CAN BE TWO COLORS.*

Ping. Another comment.

LMAO—the lechon part had me dying!! she's totally right, my mom and tito fight about cholesterol all the time she calls it having 'high blood'

That's funny.

And I click on the first comment, and hit reply.

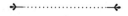

Later that morning, when my mom comes home from work, she finds me in the kitchen, in front of a sizzling pan.

"Luz? What are you doing up already?" she asks.

Her eyes grow huge as she takes in the sight of me, frying garlic rice and Spam on the range.

I arrange my arms into the "air hug" that I've been taught to give her before she changes out of her "viral-soaked" medical scrubs.

She returns the gesture with a dazed look on her face.

"You . . . cooked breakfast?" she asks.

I hand her a plate, then spin around to grab my notebook off the counter.

"So, I emailed Our Lady of the Sacred Heart *and* Our Lady of the Immaculate Conception last night. Apparently they rent out their gyms for events, and they even include chairs, and they're free for a couple dates in April. Now, before you say anything, I know you said that the priest at Prince of Peace looks like the lead singer of a failed nondenominational praise and worship band, but I emailed them, too, as a backup. I'll call later today to follow up. Okay?"

I know I'm talking fast. And I'm smiling too much.

She clutches her purse to her chest with one arm, nodding slowly.

"What's up, DebutTokers?" I say into my phone. "It's Saturday."

Because it's in the frame behind me, I've thrown my comforter over Ali's crumpled laundry pile to hide it. And I made her bed for her.

I hold up my ninety-nine-cent notebook next to my face and drum my ugly nails on its marbled cover.

"And I have good news! Items are getting ticked off The List."

After messing with it for a while, I figured out how to play music under my videos and I spent probably too much time looking for the perfect hopeful song to play while I updated the DebutTokers on my progress. But I found it.

Our Lady of the Immaculate Conception has come through for us. I always liked her better. For a reasonably affordable deposit, I was able to reserve their gymnasium for my April debut. It smells like a bleached armpit in there, so I'll be debuting in the style that I absolutely deserve. But I will be debuting. No matter what.

There's something about finding out the bad thing that I was afraid of that removed some kind of barrier in my mind.

My mom was on her way out the door for work when I told her we got the space, and she literally jumped up and down.

She stopped jumping when I handed her a Tupperware full of leaves.

"What is this?" she asked and wrinkled up her nose.

"Salad," I said. "Have you met?"

She pulled on her blazer, skeptically, but she didn't protest. I'm starting to worry about how tired she looks all the time and after poking around on NutritionTok I decided she needed to eat some spinach. Her long hair was stuck in the collar of her blazer so I pulled it out for her.

"*And*," I say to my followers—all ten of them, as of this morning. "My mom bought the plane ticket for my lola! So she's officially coming."

In my TikTok video, I'm smiling when I say this, and the comments are all heart emojis and smiley faces.

I was also smiling in real life, when I clicked "purchase" for her ticket while we were on FaceTime with Lola. Me, sitting at the kitchen table, Ali in the chair next to me, her legs tucked under her, and Mom hovering over me, holding up the phone so Lola could see my laptop screen. It was the middle of night, Lola's time. Her face was glowing in the darkness.

My mom was also smiling. She was smiling so big she made *my* face hurt.

"Confirmed," I said.

"I can't wait," Lola said, her eyes crinkling. "I'm ready to party!"

I swallowed. She doesn't know that I know, and Ali doesn't know anything. I try to hold close the peace I found in knowing. But it's a tenuous grip.

Everything is going to be fine. If I can just through this. If I can get just my debut program together. If I can just get Lola here. Then everything will be okay.

I smile now into my phone camera, and throw up a peace sign for my followers.

"So, shout-out to angelinalinaaa for the suggestion to check out church venues. Thank you, até! I highly recommend going that route if your family has already blown through your ice sculpture budget for this year. Next up: dress shopping, take two, so please pray for me. My mom and I suffer from irreconcilable fashion differences. This little-known condition afflicts one in every ten Filipinas. Please spread the word about this deadly, underreported disease."

Upload video.

"Luz, who are you talking to?" my mom calls from the bathroom, where she's putting on a full contour and highlight, simply to eat orange chicken at the Coronado mall food court.

225

Ping. Ping. Heart. Heart.

DanielaLove: OMG please tell me you're making a video of this. PLEASE!!

All that rage I felt about the sparkles and the tulle is gone. It's burned itself out. If rage about sparkles and tulle burns inside you and there's no one there to hear it, it makes no sound, it's a muffled scream, continuous. If rage about sparkles and tulle is witnessed by your TikTok followers, it flares and flares and then is gone.

Later, I scan the perimeter of the store, searching for something that I can live with. It's the least I can do for my mom, who has to live with me.

On the rack, a warm mustard color catches my eye. A little wing of a sleeve pokes out, wedged in between two big tulle ball gowns, like it's in the wrong place.

As I pull it out, Mom approaches me silently, like she's nearing a wild animal and trying hard not to make any sudden movements.

"You . . . *like* this one?" she asks.

It's a two-piece, made of a heavy, sculpted-looking material. A cropped top with large cap sleeves. A full skirt that's shorter in the front than the back.

"Do you hate it?" I ask.

The earthy, muted color stands out in a sea of jewel tones and shiny metallics.

"No, I don't," she says. "It just looks a little Filipiniana. In the sleeves."

I hold up the dress, studying it.

My mom reaches out to run her fingers over it.

"I like the color," Mom says.

She speaks carefully.

I hold it up to the front of my body, against my arm. It brings out warm tones in my skin.

"If you really like this one . . . ," she says.

She doesn't seem to trust the fact I would feel positively toward a dress. I admit, I don't necessarily trust it, either.

"Do you want to . . . try it on?" she asks.

My fingers search for the tag to check if it's even my size. Somehow, it is *exactly* my size, but the number on the price tag makes my heart sink. It's too much.

"Let's keep looking," I say.

Placing it back on the rack where it was wedged, I turn away quickly before my mom pushes it any further.

"What? Why not just try it on? Come on, I want to see you in it!"

She grabs it without even checking the price. "Please?"

And because she's looking at me like that, and because I actually kind of like the dress, I accept it from her and turn toward the fitting room.

I stand, on a literal pedestal, pulling the cropped top down my rib cage. I turn to the side in the three-part mirror, playing the part of the daughter who admires herself while her mom looks on and gushes over her, snapping a bunch of photos. Supposedly.

And even though I'm finally trying on a dress for my debut, like she wanted, Mom's not saying anything.

"What?" I ask her, laughing a little at her serious face.

She just doesn't seem *excited*, and she's not shoving some tutu number at me to try on next.

Something's different.

"It's just that you look . . . ," she says, trailing off.

Her eyebrows come together as she leans on the wall, her purse and jacket hanging from her folded arms.

"Terrible?" I ask.

I can't tell. I just know that I look different.

"Old," she says, surprising herself. "You look old."

"Like old-fashioned?" I ask. "You're saying it's frumpy? It's a crop top."

Finally, she smiles.

"No, it's just . . . you grew up so fast. I can't believe you're turning eighteen. It's your senior year of high school. And I'm still . . ."

She shakes her head, looking off somewhere else, trapped in time, because of me.

Esmé's mom looked at her this way on the night of her quince. As Esmé waltzed under the swirling lights with Mr. Mares, Mrs. Mares put her arm around my shoulders. She dabbed at the corners of her eyes with her free hand. She smelled like rose petals. Maybe she was thinking the same thing, that time goes by too fast and sometimes you don't realize it until something makes you stop, a day on the calendar maybe, something that makes you turn to look at someone, really look, and then you see it.

They've changed.

Everything changes. No matter how hard you fight it.

It just does.

"Mommy," I say.

I want to make it stop. If I could stop time for her I would. I want to stop time for her so that she can finally catch up to the version of herself she pretends to be, when she talks to her sisters on the phone. So that she can finish reading the next chapter in her textbook without falling asleep. So that she can get ahead of the next payment due. So that she can be the one to send money home when Lola needs it. When the roof blows off from the next typhoon, when the hospital bills come. So that she can throw a picture-perfect party, without asking anybody else for help.

She blinks away tears.

"Can I get it for you?" she asks.

She means the dress. She means more than the dress.

I smooth down the front of my mustard yellow skirt, and look at myself.

The dress doesn't feel like a costume. Not like the others did. In this one, I'm a different version of me, maybe. One I didn't know was there. But still me.

"Okay," I say, letting her get it for me.

The life she wants for us.

As she's ringing up the dress, the sales associate in the name tag and black blazer frowns. She runs my mom's card again.

Next to me, Mom shifts nervously from one foot to the other.

I can feel her tensing up with each swipe of the plastic in the machine.

"Ma'am, it looks like your card has been declined," she says. "Would you like to try another?"

I look at my mom for some explanation but she gives

none. She looks into her pocketbook, flipping through cards.

"Do you have a layaway option?" she asks, her voice calm, but her hands are shaking.

The sales associate smiles. "Of course."

My dress, wrapped in soft plastic, gets zipped into a black garment bag and whisked away to the back room, until it can be paid off in full.

The next thing I know, I'm following my mom across the parking lot, heat radiating off the asphalt.

"Where did I park this car, my God," she mutters to herself, waving her clicker around hopelessly.

We circle and circle but we can't find the car.

It was right here. But now we can't find it.

My heart is beating fast. Because hers is. I'm a mirror image of her. My organs play Simon Says with hers and I lose every time.

I shouldn't have let her buy the stupid dress.

I did the wrong thing.

My hands are shaking now.

"Mommy!" I say, stopping in place.

She turns, slowly, until she's facing me, her purse clutched to her chest.

"We can take it back," I say. "I don't need that one. It was too much. I should just wear something of Ali's."

"Luz, it's *fine*," she says. "I already told you."

It isn't fine. It isn't fine at all.

"But your card was declined!" I say. "That's *bad*. That's bad, isn't it?"

She takes in a sharp breath.

"You don't know anything," she says.

I clench my fists at my sides.

"Well, whose fault is that?" I snap.

Crossing my arms, I stare at her, defiant. I'm not moving.

She clicks her tongue.

"This is why you need the debut, you know," she says. "It's supposed to teach you American kids to remember our values. Like respect for your parents."

"I only respect one of my parents," I snap.

"That's *not* how you're supposed to *speak* to me," she snaps, her voice shaking. "This is exactly what I mean. You are too American. Too independent. *Every man for himself.* Well. Just because you're turning eighteen and leaving your childhood behind does not mean that you lose your respect for your elders. It doesn't work like that for *us*. I know he's not perfect, but we have to give him grace, because he's still your father."

"No, he's *not*," I say, my throat closing up, the tears springing to my eyes.

I hate all the things that are *supposed to be* but aren't, I hate the way I'm *supposed* to speak, and how I never know what that is, exactly, and how that fact freezes me in place all the times when I really need to speak, but can't.

But not now. The words are spilling out, words that I didn't know were there, it's as if I'm dislodging them from my throat, as if they'd been stuck all there along.

"Fathers are supposed to fix things," I say. "They're supposed to help you with stuff. They're supposed to take care of you, they're supposed to take care of your mom, not leave her high and dry. How can I respect him when he doesn't respect you?"

My mom looks like she's been slapped.

Her eyes are shining.

"Tama na!" Her voice quivers. "You are not supposed to talk to me like that."

There it is again. She's said the words a million times before. It's like an incantation, she keeps repeating like she wishes she could make it true by the power of suggestion. And there was a time when they would have stopped me here. *You're not supposed to.* But if nothing is like it's supposed to be, then what good are all the things I'm supposed to do?

I want to scream, *which way do you want it, Mom?* Does she want to be able to complain to me about Dad? Dump it all on me every time he lets her down, because she's too embarrassed to tell Tita Connie? That he didn't send a check like he said he would and now the water's shut off? That he forgot Ali's birthday, again? Does she want me to be her *friend*? Or does she want me to be a little kid, in a poofy princess dress, in a princess crown, who only worries about school? Because I can't be both and I'm tearing myself to pieces trying.

Can she really not see?

Leaving my childhood behind? That happened a long time ago.

I breathe deep. The air feels sharp in my lungs.

"I'm just worried, Mom," I say, my throat closing up. "Please. Just tell me what's going on. I don't want to be the reason why your credit card was declined."

Mom looks up into the thin blue sky.

"You're not," she says.

She rubs the place between her eyebrows in small circles.

"I don't know how to say this in English," she says, sighing. "I have this, like, group. We help each other."

"Okay . . ."

"We pool our money sometimes. Or, if somebody has a bill due, or a sudden expense, whoever gets their paycheck first just pays it. And then when that person's next bill is due, the next person takes care of it. And down and along the line."

"So your turn . . . ?"

"I just passed my last paycheck along to someone who needed it. So I missed a payment on my card. But my turn is next. It's fine. It'll just be a little while."

The rage and adrenaline coursing through my body dissipates, replaced with an unbalanced feeling, off-kilter, a sinking dread, shame. Suddenly, it's not just my mom in my head, hands shaking, card declined, falling asleep at the kitchen table, it's a whole city full of moms, handing their paychecks to one another, running to catch up with one another, as if in a relay race, on and on, forever, and then, the rage is back, roaring back, I'm screaming on the inside, but at who? Who can I scream at to make this rage burn itself out, to let me go?

Mom looks at me like she wants me to stop worrying.

Like she wishes she could remove the bad thoughts from my brain with her bare hands.

But she can't.

"This will work out," she says. "It always has before."

She raises her car clicker to the sky and pushes it. Miraculously, the car horn honks gently.

It was just one row over from us the entire time and we didn't see it.

The venue is booked, the dress is on layaway, but when I sit down to a fresh page of my notebook to work on my jokes for my Save the Sunshine set, I write about the Take Your Child to Work Day that Mom took me to when I was ten.

Mom was excited about it. She laid out her favorite set of scrubs on her bed. She had already started picking up night shifts here and there when I was sleeping over at Esmé's house, and she'd ask Mrs. Mares if Ali could come along, too. Ali would fall asleep between me and Esmé while we watched movies and ate popcorn with Tajín and I thought about my mom, eating lunch at midnight, and how she'd be pouring more coffee into her mug while I helped Ali with her homework in the morning.

She has always said she needed to quit the hospital. But she loved the hospital. It was obvious when we were there. She loved her patients. And her patients loved her. And she knew everybody, all the shift doctors, and the nurses, and the nurse techs, like her.

This is my daughter! She beamed, introducing me to all of them. She was so happy to show me where she worked. I was trying to be happy, but I was scared. I was scared I'd see somebody who was really sick. Or somebody dying. But I didn't want Mom to see I was scared. She did anyway.

"There's nothing to be scared of, Luz, this isn't an emergency floor. Look."

We went into a patient's room and Mom smiled at the man who was sitting up in his bed nearest to the door.

"Good morning, how are you feeling?" she asked.

His face crumpled up. He yelled for the doctor.

"Are you all right? Are you in pain?" she asked, moving closer to him. "How can I help?"

"I *said* I didn't want none of *you* touching me," he said.

And he spat on her.

He spat. On her.

And she didn't even blink.

The doctor came rushing in behind us, a doctor she had introduced me to a few minutes before.

He put his hand on Mom's back.

"I'm sorry, I should have warned you, maybe you should just . . ."

He led her out of the room.

But I was still staring at the man, who was now red in the face. And I hated him. And the doctor was talking to my mom like she was the one that needed to calm down. Even though she was completely calm. And I hated him, too.

"Luz, come on," Mom said in this weird voice—sweet, quiet.

Why was she being so sweet, so calm, so quiet? Why was she dipping her head low like that?

She pulled me into the bathroom. She washed her face.

Dabbed it with a cheap paper towel from the metal dispenser. She asked me if I was hungry.

And that's when I realized. This wasn't the first time this had happened to her.

How many times had it happened to her?

My pencil hovers over my notebook. I can't help it, I can't help that it's not funny, this is it, the kind of thing I think about. The kind of thing I still want to say. And I'm looking for the funny in it and I can't find it at all.

16

WHEN JASON PICKS ME UP FOR OUR NEXT OPEN MIC
Club outing, the other guys are already in the car with
him. Including Noah Bradford, sitting up front.

He jumps out of the passenger seat as I approach.

"You can have the passenger seat, Cruz," he says.

"Thanks," I say stiffly, as he clears the way for me.

The new information from Jason has scrambled my
usual Man Bun interaction protocol. My guard is up, but
I can't muster simple animosity for him anymore because
of what Jason said about him not being so bad really. At
least, not yet. We have a fifteen-minute car ride to the
show. That's more than enough time for him to do something that will summon it right back and make me want to
set my eyeballs on fire like he usually does. I pray for that.

"You guys okay back there?" I ask, clicking my seat belt
into place and glancing at Danny, Rahul, Russell, and now
Noah, squeezing in with them.

I wince. I *told* Jason I could just take the bus. But he
insisted.

"Sorry," I say.

"I'm very petite, Lucia," Danny says dryly. "No need to
make such a fuss."

"Oh, and I talked to the caterer!" Russell says. "All
squared away."

"And I talked to my cousin," Danny says. "The auntie feud's been put to rest. Burly Boba is in."

I feel bad that they feel like they have to report to me about all this stuff. I've been such a tyrant about the fundraiser.

But it kind of warms my heart that they've done it just the same.

"Yay," I say awkwardly. But I mean it. "Mr. Marco will be so happy. Well, he'll grunt and say that it's too much trouble. But we'll know he's happy on the inside."

"I need some pump-up music for tonight," Rahul says.

"May I?" I ask Jason.

"Of course," he says, handing me his phone.

I pull up the karaoke playlist.

And everyone immediately starts scream-singing the words to a song that was big on the radio when we were kids, which is really startling at first, but then Jason rolls down his window and lets in the cool evening breeze, everyone else rolls down their windows, too, and then so do I, and then I'm singing along with them, because it feels kind of like we're kids again, our voices spilling out into the road, into the night, and it's actually, like, fun.

According to Jason, Café Flora is a coffee shop slash performance space that serves enormous burritos with tortillas so fluffy you wish they could be your pillows, with a side of experimental community theater after hours.

When we push through the glass doors in front, there's

a bulletin board overflowing with flyers for guitar lessons and roommates wanted and Reiki healing sessions.

My stomach rumbles at the food smells, but I'm too nervous to eat anything.

I scan the room, which is lined with art for auction, worn-out couches where lots of college students from the university sit with their textbooks and laptops open in front of them, steam rising from their mugs, and potted fiddle-leaf fig trees in the windows. The mismatched chairs at the café tables have been arranged to face the small stage in the corner.

Rahul and Danny carry in an amplifier, which they hoisted from the depths of Jason's trunk.

"It's BYO," Jason explained.

I linger near the front of the café, by the counter, and I hug my backpack to my chest as I watch Noah laughing with Jason across the room.

Watching. From the side. Like all those mornings, sitting on the hood of Esmé's car in the school parking lot, surveying the crush of bodies streaming into the entrance. The soft, early light. Clutching our coffee cups, shoulder to shoulder. Jason would appear, his headphones on. And we'd start up with fan fiction. Back when he hadn't said anything yet, and there was all this possibility.

Like everyone else I'd written off already. I liked that he occupied that space. That space of maybe. It was fun, thrilling even, to imagine what he was really like. Anything outside of that . . .

Terrified me.

And even as we sat there, laughing, speculating, Esmé

was realizing she wasn't scared. Itching to jump into the ocean, as I stood on the shore.

Last time I saw her she said I didn't get it and she still wanted nothing to do with me. But I get it now. How that must have felt for her. To have this dead weight pinning her in place. She has to know that I know, but if I try to tell her to her face it'll come out wrong.

So this is my plan.

"Hey, Bombilla!"

I jump as Mrs. Mares appears, pulling me into a hug.

"Hey!" I say.

I rest my chin on her shoulder. Behind her, Esmé stands there, examining the bulletin board by the door. She's wearing an oversize green army jacket and a floor-length floral dress.

"I'm *so* glad you invited us," Mrs. Mares says. "I can't believe you had this secret comedy talent this whole time!"

"Well, *talent* is a strong word," I say.

"And my big girl here," Mrs. Mares says, putting her arm around Esmé. "Sewing all the time now, for the play. I'm so proud of you guys. You're so grown up. You're both just . . ."

"Don't say blossoming," Esmé says. "Luz will be triggered."

"Where's your mom?"

"She had to work," I say, shrugging.

"I'm sorry, Bombilla," Mrs. Mares says empathetically, as if this is a big deal.

I don't know what she's sorry for, I'm used to it, her not being there. And she'd ask me a million annoying questions afterwards anyway, if she were here, so it's much easier this way.

"Oh, I see two seats!" Mrs. Mares's eyes dart to the seats filling up. "I'm gonna go grab them. Esmío, grab me a coffee?"

"Sure, Mami," she says.

We stare at each other for a second.

"Why *did* you invite us?" Esmé asks.

"I just—" I start. But there's so much to say, I don't know where to begin, I already wrote it all into my jokes, everything I wanted to tell her. I hope the jokes will just speak for themselves. I don't know how to talk about them or explain them, I just hope she'll understand when she hears them.

"I just thought you'd be into it," I say. "It's going to be all theater-y."

She eyes me suspiciously and goes to order a coffee for her mom, saying nothing. I swallow nervously.

I watch as they place their bags on the backs of their chairs. Aside from their haircuts and clothes, they look so similar from behind. They move the same, sit up straight the same.

From across the room, I see Jason, seeing her there. His eyes are full of wonder and a little bit of fear and something like reverence.

I didn't know it was possible for me to feel worse. Maybe it's *always* possible to feel worse. What a fun revelation.

I cross the room and shout over the music into Jason's ear.

"You should talk to her after," I say.

"Who?" he asks, feigning ignorance.

I give him a look.

"Oh," he says, looking flustered. "Why?"

"Because she likes you, too," I say. "You're golden."

"Yeah?" he asks. "Really?"

"One hundred percent."

Jason's face breaks out into a smile so wholesome that I wish I'd just told him sooner. The volume on the music drops and Jason hops up on the stage, that Esmé-Mares-Likes-Me smile carrying him all the way there.

"Hey, everyone," he says into the mic. "Thanks for coming out, and thanks to Café Flora for having us."

A smattering of applause.

"We have an exciting variety program for you tonight, featuring some very cool Café Flora regulars and the Del Norte High Open Mic Club. My friend Noah is walking around with a donation bucket. Café Flora is raising money tonight to purchase a community fridge, which will be located right outside, so if anybody can spare some cash, or would be interested in volunteering to make sure the fridge is stocked once we get it up and running, Noah has a sign-up sheet as well."

As Noah stands up to wave, like the queen, he's met with clapping and cheers. My first thought is that it's not like the community fridge was *his* idea, and yet here he is soaking up all the credit and the attention about it, but then I remember what Jason said about him, and so maybe I'm wrong, and maybe, for once, I should just chill out.

The lights in the room dim. I lean against the wall, relaxing a little into the darkness.

Jason looks at ease up there. He has one hand in his pocket, even. Outfit is perfect, of course. All the hems in all the right places. Like he uses an actual tailor or something. Meanwhile I'm wearing a boxy T-shirt dress, which is supposed to look like a Dodgers jersey, but that my mom refers to as my "hospital gown."

"So, Indigenous People's Day is coming up," he says. "You know, my history teacher was actually mad about them changing it from Columbus Day. And when I said I didn't really think the dude deserved a day to begin with, this man had the audacity to suggest that 'Columbus should be judged as a man of his time and not by our modern standards.' Um, sir?"

He purses his lips and pauses while the audience laughs.

"Three hundred thousand Taínos would like a word. I do believe they will have been judging him in real time. Perhaps *they* formulated an opinion we could refer to?"

I can't help but smile when the audience claps for him. He's just so good at this. And it's so exciting to watch someone be good at something. At something *I* want to be good at. He's so good, it makes me *mad*, almost. Like I want to know how he did that, so that I can do it, too. It amplifies that little voice inside, *maybe you'll be great.*

"And okay, so you don't care what *they* thought, we get it," he continues, walking across the stage.

"But he was also *contemporaneously* considered an asshole," Jason continues. "There was this guy, Francisco de Bobadilla, who eventually replaced Columbus as 'Governor of the Indies'—so let's not give him too much credit, either, honestly—submitted a *forty-eight-page report* to the king and queen of Spain at the time, describing, in gruesome detail, all the many ways in which Columbus very much *did not deserve a day*. He wrote them like a term paper on this guy's assholery. Thesis statement: no holiday for this guy. You guys should just go to school that day, I'm sorry. And this was the king and queen who *started* the Spanish Inquisition and even *they* were like, we need to do something about this dude."

The crowd laughs as he continues on.

"So anyway, thanks for helping with my history homework. I'm Jason, let's keep it rolling for our first act!"

Noah weaves through the audience accepting cash donations for the community fridge.

One of the "Café Flora regulars" from the experimental theater is a literal sword swallower. I did not know that was even a real thing. Mrs. Mares is screaming and grabbing Esmé's arm and recording it with her phone.

After that, there's a belly dancing troupe, a fiddler, and a juggler.

"What in the commedia dell'arte is going on in here tonight, huh? Amazing," Jason says, as the juggler takes a bow. "Next, everybody please welcome our next comedian to the stage, Lucia Cruz!"

Mrs. Mares whoops loudly from the front.

Our next comedian.

Jason smiles at me when he hands off the mic.

What a fraud, that's probably what they're thinking when they see me. Right away. *How could she call herself that?* A comedian.

In my notebook, I flip past the many jumbled pages of jokes and debut plans, until I find the page that melds the two together.

Esmé crosses her arms.

With a pang of terror, I realize that Mrs. Mares is recording me on her phone.

"Uh, so, I'm turning eighteen in April," I say.

My voice shakes.

But then I close my eyes.

And I pretend I'm in the passenger seat of Esmé's grandpa's car. His rosary is swaying gently from the rearview mirror. And the world outside is a blur of neon signs outside of strip malls. And Esmé is driving.

I start again.

"I'm turning eighteen in April, and in my family, that means it's time for me to plan my debut, which is a traditional Filipino celebration for a young woman about to 'emerge' into society. So, I've been doing a lot of research on how to put this thing together, watching a lot of videos of regular people, like me, planning their debuts, but also a lot of famous wealthy people in the Philippines planning their debuts, and I think I've pinpointed that the biggest difference between me and a wealthy socialite is probably the wealth. And the social status."

I have a note here to pause for laughter, but I'm so nervous I can't even hear anything so I push forward.

"But another large barrier that I'm encountering is that I'm, uh, a loser with no friends?"

A smattering of chuckles bursts through the fog of terror enveloping my senses.

"And that's nobody's fault but my own," I go on. "I'm really quite insufferable."

I laugh at myself. *Is that allowed?* It was more a laugh of relief than anything else.

"I'm pretty self-involved," I continue. "I'm highly critical. And the last time I was forced to participate in one of these debut ceremonies, when I was ten, I ruined the entire night when I vomited from anxiety and set off a chain reaction of vomiting children in the ballroom, and the video went viral and now my mom has to be the one with the anxious-vomit child. So you see, I'm in a bit of a pickle here."

From my back pocket, I pull out the article that my cousin Maricel sent me when I asked for her help with this part, which I've printed out, and marked all over.

"Okay, let me read you this, so that you can really understand the depth of my problem. 'Step One. Decide whether or not you wish to host your debut *on your own* or with a *group of friends* with birthdays in the same month.' As you may recall I actually have exactly zero friends. A *group* of friends? Okay, *fancy*. And a group so large there'd be multiple Taurus sun signs? In the same group?"

I don't dare look at the crowd, especially not at Esmé, but there are people laughing. I can hear them. More than one person is actually laughing at this. Which is wild.

"Fun fact," I continue. "A group of Tauruses is called a Downer. Anyway—easy decision right off the bat. Step One is complete, I will be emerging *alone*. Let's see, Step Two?"

I adjust the paper in front of me.

"'Assemble your guest list and select the members of your cotillion court.' Okay, so who here is free on April twentieth?"

I shield my eyes from the spotlight and mime looking out into the audience.

"Anyone? Okay, before you agree to this, though, let me finish, and I'm quoting here, from an article on a very serious website called Occasions 4 Us dot net, very important to cite your sources: 'The most traditional Filipino cotillion dance is the Grand Waltz, a special choreographed dance performed by the debutante, eight female friends, and nine male friends.'

"Um, so if everybody could just go ahead and stand up? We can just push these chairs to the side for the auditions. There are *limited spots* in this exclusive, aggressively gendered ceremony, so please don't hold back. I can *only* choose seventeen of you. I'm *so* sorry. What else? You'll need to purchase your *own* formal wear for this event, which will be in a color that matches my motif (still TBD) and that you'll likely *never want to wear again*. We'll also need to schedule regular rehearsals for the next several . . . *months*. How are Thursdays for everyone? Actually, just clear your calendars, this is more important. *I* only turn eighteen once and it's really very special."

I've come to the end of the page.

"Okay. That's it, I guess."

Finally, I look up to find the crowd smiling at me, shaking their heads, clapping. Everybody. The sword swallower. Jason, Noah, Rahul, Russell, and Danny. The juggler. The barista behind the counter.

Mrs. Mares, giving me a thumbs-up, grinning, her phone camera still pointed at me.

But next to her, Esmé's chair is empty.

As the crowd claps, all I can do is stare at that chair. Because she isn't there.

Suddenly the room feels empty.

Because she's the one I'd been talking to the entire time.

And not just now. Always.

When Jason takes the mic from me to introduce the next act, Mrs. Mares grabs her jacket and sneaks out, waving to me, blowing me kisses.

My phone buzzes with a text.

LINDA: Sorry bombilla we had to go. U did great. X

I squeeze through the crowd and make my way toward the front door, and run outside. Look around. But they're already gone.

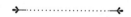

After the show, we all pile back into Jason's car, all the guys squished together in the back, Danny and Rahul sharing a seat belt, because they are the most petite.

Rahul leans forward, his face illuminated by the sign above Café Flora.

"Was Esmé Mares there tonight?" he asks, blinking innocently. "I thought I saw her at the beginning, but not at the end."

"Yeah," Jason says, looking a little forlorn as he turns out of the parking lot. "She was there."

"She saw your set before she left, though," I say. "And it was great."

"Wait," Russell says.

Oh, no, did the other Open Mic Club guys not know that Jason likes Esmé? Did I just spill the beans?

"Lucia knows about the big crush?" Russell asks.

"Thank *God*," Danny says. "I was dying to bring it up."

"Well," Rahul says. "*I* found a way to bring it up, subtly."

Noah laughs. "Oh yeah, very subtle, Rahul."

"It was!"

"ANYWAY," Jason says. "Saint, tell us more about your fancy birthday ball. Is that really happening?"

I clear my throat. "It is."

Okay, it's my big moment.

I explained the whole thing to them, in the form of comedy. From a safe distance, on the stage. Laid it all on the table. So they'd have an easy out, so it won't hurt so much when they say no, because I understand how stupid and horrible and embarrassing it all is, and I showed them that I know that, I made it very small and unimportant this way, and now all I have to do is ask them, and I will have done what I set out to do.

But asking is proving to be even harder than I thought.

"Sounds like a bringer," Jason says, merging onto the highway.

"Oh, totally," Noah says. "Totally a bringer."

"What's a bringer?" I ask.

"A 'bringer' is a comedy show," Noah says. "Where all the comedians have to bring at least one audience member in order to be allowed to perform."

"Sometimes more than one," Rahul says.

"Blue Lizard Lounge makes you bring five," Danny says.

"No way," Russell says.

"That's what I heard."

"Yeah," I say. "I guess it is like that."

"And you really still need people?" Jason asks.

My face is burning with embarrassment.

"Yeah."

"Don't your parents have, like, friends with kids they're just going to force to participate?" Rahul asks. "If my parents had their way, the Hindu Temple Society would be my entire social life."

Russell leans forward. "Yeah, JCC for me. I didn't even get to choose the guest list for my bar mitzvah. It was all my parents' friends."

"New Mexico Black Leadership Council," Jason says, nodding. "And my mom is on the board of AAPAC."

"The Chinese American Citizens Alliance," Danny says. "Unfortunate acronym withheld."

"And Noah's white," Rahul says, patting him on the back, prompting everybody to crack up.

"My parents are members of the—" Noah says.

"Don't say Albuquerque Country Club," Danny says. "I was just starting to like you."

Noah's face reddens. "My dad plays golf."

"We could tell," Russell says. "You didn't need to be part of this share."

"I know there's like a Filipino-American Association chapter here, right?" Jason asks, once the laughter dies down. "They perform every year at the state fair."

"Oh yeah," Rahul says. "That dance with the candles on their heads? Sick."

I chew on the inside of my cheek. I hadn't thought about the Fil-Am group. We used to attend some of their events when we were kids, but we haven't in such a long time. Mom said she felt bad, showing up to the events, because she couldn't ever really volunteer, because she always had to work, but they kept asking her to, and she couldn't donate any money, either, and eventually she started making up excuses not to go to events at all.

"I guess my mom's not really much of a joiner," I say.

It's weird to think of her that way but now that I hear them talking about their parents, their social circles, it's kind of true. She doesn't have anybody else to ask. She really is counting on me to assemble my court.

I look up at the roof of Jason's immaculate car, and take a deep breath.

"So, would you guys . . . ?" I ask.

God, it's so painful.

"Spit it out, Lucia," Danny says.

"Oh my God," I say. "*Fine.* Could I bring you guys? To my bringer?"

"To do the dancing ceremony thing?" Russell asks. "Like to be in it?"

"Yeah." I hold my breath.

Brace for them to make fun of me.

To say no. No *way.*

How could you even ask such a ridiculous thing of us?

"Of course we will, Saint," Jason says.

"Have you *really* not picked your color motif yet?" Danny asks. "Don't you have a mood board?"

"Do you need a choreographer?" Russell asks. "I can ask Alyssa Vasquez for you."

"Oooooh," Rahul says. "Can you now?"

He wiggles his dark eyebrows up and down.

"The master of subtlety strikes again!" Noah says.

I'm still holding my breath and my brain is still processing because somehow it sounds like they're saying *yes*, it sounds like they're going to do it, all of them, even though I outright told them how horrible it's going to be and even though I've been a nightmare about planning the fundraiser for the Sunshine and even though I never go with them to Taco Cabana after the shows. And even after the conversation moves on to whether or not Russell truly has a crush on Alyssa Vasquez from the dance team, and even after Jason puts the music back on, and drops us off at home, one by one, I still can't figure out why.

17

WHY?

When I wake up the morning after the show at Café Flora, my eyes adjust to the thin light and come into focus on the faded photo of myself and Esmé from the day we met.

Even though it's corny I keep it pinned to my cork board, over the desk. She put her arm around me for the photo, which surprised me, my shoulders scrunched up by my ears, her big smile lifting full cheeks. In the photo, she's looking at the camera, and I'm looking at her.

From that very first night, on the outskirts of our parents' work party, back when her mom was a nurse tech, too, Esmé became my friend, for no reason. She was my friend just because. Just because we both laughed at the way her little dog zoomed from under the couch to the coffee table and back again. Just because we both laughed at the grown-ups talking about boring things.

"The bank and the weather, the weather and the bank!" Esmé said, crossing her eyes and bobbing her head from side to side.

"Did you hear the bank is running for president against the weather?" I asked.

And I laughed and she laughed and it was the best sound in the world.

Is there something more to being friends than just because?

I actually did it, I want to tell her. *I joined a club*. I made new friends. Laid out all the gruesome debut details for them and they *still* said they'd do it.

They don't even know me that well. And they said they'd do it.

Just like they said they'd help me try to save the Sunshine when I asked.

Why? I ask the photo of me and Esmé. If I knew why she wanted to be friends in the first place, maybe I could figure out why she stopped wanting it. And then I could go back to doing only the first thing, and that only.

"Are you up?"

My mom appears in the doorway as I pretend to rub sleep from my eyes instead of tears. On her side of the room, Ali grumbles and pulls the comforter over her head.

"Was it 'Crazy Scrubs' day *again*?" I ask.

Mom tugs at the bottom of her ill-fitting uniform shirt, which is patterned with dancing muffins wearing birthday hats.

"Well," she says. "We have to do *something* to entertain ourselves, it's not like anything bizarre or traumatizing happens at a hospital in the middle of the night."

"Did anybody put something weird up their butt?"

"Luz."

"Well?"

"Yes," she says. "They did. Do you want breakfast?"

"Great transition," I say. "I'll make breakfast. You shower."

She lingers there for a moment before disappearing.

In the kitchen, I form the rice using a bowl and flip it upside down on the plate, like I saw on TikTok.

The eggs sizzle in the pan. Coffee drips.

Bright light floods in through the window.

"Wow, you're turning all Food Network on us, chef-chef style," Mom says, her hair plopped on top of her head and wrapped in a towel.

Ali emerges, with her school color ribbons in place, her slippers smacking the kitchen tiles. We all take our seats at the table, and break our egg yolks over our rice at the same time, forks and spoons scraping against green Fiestaware plates from T.J.Maxx, steam rising from white rice, Crouton brushing her tail against our ankles.

"Esmé's mom sent me a video of your . . . jokes," Mom says after a moment.

I freeze.

"Why did you say that thing?" she asks.

"Don't worry," I say. "I'll have the list of names for the program really soon."

She looks at me. I can't read her expression. Which is unsettling.

"I was just *joking*," I say. "Literal definition of what I was doing up there. You know, the thing with the microphone and the jokes."

"No, not that," she says. "The other thing."

"I want to see the video!" Ali says.

"I'll send it to you," Mom says, pulling out her phone.

"Mommy, *no*," I say, my cheeks burning.

She sends it anyway, and Ali scoots back in her chair,

tucks her knee beneath her chin and starts watching it, right there in front of me.

"Ugh," I say, covering my ears. "I told you, it's just some jokes, it's just for a school club thing, it's not a big deal."

Ali is laughing at the video of my Café Flora set.

"This is so cool," she says. "Look at you up there!"

Mom leans over Ali's shoulder to peer at the little screen, listening to my voice, sounding strange and backwards through the phone's speakers. Not like it sounds in my own head, at all. Mom looks utterly perplexed, watching, like she's trying to decode furniture assembly instructions she ordered from a bootleg website and they came written in Italian or something.

"Do you have to watch this *right now*?" I ask.

They ignore me.

And as I study Mom's face, scrunched up in thought, *listening* to me talk about how ridiculous the debut is, and how time-consuming, and how expensive, and how silly, and I imagine hearing all that from her perspective.

I feel ill, imagining all the things she might say.

Maybe she'd say, if you didn't make that dead rat face all the time, you'd have some friends. Maybe if you wore the clothes I bought you. If you didn't wear those pants with the rips at the bottom. If you brushed your hair. If only I'd raised you closer to my family. Then you wouldn't think like this in the first place. Then you wouldn't even have to go begging people to be your friend, embarrassing me, you'd have so many people around you, all the time, and they'd just *be* there, ready to hand you a rose. Ready to just show up. With the food. With decorations. Maybe she'd say, if only I'd never married your father. If only I hadn't left you, that one time.

Maybe then, maybe then.

I want her to say these things, to line up all her if-onlys in a row, so that I can knock them down, one by one, because I was only joking, and I didn't even invite her, because she was working, but also because I didn't want her to hear this at all.

She wasn't the intended audience.

I didn't mean to upset her.

But she just keeps staring at me. The "me" on the screen. Intent to decode me, to puzzle me out, once and for all.

"But," Mom says finally. "Why did you say you ruined Cecelia's debut when you threw up?"

I blink rapidly.

"Because I did," I say. "Because it's funny, it's a hilarious image, this chain of vomiting kids juxtaposed with the fancy clothes and the food and the ballroom and everything."

"But did you mean it?" she asks. "When you said you vomited from anxiety and you felt like you ruined it."

"Well, yeah," I say. "I guess, right?"

"You think you *embarrassed* me?" she says. "Nosebleed, ako."

She's confused, she means.

I can't figure out why.

"Well, yeah, I mean that was pretty embarrassing, wasn't it?" I ask. "Tita Connie always brings up the deposit Tita Alma lost because they couldn't get the smell out of the carpet every time she sees us."

"That's because your Tita Connie can be a real pain in the ass," she says.

Ali drops her phone onto the table and it clatters loudly.

"Luz," Mom says. "You didn't embarrass me. You were nervous. You were just a baby."

"I was ten," I say defensively.

It wasn't *that* long ago. I remember it very clearly.

I remember everything.

"You were a baby," she says again. "You didn't do it on purpose. I was worried about you, I felt so sorry for making you do that because I knew you were nervous. You hated talking in front of people. Your teacher told me. I thought you needed to just *do it*, to just face your fear, naman, but maybe you weren't ready yet, anak. Sometimes I'm a bad mommy."

Ali and I look at each other and then quickly look away.

My eyes ache.

I take her hand.

"No you're not," I say.

I can't look at her face because it's too much.

But I take her hand. She can't look at me, either.

"Looks like you're ready now, di ba?" she says. "Talking talking, on a stage in front of all those people. Like it's nothing."

I squeeze her hand. And we watch the rest of the video together.

And it's not nothing. It's not nothing, at all.

I have a calendar reminder in my phone for the day that Esmé's abuelo passed, and it's today.

He lived with them her whole life. They used to sit together in the mornings drinking coffee and doing the daily crossword. He taught her how to put red chile flakes and dark chocolate in coffee and she taught me.

I make a pot of coffee, giving the coffee maker a good smack to get it going, and make a big travel canteen of this red chile mocha coffee, and then I grab the bus to Esmé's house.

Her family is all gathered in front of the house, getting out of their cars, having just returned from the cemetery. My cheeks are burning. Maybe this was a bad idea.

It's one of those beautiful, bright desert days, the air is clean, you can hear every sound for miles, you can hear the train pulling into the station by the old railyards, and in this light everyone can probably see me, looking all red and embarrassed.

"Bombilla!" Mrs. Mares says when she sees me.

I hand the canteen of coffee to Esmé, and a sleeve of paper coffee cups to her mom.

"Oh my God, the café! Con chile? You remembered," she says. "Thank you."

"Yeah, um," I say. "Yeah."

Esmé opens the canteen and takes a big whiff of the coffee. Hot and sweet and bitter all at once. It was his favorite.

"Thank you," she says.

I look at my shoes.

Mrs. Mares looks between us both. "I'll take this inside."

Esmé hands the canteen off to her mom, who ushers it

inside along with a cluster of relatives. All small, just like her, easy to cry, and easy to laugh. Maybe Esmé learned how to be the way she is because of them.

I don't know how to start. I guess anywhere.

"Remember when you had that nightmare that the interstate exchange between I-40 and I-25 turned into a big snake and swallowed you whole?" I ask.

"I can't believe you remembered that," she says. "I'd completely forgotten it."

"I remember everything," I say.

"I know," she says. "That's because your Mercury is in Scorpio."

"I know, I know," I say. "I hold a grudge. I remember every slight."

She tucks a stray curl behind her ear, where a dangling earring glints in the sun.

"There are two sides to these things," she says. "You remember all the bad stuff. But you also remember red chile coffee."

I shift uncomfortably, feeling all the muscles in my shoulders tense, as I brace against her saying this kind of stuff, even though it's what I wanted, it's still so hard, so hard to say what I want to say, my whole body seems to be hardening against the possibility of a soft moment, of the exposure of a tender place. My body is screaming, danger, *danger*, and it hurts, kind of like how it hurts more trying not to cry than it does to actually cry.

Kind of like now.

"So," she says.

She prompts me, because I'm not saying anything, still,

and because, for some reason, she keeps trying with me, even when I give her nothing.

"You're doing your debut."

I swallow hard.

"How come you left?" I ask. "During my set?"

I wanted her to hear it, to hear everything, for her to understand that *I* understand. That I *know* what she meant when she called me a hating-ass bitch. To show her that I *know* I am. That I get it now.

She shrugs, crosses her arms.

"I guess I felt like I'd already heard that one," she says. "I've heard your Oppressive Coming-of-Age Traditions Must Be Abolished screed before. A couple times."

"It wasn't a *screed*," I say.

"It was a screed."

"Well, it was different this time," I say. "I didn't invite you just to listen to a screed. Jason Woods wanted to see you."

"What are you talking about?"

"He likes you, dude."

She scoffs. "You're lying."

"No, for real, he told me," I say. "He told me lots of stuff. We're, like, friends now."

I kick at the ground with the toe of my shoe.

"Really?" She looks like she wants to believe me, at least a little bit.

I laugh nervously. This is coming out all wrong. I had the perfect apology all planned and I'm rambling about Jason Woods. I wrote it out in my notebook, which is now completely full, front to back, so I had to write some of it on the inside cover, at the very end, on the cardboard part. I had memorized it and I even practiced it, whispering it to myself all the way here. *I'm sorry.* But when I try to remember how it started now, my perfect apology, I can't remember.

"My lola is sick," I say instead.

"What?" she says. "Oh no, Luz."

And I'm instantly, instantly crying. Like, a big ugly cry, because telling Esmé means so many things, and there's this big wave of sadness and relief and terror because now that Esmé knows, it's not just something that's happening in my mind, or at the kitchen table at Mom's apartment, but something that's happening in every part of my life, it's spreading, and massive, and nothing can ever be the same again.

"I'm sorry," I say, wiping tears away. "*I'm sorry.* For being such a bitch. That's what I meant to say before. Also, I'm sorry I'm crying, but I can't seem to stop."

Esmé pulls me into a hug.

"That's because your moon is in Pisces," she says into my hair.

And that makes me laugh, and then cry harder.

"Family stuff," I say. "Is just so fucking *hard*. I never know what I'm supposed to do, and I always feel like I'm doing the wrong thing."

She pats my back, then releases me, holds me out at arm's length.

"Can I give you my anti-screed on coming-of-age traditions?" she asks.

I nod, sniffling.

"For my parents, at my quince, it was like, they were remembering when I was born. And I was remembering with them about being little, and I was also thinking ahead about how I want the future to be, and so were they, and now we have this memory to look back on, this memory of everyone, everyone important, being together and celebrating, remembering, and dreaming, together, for once."

"That's *so* much pressure, though," I say. "Especially now. With my lola and everything."

"But that's the thing," she says. "It can't *all* be on you. That's the *point*. How could you plan one of those things by yourself? That's insane."

And she's totally, completely right.

It *is* completely insane. One person could not possibly shoulder the whole thing, it seems like, by design. Somebody brings the food and somebody brings the flowers and everybody owns a piece of it and that's the point. That's the point. And that's why it felt so hard, so impossible, and that's why it felt so unfair, and why *everything* feels so unfair, Mom trying to be everything to us and us trying to be everything to Mom.

"You're a genius," I say.

"I know," she says.

And I laugh, and she laughs, and I feel infinitely, infinitely better. I feel so much better after talking to her for five minutes than I have talking to my notebook, and myself, and my TikTok account, for months.

"Jessa Jimenez isn't stupid," I say. This was part of my perfect apology and there were a lot of other words around it but these seem like the most important, and I know she'll know what I mean.

"I know," she says.

"But Noah Bradford still is. Well. Okay, maybe one percentage point less stupid than I thought."

"What? That's extremely high praise coming from you."

"Remember when we thought there's no way he could *actually* be, like, *that* earnest about his whole Mayor of High School thing?"

"Kind of a you thing, but yes."

"Well, he might actually be. That earnest."

"Plot twist," she says.

My phone buzzes in my pocket. My stomach drops when I see Ali's name on the screen. Ali never calls me.

"Sorry, it's Ali," I say, picking up. "What's wrong?"

"Can you come get me?" she asks.

She sounds like she's going to cry, which always makes me want to punch something.

"Come get you?" I ask, my eyes flicking to Esmé.

She's already pulling out her car keys.

"Dad was supposed to come to my track meet," Ali says.

Now her voice sounds quiet, flat. It sounds more like me than her.

My insides churn. "I'll be right there."

"What's wrong?" Esmé asks again.

"My fucking dad."

That's all I have to say, and she's marching to her car parked at the curb.

The field is empty. Ali is sitting by herself on the bleachers, her blue and gold ribbon moving slightly in the breeze, hugging her backpack to her chest.

It's golden hour. The Sandia Mountains are an almost violent pink as the sun flares in the west.

Esmé and I climb up the bleachers and sit on either side of Ali. She's just sitting there, looking out at the track, which loops around and around forever, in her track hoodie and shorts, goose bumps blooming on her legs.

I've never understood why she likes to do this. Running in circles in neat lanes. But she does do it, and it's important to her, and he didn't come.

"How'd you do?" I ask her. "Did you dash all the meters?"

"I dashed," she says, laughing a little. "But they beat us anyway."

"Can't dash 'em all," I say.

Esmé puts her hand on Ali's shoulder and Ali starts to cry.

"Shh," Esmé says, pulling her into a hug. "Shh."

I stare at Ali's dusty running shoes and I feel like my blood is full of ice.

"Did he even call you or anything?" I ask, knowing that he probably didn't.

She shakes her head.

He just forgot. She knows it. I know it. But I still want to talk about it. I want to scream about it. To scream the thing he should have done. That parents are supposed to do. Because that's what they are supposed to be like. They're supposed to remember you. They're supposed to come to your things. When you don't have things to come to, it never hurts when no one is there.

But Ali has things.

"Okay, I have an addendum to my screed," I say. "A query. What do you do when your father isn't the most important man in your life, when he isn't the most important *anything* in your life?"

Esmé rubs Ali's back, and rests her chin on top of her head.

"Well, you only have eighteen roses," Esmé says.

I scoff. "Yeah, *only*."

She strokes Ali's hair as she sniffles softly.

"Maybe you don't have to give them all."

"Oh, shit," I say.

They are my *roses to give.*

The way the ceremony is, you're getting the roses. They hand them to you, one by one, until you have a full bouquet. Your dad, your brothers, your uncles, your cousins, your guy friends—if you have such things. Visually, it's them who are giving the roses to you.

But because *I* choose who gives them to me, I'm actually giving them. And I *don't* have to give them all. I don't *have* to give *any*.

I just wish I had someone to give them to.

Which is not the same thing.

My eyes are wet.

"I just wish . . . ," I say, my voice growing thick.

Ali slips out of Esmé's embrace, gently, and wraps her arms around me.

"I know," she says.

And it really does hurt, trying not to cry. So much more than crying.

My phone rings in my pocket again, jolting me out of Ali's hug. I wipe my eyes swiftly with the heels of my hands and pull it from my pocket.

"Wow, you are *so* popular now!" Esmé says. "The times, they are a-changin'."

"Shut up," I say, laughing.

The number that flashes on the screen is Our Lady of the Immaculate Conception. My debut venue. My heart stops.

"Hi, I'm calling for Renalyn Cruz?" the voice on the other end says.

"I'm her daughter, is this about the event space rental for April twentieth?"

"Yes, we tried to cash the check for the deposit but it bounced."

My stomach twists, *shit.*

Why'd they wait so long to cash it?

"There was money in the account when we sent it," I say. "I'm sorry, we'll send another one."

"I can only hold the date until tomorrow, can you pay another way?" the voice on the other end asks.

"Let me call you back. Please hold it. Thank you!"

I hang up, and rack my brain. Has Mom been paid again since she passed her last paycheck to her friend who needed it?

She's made a few payments on the dress on layaway at Macy's. Maybe we can cancel the dress and get a refund and use that money for the church space deposit?

But it's not enough. Maybe—

"What happened?" Esmé asks.

"My debut venue," I say, chewing the inside of my cheek. "I don't think it's going to work out."

Ali sits up straighter.

"Oh, no!" she says. "I'm sorry, Até."

I shake my head, feeling guilt crash down on me. *She's the one who's upset, she's the one my stupid dad let down.*

I'll figure this out on my own somehow.

"No, it's okay," I say. "I'll think of something. Are you hungry? Do you want to go home?"

"But what about the venue? Do we need to go over there or—?"

"It's fine, Ali," I say, my shoulders tensing and my jaw tightening up, *it's fine.*

"Come on," she says. "Let me help."

Esmé gives me a knowing look.

You can't do it by yourself.

And there I go again, the waterworks. I swipe tears away. Ali takes my hand and squeezes it.

"It really is fine," I say. "It'll be fine."

Ali looks off into the distance for a minute, at the volcanoes in the west, the Three Sisters. The sun, sinking lower, nearly touching the horizon, now, washing her face in a dusty pink.

"Why don't you just have it at the Sunshine?" Ali asks.

Esmé's jaw drops.

Her eyes light up.

We look at each other like, *oh my God, that's amazing, why didn't we think of this before?*

"Could I . . . do that?" I ask.

"Why not?" Esmé asks.

"Well, for one, Mom's not going to like it," I say.

"Honestly, Luz," Ali says. "If you would just act like you're happy about it, she'll be happy. I think that's all she wants."

"Well, that," I say. "And to be able to use me as a prop in her weird competition with Tita Connie and the rest of the family. I'm already a pretty disappointing debutante, my résumé is pretty thin."

"Well, *I'm* proud of you," Ali says. "You're the coolest big sister ever. You're a *stand-up comedian.* And you're single-handedly organizing a fundraiser to save the Sunshine because you love it, and it's a historical Albuquerque landmark!"

"You *are?*" Esmé asks. "When I heard it was closing I was so, so sad. That's amazing, Luz!"

"She's exaggerating, just trying to hype me up," I say, my face hot. "We might not even be able to save the Sunshine at all. It's a long shot."

"Okay," Esmé says, clapping. "Okay!"

She jumps up. The metal bleachers rattle.

"Okay, what?" I ask.

Esmé paces up and down the bleachers, golden in the sun. "Two birds, one stone!"

"Hate birds, will do anything to hasten their demise," I say. "Continue."

"You should use your debut *as* the fundraiser," Esmé says. "It'll be a way to showcase the theater, and open a new revenue stream for Mr. Marco—the Sunshine as an event space!"

"We can start promoting it right now!" Ali says, jumping up. "We can take pictures of the rehearsals and stuff."

I'm on my feet, joining them.

"Oh my God," I say. "And the bougie family is coming. On the RSVPs, I'll say, *in lieu of gifts*, donate to the Save the Sunshine Fund today!"

"Well you don't have to be *totally* selfless," Ali says. "At least ask for a microblading gift card."

"MY. EYEBROWS. ARE. FINE," I say.

"The left one is a little bit of a radical," Esmé says.

"Yeah, that left one is really marching to the beat of its own drum," Ali says.

"Okay, I have not missed this dynamic of you two ganging up on me," I say, as they cackle and hold on to each other to keep from falling off the bleachers. "Not at all!"

The sun sets as our laughter echoes across the empty field.

18

"OKAY, FROM THE TOP!" ALYSSA VASQUEZ SAYS, CLAP-ping.

Russell Bernstein snaps to attention; he's been taking cotillion rehearsal very seriously. Alyssa has, too. She was really excited for the chance to choreograph her own formal dance piece, and has incorporated segments of salsa and cumbia into the overall number, all within the constraint of the small stage at the front of the theater inside the Sunshine, which is more meant for a Q&A with filmmakers sitting in folding chairs than it is for our purposes.

"Constraint is a central tenant of creativity and innovation," she'd said.

She stands in the center aisle, wearing a workout set and white sneakers, the faded red carpet beneath her feet, movie theater chairs flanking her on either side. Mr. Marco sits at the back of the theater, his legs crossed, reading the newspaper and sipping his black coffee.

"Here's the cumbia pattern again," she says. "Start with the right foot back."

We stand in two neat lines on the stage, facing her, the movie screen, blank, behind us. My court. There's only eight of us, the comedy club guys plus Esmé and Ali. But at least it's an even number. We copy Alyssa and she repeats the steps.

Right foot back, center, left foot back, center.

I am concentrating very hard, watching her white sneakers as they move.

I've been watching everyone closely, at rehearsals, for signs of fatigue. I keep expecting them to drop out, to say it's too much commitment after all, to say it's not fun anymore.

They keep coming.

"Now, add the arms!" she says.

I can't do arms and feet at the same time. My arms and feet seem to operate independently from one another. I glance to my right, and Danny Wong is already adding the next step, hips. So are Ali and Esmé. On my left, Russell is doing zero hips and utterly too much arm.

"Russell, bro," Rahul says. "You are like, all arms."

"Jealous of the wingspan?" he asks, almost elbowing me as he flaps his arms like a chicken.

"Okay, good!" Alyssa says. "Good! I think we're ready to try it in pairs."

Esmé shoots me a look. She told me if I put her with Jason Woods she'd kill me. I told her that I'd given Alyssa Vasquez full creative control over the project. As the debutante, however, of course I had *some* say, and I've given Alyssa one specific instruction—to pair Esmé with Jason Woods.

I turn to Esmé and give her a subtle thumbs-up. She rolls her eyes.

Alyssa pulls out her phone as she reviews her notes there.

"Okay," she says. "Here are the pairs. Now, my creative vision is—"

Just then, my mom appears at the front of the theater,

followed closely behind by another Filipina lady in a blazer. She looks familiar but I can't immediately place her.

Mr. Marco jumps up from his seat and fumbles to fold his newspaper properly.

"Good afternoon," he says. "Marco Apodaca, owner."

The other Filipina lady sticks out her hand for him to shake.

"Litang Rivera," she says. "Filipino-American Association, Rio Grande Chapter, president."

Jason elbows me.

"See?" he whispers. "They found you."

That's where I'd seen her before, at the podium of those events Mom used to take us to.

"Mom?" I say. "What's going on?"

Litang Rivera sees me, and marches down the center aisle straight toward me, her nose in the air and her leather bag swaying against her hip as she does so. Even though I am standing on the stage above her, I feel instantly small, and chastised by her mere presence.

"You must be the debutante," she says, businesslike. "I was just telling your mother that I couldn't *believe* I had to hear about your wonderful endeavor through my daughter."

Ali and I exchange confused glances. We don't know her daughter, I don't think she goes to our school.

"How—?" I begin.

"She saw it on your 'TicTac' account," she says. "Which she says is very funny."

I feel Jason suppressing a laugh. There's something very funny about someone *saying* something is funny with an entirely straight face.

"My daughter also says that you and your school club are raising money to support a local small business. And I thought, why don't I know about this? So I called your Mom and told her that, didn't I? I said, Renalyn, you should have called me."

My mom laughs, clucks her tongue, as if she's about to protest, to say that she didn't want to bother her, be a burden. Litang Rivera grabs her by the arm gently, seeming to anticipate this response, and they look at each other, and my mom relaxes into her steady gaze. All of this communication is happening without words but I read it plain.

"It doesn't matter how active you've been at the association in the past," Litang Rivera says to her. "We are here now."

Jason Woods elbows me again, whispering. "Told you."

"Ethnic ladies in blazers *love* chairing associations and planning events," Danny Wong whispers.

Litang Rivera turns to Alyssa, appraising her.

"Choreographer?" she asks.

"Yes, ma'am," Alyssa says.

"Wonderful," she says, turning back to the group on stage. "So. It looks like you need some additional dancers for your cotillion. I can help with that. If you want."

It takes me almost a full minute to realize that she's addressing me.

Mom looks at me expectantly and I snap out of my daze.

"Salamat, po. But would they even want to?" I ask. "I mean, if they don't know me?"

"This is actually a very common thing, Lucia," Litang

Rivera explains. "For a debutante ball to bring young Fil-Ams and their families together who may not know one another, in celebration of our traditions, and to pass them on to the next generation."

I feel a twang of embarrassment, of guilt, for not knowing something so big about debut stuff, especially in front of Mom. I feel like I failed another test. And I feel like a phony in front of everyone else for making jokes about something that I don't even know that much about, not really, and I feel like a fake Fil-Am, and everybody knows it.

"Our association hasn't hosted a formal group debutante ball in a few years but we've done it in the past," Litang Rivera continues. "And yes, there are some youth, around your age, who I know would do it."

"I would *love* to have a full nine pairs to work with," Alyssa says. "Just visually, I mean, wow."

I glance at Esmé. This is all getting kind of overwhelming. My mom wants this, which means Lola would want this, and after all, it's how the debut is supposed to be.

The more people I involve, the less I'm responsible for, but then again, the less I'm in control.

The lights begin to feel hot on my face.

Suddenly I imagine the movie theater seats of the Sunshine, completely full, for the first time in years, with not only my family, but other Filipino families, strangers looking at me, assessing me, assessing my presentation of "Filipina womanhood."

I turn to Esmé. She gives me a little, encouraging nod.

And I look around at the guys.

They're behind me. They keep showing up. And Esmé is

here, my emotional support plus-one. And Ali is here. And we're all on my home turf, at the Sunshine, with the acid trip carpeting and the fake butter popcorn, and Mr. Marco is standing there with his hat in his hands acting like he doesn't care but he does, I know he does.

My mom is wearing her pink T.J.Maxx blazer. Her face is hopeful. Why not, I guess.

"Sure, yes," I say. "That would be great. Salamat, po."

My mom breaks out into a huge smile.

So does Litang Rivera.

"Okay," she says, clapping her hands. "When's the next rehearsal?"

"Right foot back, center, left foot back, center!"

I hang on to Alyssa's voice and steady, rhythmic clapping.

Out in the lobby of the Sunshine, my mom, Mrs. Mares, and the moms of the other participants Litang Rivera connected us with are spread out on the floor, painting a decorative banner:

HAPPY 18TH BIRTHDAY, LUZ— SAVE THE SUNSHINE!
Featuring Burly Boba

And even though I cringe to see my name there, to be the fulcrum of this thing, at least that second part is there, the Save the Sunshine part. It's not about me. But as I watch my mom laughing with the other Fil-Am association moms, and with Mrs. Mares, I remind myself that it never really was. Not entirely.

One of those other moms is a real estate agent. She and Mom started talking animatedly as soon as they met. She said she'd help her figure some stuff out. I haven't seen Mom look so relaxed in a long time.

A legion of aluminum trays overflowing with rice and glassy noodles line the ticket counter next to the register. The moms have been taking turns bringing food to each rehearsal, loading them in and out of the trunks of cars in the parking lot every week, passing them hand to hand and filling the theater with savory steam.

Everything's coming together.

The new members of my cotillion have been dutifully learning the cumbia, the salsa, and the waltz steps right along with us every Sunday for several weeks.

Ten Filipino kids, nine from Albuquerque, one from Rio Rancho, all from different schools, who I've never met before, but they all know one another from Fil-Am stuff.

When they walked into the Sunshine on that first day, past Mr. Marco's weird old monster movie posters, still there, across the acid trip carpeting, to meet us on the little stage in front of the torn movie screen, where Noah was in a push-up contest with Rahul, I didn't know what I was supposed to say to them, but I did know one thing—if any one of them uttered a single negative comment about the Sunshine, it's curtains, I'd be sending them all back to Litang Rivera.

"Hey," I said, and held my breath.

They looked at us. And we looked at them.

"This place is sick," one of them said.

And then all of them were talking at once.

"What a cool idea for a debut."

"I've always wondered what it looked like in here."

"I think your mom works with my mom at the hospital."

"Is Burly Boba really coming?"

"I'm Michael."

"Marlon."

"Jalyn."

"Jason."

"Esmé."

The Albuquerque airport must look so small to her after a layover in Tokyo and a layover in Seattle.

She looks small, too—not big, the way she feels in my imagination.

In reality she's less than five feet tall. When she comes through the glass doors and into the waiting area, Mom nearly drops the bouquet of grocery store flowers she's been clutching nervously for an hour, their petals strangled and bruised in her hands.

She insisted we be here early. She insisted we catch her the moment she walks off the plane.

She insisted we catch every moment.

They cross the cavernous room as if they are the only two people in it. They start having a conversation as soon as they make eye contact, loud and unchecked, not caring about other people or what they think or how they look, and when their arms encircle each other, they're crying and frantically speaking over each other, and laughing, all at once.

She's here.

Not confined to my phone screen. Not an ocean between us.

She's *here.*

"Ay, girls!" Mom calls out to us. "Come!"

Ali runs to them, joining their circle.

But I hang back, approaching gingerly.

Lola cups Ali's face in her hands. "You look just like your mommy," she says.

I clutch my elbows, looking at her, appraising her, terrified.

She doesn't *look* sick. Then again, she never did.

"And *you!*" Lola says, turning to me. "Why are you ignoring my calls, mahal? You are too cool-cool for your lola now?"

"No!" I say. "I'm sorry, po. I just . . . I just . . ."

My face is wet.

She shakes her head. *It doesn't matter.*

Then Lola and Mom are both pulling me into them by the arms, and Lola is looking at me, and laughing through her tears, at my baggy T-shirt and my ratty hair, which my mom was actively trying to brush while driving here and almost crashed the car doing so, but Lola doesn't care, because she doesn't care about that stuff, and she never did, and she keeps saying one word over and over—*perpekto, perpekto, perpekto,* perfect, perfect, perfect.

Alyssa Vasquez claps her hands.

"Okay!" she says. "Finally ready to put this all together in pairs, I think."

I wince.

This is the step where it stops feeling like we're just some weird dance crew and it starts feeling like it's my cotillion. Alyssa has assured me that her choreography will be classic, but not corny, there will be no lifting of me into the air, no curtsying, and no moment where everyone turns to me and drops to one knee like I'm a dictator.

She pulls out her phone to look at her notes app.

"Here are the pairs," she says dramatically. "And this is my artistic vision and I've been given full creative control by the debutante, so I won't be taking questions."

Noah gives her a salute. I wince. What if *he's* my partner? I'd only given Alyssa my explicit instruction to pair up Esmé and Jason, but had neglected to give her any guidance about *me*, which now feels like a huge oversight.

"Okay. Ali and Rahul, Danny and Russell, Noah and Jalyn, Esmé and Jason—"

"Wait, I thought I was Cruz's escort," Noah says.

Everybody looks at him. Esmé's eyebrows are raised so high they are in her hair.

"What did I just say, Noah?" Alyssa says. "My. Artistic. Vision."

Rahul stifles a laugh. Oh, Jesus. I can't handle this right now.

"I mean, I don't *care*," Noah says, sticking his hands

into his pockets. "That's just what—I mean, that's what I thought."

"That was before we got the full court," Alyssa corrects him. "And Mrs. Rivera recruited Gabriel to be Lucia's escort specifically."

Gabriel Terrado Fernandez and I glance at each other.

"Oh," I say.

At Maricel's debut in San Diego, Mom was going on and on about Mariciel's escort, how he was the valedictorian, he's going to find the cure for cancer, and so on. It's weird, this escort thing. The whole thing is weird, but this part especially. If I'm playing the part of the perfect young Filipina woman, respectful, pious and pretty, educated and demure—what is he supposed to represent, exactly?

Gabriel Terrado Fernandez is dressed all in black, with large clear glasses that frame his dark, downturned eyes. He doesn't particularly look like he's representing anything. He's just a guy. A cool-looking one, even, but just a guy nonetheless. I guess that's it. He's representing a guy and I'm representing a girl and we're representing all our parents' hopes and dreams. Tonight the part of our parents' hopes and dreams will be played by Lucia Elenamaria Cruz and Gabriel Terrado Fernandez.

"So," Alyssa says. "If there are no more questions, which I specifically said I was not taking, I will continue."

She goes on to read the rest of the pairs for the cotillion waltz. Danny and Russell are already waltzing together, weaving in and out of the rest of us while Rahul claps.

Noah is still standing there with his hands in his pockets. *He likes you*, Jason said. Well, I don't like him. And not in a he-annoys-me-which-is-actually-very-close-to-liking-him way. I should feel glee, because by not liking him back, I've finally beat Man Bun at something, I've finally wiped that smirk off his face.

I don't feel glee.

He has everything I want in some ways. An easy way with people, because he just expects everybody to like him. He walks into rooms that way, smiling, and ready to be seen, ready to be heard. I'm jealous of him, really.

I hate what he represents.

"Pair up!" Alyssa says. "We'll start at the top of the number."

I clear my throat.

"Real quick, Alyssa," I say. "Guys?"

My face is burning. Everyone is looking at me.

"Open Mic Club guys," I say.

They each look at me, Rahul, Danny, Russell, Jason, and Noah. But I can't look at them.

"Will you each be . . . one of my roses?"

"The roses thing," Noah says, clearing his throat. "The most important men in your life dancing . . . thing?"

Jason stifles a smile. Rahul elbows him.

"More dancing?" Russell asks. "You honor me."

"Yeah," I say. "That thing. We dance one-on-one and you give me a rose. It can be like a fun dance. Nothing too long."

I'm talking very quickly because I just want it to be over, it's mortifying, but there's still one more thing.

"There's a 'most important women' thing, too, the Eighteen Candles ceremony, but . . ."

The others from the Fil-Am group are looking at me curiously. Gabriel, my escort, raises his eyebrows. Perhaps they are all realizing in real time that they've been invited to be filler in the cotillion of a loser with no friends. Or perhaps they already knew that.

Fuck it. It's my party.

"Ali and Esmé, will you be my roses, too?" I ask. "Let's just do that."

Esmé is beaming at me. *They're yours to give*, she'd said.

"I *love* that," Ali says.

Mine to give. And that's who I'm giving them to.

Alyssa is furiously typing into her notes app.

"Okay, so that's seven new dance segments we'll need to work on," she says curtly.

But you can tell she's thrilled.

"Actually," I say. "I'll ask my cousin Maricel, too. And my lola. And my mom."

"Ten roses," Alyssa says for confirmation.

"Ten roses," I say.

There's a rustling sound in the back of the theater. Mr. Marco, sitting in the back row, beneath the projector, has turned the page on his newspaper.

Very loudly.

My throat closes up. Looking at his hands cradling the pages. Only his hands and hat are visible. But he's just been sitting back there, this whole time, quietly. Opening the glass door to the front of the theater every morning to let us in, his ring of keys jangling, grouchy, mumbling, balancing his black coffee in one hand, every morning.

"Mr. Marco?" I ask, calling out to him.

He doesn't lower his newspaper.

He grunts, indicating that he's heard me.

"I need to ask you a very large favor."

"I'll do it," he calls, from behind the paper. "If you need me to."

"Eleven roses," Alyssa Vasquez says.

And that's that.

There's a shuffling of sneakers against the stage floor when, to Alyssa's great relief, we finally, finally rearrange ourselves to face our partners for the waltz.

"Hand positions!" Alyssa says.

"This okay?" Gabriel, my escort, says.

"Sure," I say.

He takes my hand in his and I rest mine on his shoulder.

"I didn't realize I had an escort," I say.

"I didn't realize I was going to be your escort!" he says, laughing. "Until my mom told me I was, a few weeks ago, that is."

"Life comes at you fast."

"*Ferris Bueller's Day Off.*"

"Yes!" I say.

He grins.

Alyssa begins to count us off. "And one, two, three, one, two, three, one!"

I try to remember everything we've been practicing, but without her white sneakers to look at for reference, I keep messing up the steps.

"Wait, why are you good at this?" I say.

Gabriel's feet seem to know exactly what to do.

He laughs. "I have to confess, it's not my first ball."

"Oh, I see," I say. "So they brought in the big guns. You've done multiple debuts? *Why?*"

"One, two, three, one, two, three, one!"

"They're not so bad," he says.

"Were they your friends, at least? These other debutantes?"

He looks around the room, at the others. Waltzing. In sneakers and jeans.

"Not at first," he says. "But, eventually, they were."

"One, two, three, one, two, three, one!"

I just need to stop looking at my own feet so that I can steal a glance at Jason and Esmé. I need to know that, if we *must* do this ridiculous dance number, then at least *one* good thing might come out of it.

"One, two, three, one, two, three, one!"

My feet finally find the rhythm. Something just clicks into place.

"One, two, three, one, two, three, one! Now, spin!"

We spin, and Esmé and Jason spin past. They are both smiling in that way when you're trying not to smile super big but you can't help it and so this weird halfway smile keeps flickering on and off.

"Great cardigan," Jason is saying. "Where did you get it?"

"Off-Broadway Vintage Clothing and Costumes," she says.

"That place is the best!" he says.

And Esmé beams. And I'm scared. I'm scared that she'll spend all her time with Jason now. Shopping for vintage cardigans. Doing all the things I hate to do, like watching horror movies.

But then, Gabriel spins me, and Danny and Russell sweep into view. *One, two, three, one, two, three.* And maybe Danny was serious about going to that yoga class with him. And I could try the handstand thing again. Try and fall and try.

As we turn, again, *one, two, three, one, two, three*, Noah and Jalyn—one of my, maybe, eventually, new friends—come into view. Jalyn is laughing at something Noah says and I feel no impulse to make a dead rat face about it even though I know he's probably taking the opportunity to try out some new material.

I have new material, I realize. A lot. I have *so* much new material to try. About the debut and my mom and how I got everything wrong. And I could share it with Noah and Jason, and we could go back to that horrible open mic and try again, or maybe start our own, right here on this stage, and say No Assholes Allowed on the flyer.

Out in the lobby, a wave of laughter from the moms and Mr. Marco. As I turn, I can see him, through the propped-open door, animatedly telling them a story, and I can imagine this place full again, and the strip mall parking lot of cars outside, and the marquee glowing the dark, *tonight, perpekto, tonight, perpekto.*

Renalyn Abasta Cruz, mother of the Debutante,
welcomes you to

LUCIA'S 18TH BIRTHDAY

A FUNDRAISER FOR THE SUNSHINE THEATER

Tonight's Program

INTRODUCTION OF THE DEBUTANTE, HER ESCORT, AND HER COTILLION COURT

Rosali Cruz, Esmé Mares, Jason Woods, Noah
Bradford, Danny Wong, Russell Bernstein, Rahul
Mathur, Jalyn Colleen Morales, Joshua Celebrado
Dalandan, Angel Mabanglo Bollosa, Che Kalanduyan
McKay, Teresita Christina Pasajol, Michael Bungcayao,
Joseph Dupaya, Marlon Benitez, Baby Fontanilla, and
Gabriel Terrado Fernandez, escort of the debutante

TOAST IN HONOR OF THE DEBUTANTE

WELCOME REMARKS

Renalyn Cruz

PRAYER

Litang Rivera, Filipino-American Association,
Rio Grande Chapter, President

GRAND COTILLION WALTZ DANCE

Choreographed by Alyssa Vasquez

Rosali Cruz, Esmé Mares, Jason Woods, Noah Bradford, Danny Wong, Russell Bernstein, Rahul Mathur, Gabriel Terrado Fernandez, Jalyn Morales, Joshua Dalandan, Angel Bollosa, Che Kalanduyan McKay, Teresita Christina Pasajol, Michael Bungcayao, Joseph Dupaya, Baby Fontanilla, and Marlon Benitez

18 ROSES DANCE

Maricel Magdelena Rosalía Cruz Diaz, cousin of the debutante; Rosali Cruz, sister of the debutante; friends of the debutante: Marco Apodaca, Linda Gonzalez Mares, Jason Woods, Noah Bradford, Danny Wong, Russell Bernstein, and Rahul Mathur; Esmé Mares, emotional support plus-one of the debutante; Renalyn Cruz, mother of the debutante; and Joséfina Cruz, grandmother of the debutante

SINGING OF THE BIRTHDAY SONG

CUTTING OF THE CAKE

TIME TO PARTY!

Live music by Burly Boba

EPILOGUE

"WHAT'S UP, DEBUTTOK?" I SAY INTO THE CAMERA ON MY phone. "So, here's how it went down on the big night."

There are no ice sculptures of me.

No drone shots of any palatial grounds.

No father, no father-daughter dance.

No new car waiting outside with a big red bow on top.

Just me, in a mustard dress, coming out into the spotlight, squinting, trying to find my mom's face in the theater while Burly Boba plays my entrance song, the drum kit so close to the stage that I feel the vibrations in my bones.

There she is.

Smiling, and inexplicably holding up her iPad with both hands, recording me, and it's *so* corny and embarrassing that I want to cover my face with my hands.

But I'm glad I don't, because right next to her is Lola. Because she's still here.

Still here with us, for now.

Surprisingly, she chose to wear this really amazing tailored suit.

I don't know why I didn't think of that. *A suit.* So much agony for so many months and my lola was just a video call away the whole time with the answer. Esmé has not stopped asking my lola questions about the suit since she set eyes on it, and is now planning to replicate the look for herself to wear to graduation.

When the spotlight falls on me, I try not to make my dead rat face.

It's hard. But I stand there anyway.

My relatives from California, including Tita Connie and Tito Nelson, look incredibly confused to be wandering into a movie theater, in a strip mall, in Albuquerque, New Mexico, for a debut. But after a few minutes, and after Mr. Marco hands them each a bag of popcorn, they're just happy to be laughing, and to be together with the whole family, just like at all the others, and shaking hands with Litang Rivera and the other members of our Filipino-American chapter, all the "youths" bowing and pressing their foreheads to their elders' hands, as a sign of respect.

I give the signal to Mr. Marco.

"As all you fine DebutTokers know very well," I say into my phone camera. "This is more than a party."

On my signal, a smoke machine fizzles to life.

"It's a chance to be together," I say. "With your people. Whoever those people are."

The song starts, and with it, my Eighteen Roses dance. After some back and forth with Mom, the Eighteen Candles ceremony was officially struck from the program, for fire hazard reasons, and also because this is a made-up tradition and that means we can do whatever we want with it, and we don't care what Tita Connie says, she's a pain in the ass.

For my TikTok video, I use footage taken from Mom's iPad.

It starts with me, alone, pumping my fist in the air.

As the bass line pulses, my cousin Maricel joins me on

the dance floor, smiling like Miss Universe, pressing a long-stemmed rose into my hand. Shoulder to shoulder, we rock back and forth, in sync, dancing a dance she taught me. I took her to Golden Pride Fried Chicken and Burritos as soon as she got off the plane for a number nine breakfast burrito with green chile. She said it was good, but not better than In-N-Out. She is wrong, but I respect her for her loyalty to her regional cuisine.

Next up is Mr. Marco, in a tan suit, cowboy boots, and a bolo tie.

He grumbled the whole time we were practicing this. Throughout every rehearsal. Every time he unlocked the front door and let us all descend on him. He said there's no way we'd raise enough money to save the theater. He said he was ready to retire. He let us do it anyway.

Now his rose joins Maricel's in my palm, the ghost of a smile on his face.

The crowd cheers as we surprise everyone by doing the cha-cha, which he taught me. Alyssa Vasquez was impressed.

Mrs. Mares is straight up crying when she gives me her rose. Looking at me like she looked at Esmé at her quince. And my eyes hurt. And I might cry, too. Not a single, perfect tear either, like my cousin Cecelia. The comedy club guys cheer for one another as they add their roses to my bouquet, one by one, each of them doing a different section of the "(Crank That) Soulja Boy" choreography with me, made famous by our appearance at St. Lucia Independent Living.

The cheering in the crowd swells as my lola spins herself onto the floor in her slick black-and-white suit, bumping hips with me as she bites the rose stem between her teeth. She beckons to my sister.

Ali, who has changed into a cute little dress that matches mine, joins us.

When she hands me her rose, I spin her around, and I hope, in a few years, for her debut, we will all be together again.

And I don't know that we will be.

And so I pull her into an extra-tight hug before I release her.

Next, my mom, in stilettos and a dress I'd never wear, but that's okay, clutching her rose to her chest.

She looks between Lola and me, her eyes filling. Lola pulls her into a hug.

She and Mom have been arguing nonstop since she got off the plane. About everything. Too much vinegar in the adobo sauce. How could Mom let me walk around inside with no socks or slippers on? Why didn't we charge the karaoke machine before she got there? And so on.

It's great. It is perfect.

The song rises. When the hug breaks, Lola holds her daughter out at arm's length.

"Thank you," Mom says to her.

Then, she turns to me, hugging me close to her.

"Thank you," she says again, whispering it.

This is her way of saying *I'm sorry* and *I love you*, all at the same time.

I clear my throat.

"Ready?" I ask.

Lola puts her hands in her pockets and steps aside as my mom and I raise our arms to the ceiling in unison for our planned performance.

It's Mom's favorite song, "I Wanna Dance with Somebody (Who Loves Me)," by Whitney Houston, 1987, another staple of our apartment karaoke days. And as we clap, jump, slide from side to side, childhood may be over, but it's like being kids again. All of us, even Mom.

When it's Esmé's turn, everything feels like it's in slow motion. She's holding the rose in front of her with both hands. My eyes fill with tears, finally, and my face crumples into what I know is an ugly cry.

"Maybe somebody should do a video on how to cry gracefully," I say into the camera on my TikTok video. "But my advice to you, if you're planning your debut, is to just go ahead and ugly cry. Do what you need to do. Scream at your mom. At your own risk, of course. Laugh with your mom, if you can. Make up with your best friend. Because before you know it, it'll be over."

Esmé crosses the dance floor and I hug her tight, swaying her side to side. My mom is still clapping, the whole theater is clapping.

"It'll be over, and whether everything went perfectly or horribly, or some mix of the two, things will go on changing."

Esmé adds her rose to my others.

There aren't eighteen of them, but it's a beautiful bouquet.

It's full.

ACKNOWLEDGMENTS

THANK YOU TO MY AGENT, SERENE HAKIM, FOR FIELDING all of my baby author questions (read: meltdowns) with grace. I'm so grateful to my editor, Kat Brzozowski, for helping me bring Luz's inner world into the light, and I apologize to her for putting so many characters who wink in my books (*wink*). Thank you also to the entire team at Feiwel & Friends. I put them through a lot during the editing process because I never know what day of the week it is supposed to be, and I insist the sun must always be setting for important literary reasons (reasons = sunsets are pretty).

Endless appreciation to my MFA program mentors Francesca Lia Block, Naima Coster, Aditi Khorana, and Aminah Mae Safi for your invaluable feedback on this manuscript—for showing me when to speed up, when to slow down, when to turn away from the pain, and when to let it breathe. Thank you to my MFA workshop group (Regan Humphrey, Amy Klipstine, Alisha Mercier, Aldo Puicon, Debbie Wright, and Lizzy Young), who encouraged me to stick with this story, and who empathized with Luz, even though she's . . . Luz.

Thank you to my friend and writing partner, Elizabeth Dwyer, who combed steadfastly through several drafts of this manuscript when I asked her to—because she's a Leo, and Leos are very loyal—and also for marking all the typos that I didn't notice because I'm a Sagittarius, which means that I'm actually very fun and carefree (I swear!).

Gratitude forever to my writing crew: Randi Burdette, Sara Lord, Phoebe Low, Rosemary Melchior, Elishia Merricks, Gigi Rodriguez, Theresa Soonyoung Park, Carolyn Tara O'Neil, Samantha Panepinto, and especially Jennifer Poe, who said an early draft of this book was *hi-lar-ious*, which is the highest-level praise you can get from a New Yorker. Thanks to Justin Earley for various creative consultations related to management of The Brand.

My research while writing this book included studying Evelyn Ibatan Rodriguez's *Celebrating Debutantes and Quinceñeras: Coming of Age in American Ethnic Communities*, and the documentary *The FMA Debutante Ball: 43 Years of Filipino-Minnesotan Coming of Age*. It also entailed sitting down with the very funny Sarah Kennedy and Kelli Trapnell, who generously answered my questions about stand-up comedy and specifically the comedy scene in Albuquerque, New Mexico. It's because of them I know what a "bringer" is, and a lot of other things about community.

Thank you to my many creative and funny friends. Your humor, vulnerability, and friendship could have inspired several more novels beyond this. Thank you to Adam for making me laugh when I'm crying over being "[Redacted], The Scrivener." Thank you to my family for hyping me up in the group chat and IRL—even though it makes me very uncomfortable and I'd prefer not to be perceived in any way, please know that I do appreciate it.

Thank you to my mom for not making me have a debut when I turned eighteen but insisting that we at least have a lechon. Thank you to lechon, as a general concept, for being something that my mom and I can agree on 100 percent.

Thank you to my Lola Awang, who never would have made me wear a dress to anything. You were the coolest there ever was.